Review Quotes for ***Our Rae of Hope***

Quirky. Fun. Romantic. This sweet story is small-town quaint on every page. The female lead, Rae, is terribly likable and a chuckle a minute. The author's voice is clean and fresh, and utterly adorable. *Our Rae of Hope* will be a lovely addition to the library of fan Christian romance.

April W. Gardner, award-winning author of *Creek Country Saga*

Our Rae of Hope is a heartwarming story of a woman unafraid to take a chance in a new town where she invested in business, new friends, and a personal relationship. The author captured my attention with her first-person viewpoint and character's faith. This is an enjoyable read.

Alfred W. Bates author of *The Wickie* and *Spirit of the Lighthouse*

Our Rae of Hope offers delightful characters, including two adorable dogs. I'm a fan of Bed and Breakfasts, so I was thrilled the author created this setting. This story satisfied my appetite for the drama of an old-fashioned love story.

June Chapko author of *The Legacy Series*

Our Rae of Hope is an engaging story of the problems opening a bed and breakfast in a small town. Rae finds small-town living different and unique. She establishes new friendships and her dog, Puffs, helps her find romance. Love how Terry Beard infuses humor and faith in the story.

Cathey Edgington author of *Journey Out of Loneliness*

Our Rae of Hope is a delight for the senses. Terry Beard brings her characters to life through the sights, sounds, and smells of small-town life. Change, family, friendships, and romance. Every aspect of this book made me want to go live in Hope!

Monica Clegg, Freelance Writer

Our Rae of Hope

Terry M. Beard

Our Rae of Hope

Terry M. Beard

Beard, Terry M.
Our Rae of Hope

ISBN: 978-1-7333102-0-8 paperback
ISBN: 978-1-7333102-1-5 ebook

Hope Series Book 1
First Edition
Christian Romance

Library of Congress Control Number:2019910245

Contact the author at terrybeard.wordpress.com
franklinscribes.com/terry-beard

Published by Terry M. Beard
Universal City, Texas 78148

Publishing services provided by
Franklin Scribes Publishing Consultants
Front and back book covers by Thompson Printing Solutions
Cover photo by Rachel Beard

This book was printed in the United States of America.

Acknowledgments

Thank you, Jesus, for sparking a desire to write in me and carrying me through each step of the way. You are my Comfort and Rock. My family from parents to grandchildren have inspired me to write and laugh during our fun-loving storytelling adventures. My oldest granddaughter, Audrey, graces the cover of Our Rae of Hope. I love you, Peach.

Christian Writers Group of Greater San Antonio prayed, critiqued, and encouraged me as they perused my pages to completion. You are a blessing. Writers for Him makes Monday morning fabulous. Your expertise and prayers bless my life. Thank you, Franklin Scribes Publishers, owners Judy Watters and Sandra Cleary, for your professional advice, valuable knowledge, and heartfelt assistance. Y'all are the best. Carol Holland, thank you for being my Beta Reader at a moment's notice. I'm so happy we share the same Heavenly Daddy. Casey, Rach, Chris, Carl, Stef, Audrey, Joshua, Elizabeth, and Abigail, you bring exuberant joy to me. Aunt Sue Mohacsi, I am so grateful we're related because of Jesus!

I'm thankful for you, Barry Beard, and am glad God led us to Beaufort, South Carolina, where we met.

Dedication

I dedicate this book to my best friend, a true southern gentleman, and husband, Barry. His faith-filled heart, encouragement, and love blesses me beyond words.

I love you.

Chapter One

Hope. Quite an appropriate name for this Piedmont town nestled near the mountains for fall foliage, yet close enough to the beach for summer vacations.

Driving down the manicured, tree-lined, brick street, I passed the cream-colored library to the left. Oh, so southern with its raised foundation and wraparound porch. My eyes scanned past the library as the road curved to the right; the sight took my breath away. The French-doored, twinkle-lit shops along main street drew me closer. The warm glow of light peeking through each shop and restaurant window said slow down and come on in. I longed to stop, explore, and sip a cup of hot tea at one of the tiny bistro tables lining the sidewalk in front of Molly's Restaurant.

However, Puffs, my Chocolate Labrador, began to whine. "Hang on, girl. I'll stop." I parked and reached back to clip the leash onto her red collar. Wrapping its extra length snuggly around my right hand, I wondered again as to my thought process when I bought my VW Beetle. But I fell in love with the shiny red bug at first sight and envisioned myself driving the highway with the top down and the breeze blowing through my hair. Considering a retractable leash would have made it easier to control Puffs, too.

Puffs squeezed between the driver's seat and the door and she was off. I managed to hang on as she pulled me across the brick street toward the lake. Much to my chagrin, she spotted a squirrel, and her doggy senses jumped into hunter mode.

Tugging on Puffs' leash, I tried to coax her back across the street to the car. But she had been in the car way too long. She would not be drawn back without a fight. Then her eyes darted from squirrel to duck. One last jerk and she pulled out of her collar as she lurched toward the water to retrieve a duck floating on the ripples from the passing paddle boat.

"Puffs! Get back here! No girl. Come back!" Since this was my first time in Hope, I didn't want people to think my lab and I would be nuisances. I cupped my hands around my mouth telling myself that only Puffs would hear this screaming lunatic. But it looked as though Puffs was winning this battle.

It was hopeless. Once my dog made up her mind to retrieve a bird, nothing could stop her. Except another dog.

A sudden splash soaked my shoes. The Great Dane paddled his four paws with ease, focusing on my daughter, not the bird.

"Hurry up, girl! Get back here! Come get a treat!" I yelled—no hands cupping my mouth this time. I decided I didn't care what people thought. I wouldn't let that huge gray pony-sized dog get my sweet three-year-old pup.

The deep voice behind me startled me at first as the brute's master called to him. "Here, Buddy. Come on, boy."

Buddy immediately turned his enormous body toward the shore.

How does he get his dog to listen at first try and mine is still going after the duck?

My eyes dashed from the large dog to Puffs. A nearby paddle boat glided close to my weary baby and stopped beside her. The young teen handed the driving lever to the girl riding with him and jumped into the water to rescue Puffs who gave no resistance. The young lady peddled vigorously toward the shore while my hero held onto the side of the boat with one hand and Puffs with the other.

The girl tied the boat to the dock and grinned from ear to ear as her friend pulled himself and Puffs out of the water onto the bank. After risking life and limb to save a drowning dog, he became not only my hero, but also, a hero to this young lady.

I rushed to Puffs and slipped the collar back on her, wrapping the long leash around my hand again. "Thanks so much," I said. "She's not accustomed to swimming in a lake. You saved her. Let me pay to have your clothes cleaned. Wait here; my purse . . ."

"No, ma'am. Your dog helped me, too." He gave a quick smile as the girl gave him a peck on the cheek. "By the way, Puffs sure is a funny name for a Chocolate Lab."

I started to explain how I'd chosen her name, but he walked away quickly with his friend, uninterested in what this old woman of twenty-eight was about to say. Young love—oh, how sweet.

Out of the corner of my eye, I spotted the man with the deep voice. His huge Great Dane's body shook with gusto from the top of his ears to the tip of his whip-like tail. Water flew everywhere.

The man gave an enormous belly laugh as the lake water made its way from the dog to his pant legs. Soaking them. Soaking him.

Our eyes met for a second; we diverted our attention back to the dogs. Attempting to keep them at a distance from each other was hopeless.

He spoke to his dog. "Hey Buddy. Who'd ya meet here?"

With my head tilted back, I shielded my eyes from the sun to look up at him. "Her name is Puffs."

The sun warmed my face as he bent down to look at me, and I got a peek at his green eyes. He grinned. Maybe it wasn't the sun that made my face feel so warm.

Before we uttered a word, Buddy gave his master an extra tug toward a Crepe Myrtle near the sidewalk. The man turned and glanced in my direction. "Great meeting you, Puffs. By the way, I'm Joe Byer."

I raised my voice a tad so he could hear me. "Glad to meet you, Buddy and Mr. Byer. I'm Rae Long."

His deep voice carried in my direction. "Hi, Ms. Long."

I rushed Puffs to the car, found an old towel I kept in my VW for such times as this, and fluffed her hair. She leaped into the back seat. After numerous circling in the same spot, she finally laid down. As I closed the passenger door and walked to the driver's side, a dark-haired guy jogged by. He gave me a quick wave and slowed down just a bit. He turned and did a slow jog backwards, yes backwards.

"Hi, I'm Mick." His grin was contagious.

"Hi, I'm Rae."

"Have a great day." Mick jogged a bit farther down the sidewalk and entered one of the shops.

Hmm—this cute little town had some very interesting possibilities. Not just the bed and breakfast I'd researched, but in many other categories, too.

I pulled out of the parking spot just as my stomach growled. Slowly driving down main street, I scanned the shops for a fast food drive through, but to no avail.

"The peanut butter crackers will have to suffice for the moment, Puffs." I took two nibbles and felt a wet nose on my shoulder. "Here you go, girl." I held a cracker up to her that she quickly devoured. "Hang in there, Puffs. The trunk has your doggy food. We'll be at our rental soon."

For I know the plans I have for you . . .
Jeremiah 29:11

Chapter Two

Morning light streamed through the half-opened window while the sheer curtains flowed slightly in the soft breeze. Puffs slept at the foot of my bed, and when she felt me stir, she slowly stepped onto the floor with back swayed and legs outstretched. My yawn was almost as big as hers. Stretching my arms above my head, and arching my back slightly, I slipped from under my cozy blanket. The wooden floor, warmed by a ray of sun, made my feet even warmer.

Leasing the small, two-bedroom home online before I arrived in Hope was easy. This would be only a temporary stay, since Puffs and I planned to move into the bed and breakfast soon.

After showering and dressing in my gray slacks, yellow cable knit sweater, and gray boots, I added a gold clip to my hair—a gift from my grandmother.

Puffs and I felt the cool air as we walked down Pecan Street. Thankfully, Puffs didn't notice the black cat sitting on my neighbor's porch as we strolled past.

We meandered toward Bitty's Buns, a tiny bakery I'd noticed the day before on the main street. I chuckled to myself as the shop's name gave me a funny visual.

Puffs' leash wrapped easily around the hook near Bitty's front door. She sat contentedly and sipped water from a community doggy bowl. The fragrance permeated my nostrils as I entered Bitty's—heavenly. Two people stood in line ahead of me. An elderly gentleman, with laugh lines burrowed deeply into his face, carefully bent his arthritic knees so the little girl with him could place her order. Her bright pink hair ribbon bobbed up and down as she giggled. "Papa, can I have hot chocolate with whipped cream?"

He nodded to the child, then noticed me behind them. "I don't believe I've met you, young lady. I'm Ike Wood and this is my granddaughter Penelope. We all call her Penny. Are you visiting Hope?" Ike Wood gave me a toothy grin.

Hmm . . . I wonder if those are his real teeth.

Penny turned around while still holding on to her Papa's hand and flashed a grin, just like her Papa's. *Question answered.*

Penny squinted her hazel eyes and pointed outside the door where I'd leashed Puffs. "Is that your dog outside? What's her name?"

I loved hearing her sweet southern accent.

"Yes, she sure is; her name is Puffs. My name is Rae."

Mr. Wood, Penny, Puffs, and I sat at an outside table and enjoyed the September weather and conversation. Puffs nuzzled up to Penny, placed her muzzle on Penny's lap, and did the best doggy begging I'd ever seen. When she gave Puffs a couple cinnamon bun nibbles, they became instant friends.

The pastry tasted divine. Perfectly round with lots of cinnamon and an extra helping of pecans scattered on top.

Natalie, the owner of the shop, said I got more because I was a first-time customer of Bitty's. I glanced at Ike's and Penny's; they had just as many pecans as I did. But I had an added helping of icing. Being a newbie certainly had its perks!

"Mr. Wood, are you familiar with the bed and breakfast on Charleston Street? I'm buying it. I can't wait to see it. For now, I've rented a small house on Pecan Street and can't believe I smelled the cinnamon buns from there."

Ike motioned that his mouth was too full to speak, but I did notice his Adam's apple bob as I mentioned the bed and breakfast. After he finished his bite, he took a large gulp of his cooled coffee. "Hmm—I hope that works out for you. It sure was nice meeting you, Rae. I need to get Penny to kindergarten. See you again." Ike scooted out his chair and handed Penny a napkin to wipe icing off her cheek. "Have a great day."

Penny gave Puffs a big hug. "Bye, Miss Rae. Have a fun day, Puffs."

She ran ahead of her Papa before I responded. I watched Ike Wood stretch his long legs as he attempted to catch up with Penny. His reaction to my buying the bed and breakfast seemed strange. Maybe he was afraid Penny would be late to school. But that was all right since I had an appointment to meet with the real estate agent soon.

***

The real estate office stood a few doors down from Bitty's Buns so there was no need to rush. I finished my cinnamon bun then Puffs and I took a leisurely walk down to Tweeters Realty. *How did they ever come up with the name Tweeters? Sounds like the name of a pet shop.*

I wrapped Puffs' leash around the historic hitching post in front of Tweeters. She gave me her big-eyed look and lay down outside the door. I didn't want to assume dogs were welcome inside.

A silver bell on the door jingled as I stepped inside. The nameplate on the first desk to the right told me this was Jamie Brown's desk. The desk behind it—Brittany Brown. I hadn't hired either of these Realtors. Both ladies were involved in phone conversations.

"May I put you on hold one moment, Mrs. Johnson?" Jamie asked into the phone. Then she smiled at me.

"Hi, I'm Rae Long. I have an appointment with Mr. Treavor. Is he here?"

The silver bell tinkled behind me and the jogging guy I'd seen the day before entered. The fingers on his left hand raked through his dark, wavy hair. Trying to smooth out those waves was hopeless. He fumbled with his rolled-up cuffs and grinned.

Jamie Brown stood and started to introduce him to me. "Ms. Long, this is Mick . . ."

Mick interrupted Jamie, "Rae and I met yesterday. Well sort of."

Jamie smiled and returned to her phone call as Mick straightened his tie. "Are you ready for the tour?"

"The tour? No thanks, I have a meeting with Mr. Treavor. I'm here about the bed and breakfast on Charleston Street."

Mick walked to the large modern desk, picked up the nameplate and held it under his chin. “Hi, I’m Mick. Mick Treavor.” He put down the sign and offered his hand.

My cheeks felt warm. “You’ve got to be kidding me. You didn’t say your last name when I saw you jogging yesterday. I expected someone much older.” Oops, there I’d said it. No taking it back. Now my cheeks felt even warmer. “Uh, you know what I mean.”

Both Brittany and Jamie, now off the phones, snickered. Brittany added, “Yes, we know what you mean.”

Mick cleared his throat and took a quick glance at his watch. “Let’s change the subject, ladies. Just for the record, I thought you’d be older, too.” He grabbed his leather case. “Want to see the property, Miss Long?”

“Of course.”

Mick waited as I retrieved Puffs’ leash. She trotted between the two of us in the direction of our cars.

I should have noticed a red flag when Mr. Treavor’s conversation began with, “I really wasn’t sure you’d be here this morning after seeing the bed and breakfast yesterday. You did see it when you drove into town, didn’t you?”

“No. I didn’t.” I nervously bit my lower lip.

“Well, then, guess you’d better look at the place. I’d offer you a ride, but I don’t think you and your dog can fit in my car.” He chuckled. “Just follow me.”

Puffs jumped into the backseat of my convertible. I put the top down and followed Mick’s car as he crept along Beaufort Street. Puffs always sat up tall in the back seat when the top was down; when traveling at higher speeds, the wind blew her ears so they stood out to the sides.

The curve at the end of the road led to the right. It would be easy to follow the brick road since it naturally circled the lake and majestic homes. However, we turned left down Charleston Street. It wasn't a street at all, but a driveway with a name attached to it.

The overgrown tree-lined driveway didn't possess the beauty of a French alley. The kudzu-entwined telephone poles stood spaced unevenly along the right side of the gravel drive. The wires sagged from the weight of the invasive vine. I wondered if the phone worked at all.

Mick pulled over. He motioned for me to park beside his car, which I did. Reluctantly.

He lowered his window. "Rae, as you can see, this property needs work. It'll be easy to clean up if you hire the right people." Sheepish grin.

I accelerated my car and passed his. I didn't need a lesson on how to clean up this mess.

Inching along the driveway, I felt Puffs' hot breath on my neck. For a moment I had forgotten she was in the back of the car. Even though it was a little cool outside, I felt hot under the collar. No pun intended.

"Please help me, Lord." Those words I spoke out loud as I saw what lay ahead. The Bed and Breakfast of Hope should have been named the Bed and Breakfast of Hopeless. I'd been deceived when I viewed the B&B on the website and trusted the pictures to be current. I placed the car in park and put my head down on the steering wheel. Eyes closed. Silent prayer.

Mick's car skidded on the flattened gravel as he followed close behind me. Almost too close. He jammed on his brakes, stopping within inches of the back of my car. He approached my VW.

His smile looked a little forced. "Are you getting out to look?"

I shook my head, "No. You duped me."

"Miss Long, I have another client lined up to see the property in the next couple of days. Should I assume you're not interested?"

I said a quick prayer, and I mean, a real quick prayer. "I'm so disappointed. What happened to the gorgeous bed and breakfast on the website? Am I at the wrong place?" I cleared my throat. "This can't be it."

His slight grin gave him an air of confidence. "You must not have looked at the small print."

"Small print?" My head cocked to the left. "Are you kidding me?"

He shook his head slowly. "The pictures on line were from years ago. The place thrived back then. Now it needs a little repair." He stepped back from my car door.

"A little repair? Are you crazy?" Good thing he'd stepped away from my car because I flung open the door, just missing Mick Treavor. Secretly I wished the door had hit him. *Please forgive me, Lord.*

He stood in front of me with his arms folded. "Do you want a tour or not?" His eyes twinkled.

Is he teasing me? Bet this isn't the place after all, and he's just pulling my leg. I'll go along with his little skit. "How dare I be so picky. This place is absolutely fantastic, and I can't wait to sign the papers to make it mine." I kicked the dry red dirt beneath my feet.

Mick uncrossed his arms and looked a little more relaxed. "I brought the papers with me. I'll get them out of my car."

"You're kidding, right?" I cocked my head to the side again. "When are you going to show me the bed and breakfast listed online?" I gave him a silly little smirk.

The sullen expression on his face made me uneasy; I stopped kicking the dirt.

Mick squirmed, stopped in his tracks then opened his car door. "Rae, this is the bed and breakfast. Like I said, fine print."

I couldn't believe my ears. No way! I left my cushy job in Maryland—for this? It couldn't be the same place my grandparents visited years ago and loved. "Your website is deceptive. I've wasted my time coming here."

He stood still. Didn't say a word.

I slid inside my car, started the engine, and sped down the driveway.

Small rental abode on Pecan Street here I come.

. . . in all your ways submit to him,
and he will make your paths straight.
Proverbs 3:6

Chapter Three

Chocolate. I needed chocolate. After changing into jeans and a blue flannel shirt, I gathered my computer, a thermos of hot chocolate, and doggy treats. With those items tossed into my backpack, Puffs trotted beside me as I walked out the door. The lake seemed to beckon us.

“Hey girl, let’s go in a different direction. I can’t stand the thought of walking past Tweeters.”

Puffs couldn’t care less which direction she went. Her doggy senses already discovered the joy of trees—with squirrels attached to them.

A white, two-story home with an American flag flying proudly on the porch pillar, caught my eye. Children rolled in piles of colorful leaves. I stopped in front of the home.

The boy in the yard picked up some leaves. “Hey, Dad! Since there’s no snow for a snowball fight, let’s have a leaf fight! Guys against girls.”

The boy’s dad gave his son a high five and cheers erupted from the two girls and Mom. Two guys against three gals. Family. Fun.

Their extremely contagious laughter triggered a belly laugh from me. Puffs’ ears perked, and her eyes looked upward at me. The mom tossed leaves at the dad, wiped her hands on her jeans, and walked to where I stood. Her picket fence stood between us.

"Hi, I'm Fran and you must be Rae. I heard you rented the house down the street and are looking at the B&B. It's been such an eyesore for years."

"Yes, I'm Rae. News travels fast in this town. It's good to meet you, Fran. I haven't decided on the B&B yet. It's quite a mess."

Her welcoming smile made me feel at ease and I subdued a chuckle when I noticed two maple leaves stuck in her hair. Her children ran to where we stood, and the smallest girl giggled then pointed to her mother's head. Fran realized what was going on and played along with the teasing. She grabbed at the top of her head, just missing the leaves, as her youngest daughter laughed non-stop. The two other children shook their heads and threw a barrage of leaves on their little sister.

Fran snatched the leaves from her hair. "My husband George and I are the proud parents of these rascals. Clark is twelve, Zoe is six, and Olivia is four."

"It's so good to meet you. This is Puffs." I patted Puffs' head. "I love your place. It makes me feel like I'm home in Maryland."

"Thanks! What brought you to South Caro--?" Olivia's cry caught Fran's attention. "Oh sorry, I'd better go before they all start crying. Look forward to seeing you again." With that, she turned and chased the three into the backyard like a mother hen. I caught a glimpse of Fran tending to the upset child.

Maybe someday . . .

Puffs and I picked up the pace. We crossed Beaufort Street and claimed a bench under a Weeping Willow. Occasionally, I felt one of its leafy branches brush the top of my noggin.

With my computer teetered on my lap, the hot chocolate-filled thermos balanced on the bench, I noticed Puffs had settled quickly. She lay on the ground next to me, with her eyes closed, and slowed breathing that indicated slumber. Her paws twitched. I knew she was dreaming about those pesky squirrels.

Computer activated. Letter to Tweeters. The words sputtered in my mind as I searched for just the right thing to say. I typed a list of all the negatives of the property and the deceptive website. Words flung from my fingertips onto the computer screen until I casually looked up and spotted the most magnificent sunset I'd ever seen. With the save key punched, I quit typing, took a sip of the hot chocolate, and took in the beauty. It took my breath away. With my legs crisscrossed under me, I relished a slight breeze tossing my hair to and fro. Several sips of the chocolate warmed me from head to toe and I felt peace. Something I rarely felt. Surreal.

After sitting for quite a while and enjoying myself, I felt a few sprinkles of rain.

With my bag slung over my shoulder, Puffs and I did a marathon walk back toward the house. We took the shortcut by Tweeters. Unfortunately, Mick spotted us and opened the office door. "Rae. You and Puffs can come inside."

I waved. *No way. I'm not going into Tweeters.* Then Puffs' leash dangled in front of my right leg, my foot caught the leash, and away I went. Not the most graceful maneuver. I landed hard on my fanny. "Ouch!"

"Rae, are you all right?" Mick, yes Mick Treavor, came to my rescue. "Here, let me help you." He unwound the leash from my ankle.

Puffs whined and licked my face—canine remorse.

I patted her head reassuringly. "It's okay girl." I rubbed my ankle. "I'm all right, Mick. Thanks." I stood and fell against his right side as I tried to steady myself.

"Come in. I can get you a glass of water and look at your foot." He gently assisted me while holding onto Puffs' leash.

Before entering Tweeters, I saw Joe and his mammoth dog trotting in my direction. "Rae, are you okay?"

I didn't say a word because Mick answered him. "She'll be fine. I can handle this." He opened the Tweeters' door and escorted me inside.

Joe and Buddy followed close behind. I positioned myself in the chair next to Mick's desk and rubbed my ankle. Joe, Buddy, Mick, and Puffs stood around the chair and I began to giggle, which turned into a belly laugh. Mick and Joe looked bewildered as Puffs and Buddy licked my cheeks. The doggy kisses didn't stop my laughter. Instead they made me giggle even harder.

Mick shrugged his shoulders. "Why are you cracking up? I thought your ankle hurt."

I sounded ridiculous, but I couldn't stop. The picture of these two men of Hope, a mammoth gray dog, and my Puffs staring at me—priceless.

Joe stepped back from the chair and roared with me. He caught his breath and his words escaped sporadically. “I don’t know why you’re laughing, and I really don’t know why I am either.”

I planted my face into Puffs’ brown fur and finally regained composure. “Sorry, guys. When I looked up and saw the two of you like knights to the rescue and two huge dogs standing at your sides, it just struck a funny chord. For one thing, it made me forget my ankle.” I gently twisted my foot from side to side and cringed a little as I slowly stood. “Thanks. You’re both terrific.” What was I saying? Mick and his website were far from terrific.

Mick offered to drive Puffs and me home. “Thanks for the offer. There’s no way three of us will fit in your sports car.”

“Guess you’re right.” Mick sat behind his desk and opened his laptop. “Maybe Joe can give you a lift.” He snickered. “I’m sure you have room in that truck of yours, Joe.”

“Sure do. My truck looks like junk, but it gets me where I need to go.”

I exited Tweeters. “Thanks, again, guys.”

Joe and Buddy followed Puffs and me outside. “Rae, my truck is at home. I’ll be glad to jog home and get it.”

“We’ll be just fine. I appreciate you and Buddy checking on me.” I gave him a slight wave as Puffs and I proceeded down the sidewalk toward home

***

When I crawled under my comfy covers that evening, the soft tapping of rain drops lulled me to sleep. Drip, drop, drip. Splish, splash, splosh.

Puffs' breathing moved the bed slightly. A tin roof, a soft feather pillow, sleep.

. . . Be still and know that I am God . . .
Psalm 46:10

Chapter Four

With my bedroom at the front of the house, I heard almost everything and everyone who passed by. Puffs woke before me and did her usual morning whine. I carefully stepped onto the hardwood floor and felt only a slight ache in my ankle.

I carefully walked downstairs and breathed in the heavenly smell of coffee. My habit of setting the coffee to brew the night before was never more appreciated than it was this morning. I let Puffs out and then back in. I reached for a mug and filled it with fragrant java. Cup in hand, I limped outside onto the front porch with Puffs close behind.

Sitting comfortably in a wicker chair, I sipped my java slowly and watched the children walk and skip to school. They waved at Puffs as they passed the house. With a break in pedestrian traffic, I tilted my head back against the chair and closed my eyes, savoring this sweet moment.

Until I heard my name.

It sounds like him. It can't be him. I'll die if it's him.

Joe stood on the sidewalk in front of the house. His backpack hung over his left shoulder with a laptop case in his right hand. The Navy-blue dress shirt and solid red tie made him look even more handsome.

"Good morning, Rae. The coffee smells good."

My head tilted downward as I slumped into the rocker trying to hide myself. It didn't work.

"Hi, Joe. Would you like a cup?" *Did I say that out loud?*

His crooked grin made my cheeks warm. Again.

"You know, I'd love some. My mug's in my backpack so you don't have to use any of yours." He started to remove his backpack.

"Don't bother. I'll just grab a Styrofoam one inside the house. I'll be back in a minute." *No way can I take his mug or even get close to him. Not the way I look.* I glanced back in his direction. "By the way, how do you take your coffee?"

"Just black."

My heart skipped a beat as I slinked into the house. Carefully walking upstairs, I threw off my robe, pajamas, and pulled on my jeans and a gray sweater. After looking in the mirror, I ran my brush quickly through my hair, zipped my toothbrush along my teeth, and stepped cautiously down the steps.

With filled coffee cup in hand, I opened the door, and headed toward the picket fence. There he stood. Patiently awaiting the java. Or awaiting me?

Puffs got under foot and almost tripped me again. Joe reached across the fence and grabbed my arm, rescuing me and the steamy drink.

"Thanks."

"Thank you." He held the cup in his free hand. "Your ankle feeling better?"

"It sure is."

"Glad to hear it." He gave a thumbs up. "Tonight's the Hope High School football game. The whole town will be there. Want to go? The Bulldogs play every Friday night." He tripped over his words; I noticed his ears turned red.

"I heard about the game. Not sure I'll be able to make it."

"If you decide to go, I can stop by and get you at 6:30; we can walk to the school. They have hot dogs so there's no need to eat till we get there. Unless you don't like hot dogs." He spoke without taking even a slight breath.

I suppressed a giggle. "I love hot dogs with lots of mustard."

He smiled and took a drink. "I better run, I'm a professor at the university and class starts in fifteen minutes. Thanks for the coffee."

With the bed and breakfast purchase in limbo, a relationship wasn't on my radar. My mind told me, NO, but my heart twittered at the possibility of going to the game with the professor.

The Lord has done it this very day;
let us rejoice today and be glad.
Psalm 118:24

Chapter Five

After the coffee exchange with Joe, I donned gardening boots and bug spray. My loyal companion and I walked to the tumbledown B&B. I knew better than to go alone, but I didn't need Mick telling me what to do with the place. Together, Puffs and I weaved through the wooded area. I carried a tall stick to scare away anything treacherous. Poking the weeds in front of me and Puffs at my side, I discovered eight little cottages scattered on the land near the main dwelling. From a slight distance, they appeared in better shape than the main building.

Four pecan trees lined the backyard. The ultimate squirrel heaven. I picked up a few pecans, grabbed a stone and shattered the shells. The meat inside tasted scrumptious. *Hmm—Possibly sell pecan pies? Am I crazy? Salvage this disaster area? Nonsense!*

As we trudged closer to the main house, Puffs' bark scared me to death. Hackles up and teeth barred, she placed herself between me and it. I'd heard it said before, never come between a mother bear and her cubs. The huge black bear lumbered from the back of the main house. I released a blood curdling scream. The bear stood on her back legs, swung her head from side to side with saliva dripping on Puffs' back. That's all it took. Puffs charged, biting at the animal's leg as the bear's right paw dropped on top of her. I arched my back, grasped the stick with both hands, and swung it full force onto the bear's back. The stick broke, the bear bellowed, her cubs ran out from under the front porch and raced into the woods behind the house, with mother bear galloping behind her babies.

I spotted Mick's sports car parked in the driveway.

He jumped out of his vehicle. "Are you okay? I yelled for you to get in the car, but you didn't hear me."

Mick jogged toward me as I ran to Puffs. Her shallow breathing and the laceration on her back made me queasy. "Puffs. Puffs. Thank you for saving me, girl. Puffs."

I desperately shouted to Mick as he turned, then ran in the opposite direction of Puffs and me. "Mick, where are you going? Call for help—please." Tears fell from my eyes as I knelt next to Puffs and gently patted her head.

"I'm calling now." His phone pressed against his ear. When he ended the call, he jogged to a car parked behind his. After speaking with the occupants, the car sped off spewing a little dust in its wake.

Mick jogged back to me. "Val will be here any minute. She's a great vet and will take good care of your dog." He gently patted my hand.

Waiting for the vet and her crew seemed like an eternity. I found out later they arrived in less than ten minutes.

***

I rode in the back of the rescue truck with Val and Puffs. She softly petted Puffs as she called Animal Rescue concerning the bear family. As we passed down the main street, neighbors gave a thumbs up or pointed upward to let me know they were praying. News traveled fast in a small town.

Val gave me a reassuring smile as the vehicle sped to her animal hospital. "She'll get good care, Rae."

Mick followed us in his car. As the rescue crew took Puffs inside, I entered the waiting area.

Mick tapped my shoulder. "Can I get you anything? Something to drink?" He pointed toward the coffee pot on the counter.

"Thanks. I don't need anything right now."

Val opened the door to the waiting area. "We'll take care of Puffs, Rae." The door softly closed behind her.

I filled out paperwork, paced back and forth in the waiting area, then finally flopped into a chair.

Mick sat nearby and scrolled through his phone messages. "Rae, I hope all goes well. I need to run. Jamie's text said my clients have arrived." He zipped up his black leather jacket and leaned down to give me a quick hug. "Take care."

"Mick, thanks so much for helping Puffs and me."

"No problem. Be well."

I stood and watched out the window as he sped off in his car. Ah, it felt so good to get the blood circulating again from the tips of my fingers to the tips of my toes. As I approached the coffee cart, I took another glance out the window. In the distance, I spotted a clunky old truck barreling down the hilly road toward the Animal Hospital.

I picked up a paper cup and poured a cup of steaming hot coffee. As I added cream and took a careful sip, the outside door opened.

"Joe, how did you know I was here?" I turned toward him with a sincere smile on my face.

"Small town, remember?" He gave a slight nod. "How's Puffs?

"She's in there." I pointed to the doors. "Puffs tried to save me."

He patted my shoulder, straddled a nearby chair, then listened to every word I said about the incident.

After some time, Val walked through the automatic doors from the operating area and removed her head cap. She pulled up a chair and sat eye to eye with us. "The antibiotics will help. We thoroughly cleaned the wound and did the best repair job we could. She should be just fine, but we want her to stay with us a few nights. Puffs needs a lot of rest to heal." She nodded in my direction. "You need to take care of yourself, Rae." She patted my knee. "Do you have any questions?"

"Is it okay if I see her before I leave?"

"Absolutely. Come this way. Joe, you're welcome to come too if it's okay with Rae."

"Yes, would you like to come, Joe?"

He followed me into the recovery area. My sweet dog slept on a stretcher and breathed with assistance. I leaned down, kissed her nose, shed tears, and patted my injured pup gently. "Good night, girl." I turned toward Val. "Thank you so much, Val. I really appreciate all your help." I hugged Val then proceeded to the waiting area with Joe at my side.

The Animal Hospital sat on farmland and rolling hills. The perfect location for convalescing animals of every shape and size. However, I lived a distance from the locale.

Joe helped me with my coat. “Please let me give you a ride.”

“Thanks, Joe. I know there’s a football game tonight. You can’t miss it. Val said one of the techs can drive me home.”

“I don’t care about the game. I’d be glad to take you home or maybe we could grab something to eat at Molly’s.”

I patted my stomach. “You know what, I didn’t realize how hungry I was until you mentioned Molly’s. I’d love to get something to eat. I’m famished.”

He drove us in his red truck. It needed shocks and washing, but I didn’t care. I glanced at the back seat and noticed an old blanket covered in dog hair.

“Is that Buddy’s official seat?”

“You bet. You’ve seen how big he is. The crazy dog curls up to fit on the seat and loves going places with me. Sorry for the dog scent, but this is as much his truck as it is mine.”

“I know exactly what you mean. Puffs sleeps in my back seat and her blanket is hot pink. Talk about a spoiled dog.”

***

Molly’s Restaurant served three entrees on Friday nights. Almost everyone in town attended the game and afterwards invaded the restaurant. I chose the taco plate. Joe chose the hot dogs. Hamburgers—third choice.

Molly’s husband, Henry, served us. “The meal is on me, Rae. Sorry your dog got hurt. How’s she doing?” He placed our dinners in front of us, "I heard they caught the bear and cubs and transported them back to the mountains."

"Puffs is in good hands and doing fine when I left her. I'll call to check on her when I get home." I looked around the cozy restaurant. "You and Molly have a fabulous restaurant; I love it already." I smiled and hoped I didn't have lettuce or something taco-y stuck in between my two front teeth. Cheese!

"We aim to please." He smiled then approached the booth behind us.

I took another bite of my taco and a sip of my soda. "How's Buddy doing? Is he an inside dog?"

"He's doing great and yes, he's an inside dog. I called my folks and asked them to watch Buddy before I went to see you. He's having a sleepover." Joe laughed till he almost choked.

That crooked grin of his. *Captivating.*

I laughed, too, "Does your family live here?"

"Born and raised here but traveled stateside and overseas. Where are you from?"

"Military dad, so we moved all the time. It's one reason I wanted to buy this B&B. I crave roots." I crunched another bite of my taco as the shell cracked and spilled all the contents onto my plate. "Guess I've turned this into a taco salad." I chuckled as I scooped up the contents with a broken piece of crispy tortilla.

"I hope you decide to put down roots here." Joe grinned, devoured the last bite of his hot dog, and finished his shake. The chocolate mustache curling across his upper lip caused me to snicker.

"What are you laughing at?" He winked. "You don't like my 'Stache'? I've been trying to grow one for years, now I'm successful and you chuckle." He picked up his napkin and gave his lip a cleanup. "Better, Miss Rae?"

Whew. I averted my eyes from his and smiled sheepishly. Be still my heart.

The chatter at our booth ended much too quickly. This taco/hot dog dinner eased my stressful day.

***

Joe parked his truck and walked me to my door. It seemed strange that Puffs didn't greet me with her familiar bark.

I reached up and gave Joe a hug, "Thank you so much for everything. You really brightened my day." He smelled like the outdoors. *Fresh—masculine.*

"Let me know if you need anything. Rest well. Prayin' for Puffs." He stepped off my porch steps in one long stride, put his hands in his jacket pockets, and whistled as he headed to his truck.

I appreciated that word prayin'. I knew he meant it.

***

After calling, the vet told me Puffs continued to sleep. She urged me to call anytime because the staff stayed on duty twenty-four hours a day.

I slipped into a warm bubble bath and startled myself when I almost dozed. Dressed in my cozy flannel gown, I brushed my teeth, dried my hair, and slid into my downy bed. It enveloped me. No sweet pup warming my toes, but Joe's earlier hug still warmed my heart.

Good night, my sweet Puffs.

. . . but those who hope in the Lord will renew their strength.
Isaiah 40:31

Chapter Six

My squeaky screen door swung open easily as I stepped onto the front porch to water the potted geraniums. On the wicker rocker, I spotted a bag tied with a red ribbon. A homemade card dangled from the ribbon, and I peeked inside the bag to discover dog treats. The card read: *I hope these make Puffs feel better. Love, Penelope, and Papa.*

Tears streamed down my cheeks as I clinched the precious doggy gift and settled into the chair. After several nose wipes on my sleeve, I noticed five little boys tossing a football while walking on the sidewalk in front of my house.

"Is Puffs okay, Miss Rae?" They spoke in unison.

"She's doing just fine, fellas. I'm going to see her shortly."

One of the boys opened my wooden gate and approached the porch carrying a yellow mum in his pudgy hand. He handed me the flower and smiled an adorable smile. Minus his two front teeth.

"This is for you." He turned and ran through the open gate.

"Aww, thank you!" My exuberant wave didn't end until he and his friends were out of sight. I placed the mum in my jacket button hole. A wonderful way to begin my day.

***

I arrived to see my girl. Her tail wagged non-stop as she lifted her head, smiling. Yes, she smiled. Val told me I could offer her one of Penny's treats. Puffs sniffed, licked, and laid her head back down.

"Rae, don't worry about the treats. I think you'll take Puffs home on Monday. She's responding well to the antibiotics and even smiling for the staff." She chuckled and gently stroked Puffs' ear. "Oh, by the way, Joe came by to check on her at seven this morning on his way to coach the kid's football team. I thought you'd like to know." She grabbed a clipboard from the shelf. "Take your time with Puffs. I need to make my rounds." She pushed the door open and spoke over her shoulder. "By the way, Mick called about Puffs this morning." She shook her head and gave a slight grin as the door closed behind her.

I sang songs to my sweet girl and the staff filled in the words I failed to remember. She snored loudly. Time to exit.

***

I sat in the car and finished scanning phone messages. My thoughts centered on Joe. Was his team still practicing? Instead of driving home, I opted to get out of the car and jog along the narrow gravel road that led to the football fields. The crisp morning air and changing leaves put my senses into overdrive. A nearby concession stand selling coffee and sweets caught my attention. I caved and purchased the extra strong liquid and cinnamon bites. Clinging to a bag of bites in one hand and my cup in the other, I maneuvered up the bleachers to a vacant spot. Then I realized practice had ended and the junior varsity readied to annihilate the enemy.

I spotted Fran and George sitting on the bleachers a couple rows down from mine. Their daughters, Zoe and Olivia, turned around and energetically waved to me. Precious girls.

Mick sat at the end of the row. He started to stand up and approach me but couldn't navigate through the crowd. We nodded and immediately focused on the opposing team's touch down.

Out of the corner of my eye, I caught a glimpse of Joe two benches down. His red baseball cap sat precariously on his head and his muddied sweatshirt needed a good washing. *Definite proof of a great football practice.* His eyes were glued to the game on the field.

I glanced Joe's way again and noticed his focus shifted to a cute blonde sitting next to him. Her ponytail flipped easily and her purple turtleneck sweater snuggled every inch of her frame. She shouted the right encouraging words to the players on the field and gave Joe a friendly punch on his shoulder as the home team scored. He pretended to agonize over the punch and the two of them roared with laughter.

Get a grip girl. You've only known him a few days.

During the last quarter, when residents of Hope stood and applauded a touchdown, I managed to navigate down the bleachers. I tried to be discreet as I made my final descent and stepped onto the ground. It didn't work.

"Rae! Come up and join us!" Joe shouted as he saw me. "There's room next to Emily."

I motioned I needed to go and gave him a wave of thanks. He waved back. Emily did, too.

I jogged toward the Animal Hospital and felt like a fool when I slipped on the gravel road and skinned the palm of my hand. I hoped my clumsiness eluded Joe and Emily's sight.

After washing my scrape at the hospital restroom, I checked on Puffs. Her paws did their usual twitching while dreaming. *Sleep peacefully, my pup.*

***

I drove back to the house, changed clothes, then walked to Beaufort Street craving sustenance since I didn't finish the cinnamon bites at the game.

Orange and yellow mums lined the steps to the wreath-laden doors of Bitty's Buns. I couldn't wait to step inside.

The hostess approached me. "Welcome, will you be dining inside or alfresco today?"

"Alfresco, please."

"Just make yourself at home. As you probably noticed, we have heaters outside for your comfort. We'll bring your order to you." She carefully adjusted her crisp, white apron. "Now what would you like this lovely day?"

I placed my order and returned outside. The nearby heater zapped enough of the chill in the air to make me quite cozy.

Shortly after perusing my phone for emails and text messages, my meal arrived.

I closed my eyes and savored the first bite of the warm avocado and egg croissant as it melted in my mouth. When I opened my eyes, Mick stood in front of me.

"Can I join you?" He didn't wait for my answer, but placed his plate full of eggs, bacon, toast, and a side of grits on my table. He sat in the vacant seat, adjusted the collar on his brown leather coat, and made himself quite comfortable.

I gave him a sideways glance. "Guess you've invited yourself."

"Ah, I'm sure you don't mind." He cocked his head. "I was sitting inside when you ordered and decided to come out here and join you." He brushed his hair from his eyes, gave me a quick grin and took a mouthful of eggs, followed by a gulp of whatever he was drinking.

He wiped a rogue crumb from his chin. "I don't come here often. It's weird that we're here at the same time." He took another bite and waited for my response.

"Guess so." I blew on my coffee and took a sip, "Thanks for checking on Puffs this morning. Val told me you called." I took a small bite of my croissant.

"Glad your dog's doing well." He picked up his glass. "I'm getting a refill, want one?" He shoved his chair back and waited for my answer.

"No, I'm fine."

Mick went inside, returned with a filled glass, and finished his breakfast in a flash.

Our conversation ended as Joe and Emily approached. Joe nodded at Mick and me. "Looks like you're both enjoying a hearty breakfast."

I grinned, and Mick began a conversation with Joe and Emily about the game. I felt like a third wheel for a couple minutes and continued to finish my meal. The discussion paused, and Joe asked me about Puffs. Emily did the same.

"Thanks for checking on her, Joe. Val told me you went by earlier this morning."

Emily squirmed. "I did, too. Didn't Val tell you?" Her bubbly personality made her even more adorable. I hated it.

Emily got sidetracked, and I didn't tell her Val neglected to mention her visit to see Puffs. Joe and Emily sat at the little bistro table near Mick's and mine.

We chatted back and forth about the Hope Bulldogs and the upcoming Homecoming game.

Mick pulled up his jacket sleeve and checked his watch. "I need to go. Lots on the agenda today for us real estate agents, especially since the bed and breakfast is still on the market. I'll give you a call later to check on Puffs." Off he dashed.

Joe glanced my way. "Rae, can I walk you home?"

I was shocked. Emily stood next to him and didn't flinch.

"I can take myself home. You and Emily need to order your food."

"We aren't going to eat here." Joe took off his cap. He fumbled with it and shuffled it from one hand to the other. "Emily's got to get back and take care of the kids."

Okay. Where is he going with this? He never told me he was married. Why is he offering to walk me home? Scoundrel.

He noticed my awkward expression; I noticed his.

"Emily's a Nanny for the Rodriguez family. I thought I mentioned that last night but guess I didn't."

Emily grinned and waved. “I’ve gotta run. Great meeting you, Rae.” She gave Joe a quick hug and off she went.

“You too, Emily. I need to go, too.” *Alone.*

Emily walked in one direction. I walked in the other.

I looked back and could faintly hear Joe shouting something to her. I didn’t care.

***

As darkness crept in, I called to check on Puffs. Another good report. With a hot cup of cocoa topped with whipped cream, a good book, and pink flannel pajamas, I curled up in the chenille-covered chair.

Until the doorbell rang. It startled me. Puffs’ bark always alerted me to visitors. I looked through the peephole and there stood Emily shivering with Buddy at her side.

I opened the door. “Come on in. You must be freezing. It’s so good to see Buddy. You, too.”

“I thought I’d jog over and apologize for running off today and leaving you and Joe. Sorry. I wanted to call you after putting the children to bed but didn’t have your cell number. Buddy needed exercise, so I decided to head your way.” Her smile was infectious and her nose as red as a beet.

“Please come inside.”

“I’ll take a rain check. Hopefully I’ll see you tomorrow at church.” She turned and scurried towards the gate with Buddy leading the way. “Oh, by the way, my brother went back to see Puffs tonight.” She shouted over her left shoulder.

“Your brother? Who’s your brother?”

"You don't know? Joe's my big brother." She laughed and shivered at the same time. I heard Emily call out to my neighbor as she passed Doris' home. Her flashlight swung from left to right as she ran down Pecan Street.

I closed the door and flopped onto the sofa. *I feel like a fool. I feel relieved.*

Do not be anxious about anything . . .
Philippians 4:6

Chapter Seven

The drive to church curved along Vine Street and dipped into the valley below. Nestled in the center of a grove of Oak and Maple trees the white church steeple peered above the highest treetop. The colored leaves made a quilt of such an intricate design.

I thought I'd be discreet by sitting on the back pew. However, the congregation stood, shook hands, and welcomed everyone to the service. Including me.

Joe wove through the crowd and scuttled toward me. His smile immediately caught my attention.

"Come join us up front. You can meet my parents." He took my hand and guided me to the second pew.

"Dad and Mom, this is Rae. Rae, Grace and Lance Byer." The quick introduction made me a little nervous as Grace snickered, nodded, and returned to her seat. Lance, on the other hand, gave me a bear hug.

"Mr. and Mrs. Byer, it's nice to meet you." The music stopped and so did our introduction.

Grace and I sat next to each other. Tension. I tried to absorb the pastor's message to no avail. Folding my hands in my lap and making sure I didn't shift in my seat, made me uncomfortable instead of reverent.

Grace rummaged through her purse, checked her watch, and elbowed Lance when the preacher shared a comment she thought applied to her hubby. Lance responded to Grace's ribbing with a whisper in her ear.

The service ended, and Joe walked me to my car. "Would you like to join us for lunch at Fenster Haus? A group of us are going."

"I don't even know where it is, Joe. Is it in Hope?"

"It's at the curve in the lake near the library. Ride with me?"

Ascending into Joe's truck required finesse since I wore a pencil skirt and heels. I finally squirmed my way onto the torn velour seat.

"Why do they call the restaurant Fenster Haus? Doesn't it mean window house in German?"

"Sure does. It used to be a green house owned by a prominent German family. The Rodriguez family bought it six years ago, kept the name, and converted the green house into a five-star restaurant." As he finished his explanation, we arrived.

We entered the restaurant, and I noticed a large group of people at the back seated on both sides of an enormous community table.

The ambiance—extraordinary. Huge windows covered each wall, and everywhere I looked gave me a full view of the colorful leaves outside. Shelly Rodriguez guided us to our places. As we meandered around the tables, an enormous stone fireplace caught my attention. Sauntering toward the waiting diners, we passed several small white tables adorned with mums in silver cups. The wooden floor creaked with every movement. Charming.

Joe pulled out my chair as Shelly handed us our menus.

"Y'all take your time choosing. Joe, I haven't met your date."

Grace quickly interjected. "She's not Joe's date. Joe invited Rae because she visited the church." Grace made sure everyone at the table knew.

"Great meeting you, Rae. Hope you buy the B&B." Shelly smiled and mingled amongst the other guests at the table.

Emily sat to the left of me. "What do you suggest? Everything sounds delicious."

She quickly gave her suggestion. "Blackened chicken and rice pilaf. My favorite." She turned and introduced me to the young man next to her. "Rae, this is Blake Wayne, my boyfriend. He teaches Math at the university." She squeezed his hand.

Blake pushed his chair back and stood to greet me. "Emily hasn't quit talking about you buying the old bed and breakfast." He sat back down and perused the menu.

"Great to meet you, Blake."

With orders placed, the waitress brought fragrant buttered yeast rolls to the table. We all nibbled on them while waiting for our meals.

Joe's dad, Lance, stood. "I don't know if y'all have met Rae Long. She is in the process of purchasing the bed and breakfast. Hope everyone in Hope makes her feel hopeful about her endeavor." He grinned from ear to ear.

The crowd rolled their eyes at his over- one references to the word hope. Grace punched his arm gently.

Molly spoke loudly so all could hear. “Lance, you’re behind the curve. All of us know Rae. She’s bringing hope to Hope.” She grinned at Lance and winked at me.

The others at the table welcomed me and made the meal enjoyable, in spite of Grace’s cool demeanor. I refrained from telling everyone I hadn’t made my decision about buying the property.

The wait staff placed our dishes in front of each of us and the aroma of blackened chicken tickled my nostrils. Instead of rice, I opted for garlic mashed potatoes. *Divine.*

Lance Byer said the blessing and then we nestled into our chairs for a tantalizing meal.

Joe offered me a bite. “Steak is one of their specialties, Rae.”

Instead of taking a bite from his fork, I offered him mine and he placed a piece of juicy steak on the tines. The steak melted in my mouth; I savored the flavor.

“Delicious.” I gently dabbed my napkin on my lips, “I’ll have to order it next time.”

Emily looked in my direction. “Rae, I work for the family who owns this little bit of heaven. Sunday is my day off because their children spend the day with grandparents. They’re a great family.”

Emily took another bite as I continued the conversation. “I see why you love your job. If the Rodriguez family cares for you as much as they do the restaurant, you must be pampered.” We both nodded and continued eating.

“I absolutely love spending time with the children.” Emily turned toward Blake. “Blake helps tutor the kiddos when they need a little boost with math. Don't you?" She kissed his cheek.

Blake shifted in his chair. "The oldest Rodriguez child is in the fourth grade. Anyone can help with fourth grade math." He reciprocated a kiss on Emily's cheek.

They looked like an adorable couple. For a split second, I wondered how long they'd been boyfriend/girlfriend.

As members of the church finished their meals, they approached me. I knew some of them already while others introduced themselves.

"Rae, it's so good to see you again. I'm Natalie and this is my husband, Sid. I met you when you came to Bitty's Buns."

Joe interrupted, "Not only do Natalie and Sid own the bakery, they provide all the desserts for Fenster Haus. The best desserts anywhere."

Sid's belly laugh shook the floor—just a little. "Thanks for the free advertisement, Joe. How much do we owe you?" He took Natalie's hand as they waved, then walked toward the main entrance.

Joe leaned toward me. "We all try to meet once a month after our churches let out. Since Fenster Haus is the largest restaurant here, we've made this our meeting place."

I appreciated Joe. He kept me well informed.

Grace and I exchanged a minimum of words since our introduction at church. Her attention scattered, and it seemed she attempted to avoid eye contact in my direction. I must admit, I felt a little uneasy sitting across from her. Several times, Emily tried to bring her mom into our conversation; however, Mrs. Byer's participation was minimal at best.

Grace moved her chair. “Excuse me.” She got up, walked to the end of the table, and spoke to a young lady, about my age. The beautiful brunette gave Joe’s mom her undivided attention until Grace returned to the seat across from mine. “Rae, have you met Amber? She and Joe dated for a few years. Come, let me introduce you to her.”

“I’d love to meet Amber.” *What else could I say?*

“Mom, I’ll introduce her.” Joe stood and pulled my chair out for me.

Amber smiled as I walked toward her. “Hi Rae. Good to meet you.”

“Nice to meet you, too.”

Amber blotted her mouth with her napkin and placed it next to her plate. “I sure hope you buy the bed and breakfast then turn it into something fabulous. Mick’s been trying to sell the place one minute and the next he wants to keep it.”

“That’s the first I’ve heard Mick’s interested in the renovation.” I stepped a little closer to her chair. “There are a lot of things I’m taking into consideration before I take the final purchase plunge.”

Amber smiled. “In all honesty, the place appeared on line a couple years ago and I know people weren’t in line to scoff it up.” She giggled. “Best wishes, though. Heaven knows we desperately need a decent place for visitors to stay in Hope.” She folded her napkin. “Maybe we can have lunch together sometime. I’ll tell you everything about Joe, the History professor.”

Joe didn’t respond but bent down and gave her a quick hug.

"Lunch sounds good."

The second I returned to my seat, Grace cleared her throat and spoke to me. "Where are you from, Rae? I know you're not from here since I know everyone in Hope." She sipped her water. "Do you really think you'll buy the bed and breakfast? It's really a monstrosity."

Grace—bless her heart. "My grandparents left me money to purchase the property."

"How did they know the place existed?" Grace sat erect in her chair, inquisition style.

"They drove through Hope years ago and stayed at the bed and breakfast. Grandma and Grandpa cherished Hope."

"Interesting."

Joe interjected. "If Rae gets the place running, it's going to be great."

Grace nodded at Joe. "Sure." She fidgeted with her fork for a moment. "Go on. I want to hear more."

"After I graduated from college with a major in Interior Design, Grandma and Grandpa reminded me of this little piece of heaven, as they referred to the Hope Bed and Breakfast. They gave me my inheritance immediately after noticing the listing on the website." I took another sip of my water and waited for Grace to say something. She didn't. "They passed away before I visited Hope. I miss them every day."

I talked way too much. My large goblet of water sipped dry. Thankfully, a waitress noticed, refilled the cup, then put a water pitcher nearby on the table.

Grace squirmed in her seat and added, "I didn't mean to pry. I'm really sorry to hear about your grandparents." She looked up at Lance who hadn't heard a word of our conversation. "Shall we order dessert, dear?"

Lance patted his ample waistline. "I think I'll pass on dessert. Maybe another time."

She nodded in agreement.

Joe looked at his mother and cocked his head. "Rae had wonderful grandparents, didn't she, Mom?"

"Yes."

That ended our conversation. Grace didn't glance my way again.

The church lunch crowd dispersed. Joe and his dad chatted as they retrieved our coats from the entryway, and Mrs. Byer hung on every word.

I hung behind a little and felt a tap on my shoulder.

Amber spoke quietly to me, "Rae, obviously, Joe's a great catch." She flashed a beautiful smile. "We dated on and off and now I'm dating his long-time friend, Jack. Grace hasn't accepted that fact." She smiled and put on her winter hat.

Joe arrived with my coat and looked at Amber and me. "What are you two talking about?" Crooked grin. "My mother's match-making tactics with Amber and me?"

Amber gave a thumbs up.

I gave her a hug. "Thanks."

Amber pulled on her gloves and coat and left with the last of the community table entourage.

My arm caught in the sleeve of my coat as Joe assisted me. "I enjoyed the time here." I squirmed a little and eased my arm into the sleeve.

"Even after my mom grilled you with a ton of questions?"

He didn't wait for my answer as we walked to his clunky Ford, and he helped me in his truck. The unseasonably cold temperature outside left a sprinkling of ice pellets on the windshield.

Freezing. Literally.

"In answer to your question, I enjoyed meeting your folks."

"Well, I'm glad you came to lunch with us and hope we can do this again."

"Me, too."

The truck sputtered toward the church. This tiny town left very little time for conversing while driving from one location to another. I wanted more time to talk with Joe. Maybe he felt the same way. We arrived at the church much too quickly, and I jumped from Joe's truck into my car.

***

I arrived at the Animal Hospital expecting to see Puffs lying in her kennel.

Instead Val's smile greeted me. "Glad you're here, Rae. Puffs is ready to go home if you want to take her. Her vital signs look great. We don't have any reason to keep her another day like I thought in the beginning. We're all going to miss her smiling face."

"That's great news. I really appreciate everything, Val. You're the best."

"Puffs is a wonderful patient." She handed me a print out and filled prescription.

I paid my bill and within minutes, Val helped walk Puffs to the car for a quick ride home.

***

Later that evening, Puffs gobbled her meds in a smidgen of hot dog and carefully stretched out on her cushy bed. "Good night, sweet girl. I love you. Thank you, Lord, for this day."

The morning at church— a blessing. Lunch at Fenster Haus—beautiful. The ride with Joe —a beginning. Home with Puffs—the best.

Many, Lord my God, are the wonders
you have done . . .
Psalm 40:5

Chapter Eight

Morning has broken . . . The tune swept through my mind as my trusty four-legged friend and I drove to Charleston Street.

I remembered my last visit to the bed and breakfast and refused to get out of the vehicle. Although the bear and her cubs resided in the mountains now, I recoiled at the idea of taking any chances.

With the engine running, I sat in the car for almost fifteen minutes. Turning the engine off after the car warmed, starting it again when it cooled, probably used more gas than necessary. I didn't care. My mind raced as I daydreamed about the property's potential.

The sound of Puffs' breathing became peaceful and hypnotic. I nodded off until a low growl from Puffs and a soft tapping sound on my window startled me.

"Are you okay?"

I lowered my window. "Mick, you scared me to death! What are you doing here?" Puffs attempted to lift her head with as much strength as she could muster.

"I'm asking you the same thing. I have a couple who are interested in the property and they just texted me that they'd meet me at Tweeters instead of here. Their plan is to demolish most of this and start from scratch." He shielded his eyes from a beam of sunlight. "I thought you lost interest since the bear incident."

Someone else interested in the bed and breakfast? Unbelievable.

"I never said I wasn't interested in the place, Mick. Of course, the bears shocked me."

"Well, you need to think quickly about the purchase because they'll be at Tweeters in a minute," He looked at Puffs in the backseat. "Good to see her out of the hospital." Mick tipped his hat at me and proceeded to his car. He tripped on a piece of ice, almost fell, reached his door handle in time, and regrouped. I laughed to myself as he revved his car engine and skidded on a patch of ice. Macho Mick.

While burrowed into the heated seat, I made a to-do list of things to make this property somewhat livable. If I really craved this money pit, I must hire an inspector, architect, contractor, etc., etc.

I started the engine again and a thought popped into my head. *I moved here to buy the B&B. With funds, nothing stops me except my silly fears of commitment and lack of faith in this huge endeavor. I prayed about the entire thing before leaving Maryland.*

***

A huge pot of red mums propped open the door to Tweeters as Puffs and I walked inside. Brittany and Jamie chatted on their phones.

Mick motioned for me to sit in the ergonomically correct chair in front of his desk. "I didn't expect to see you this soon, Rae."

"I didn't expect to be here this soon either, Mick." I glanced down at Puffs. "I guess I should ask if you mind Puffs being inside."

"She's a celebrity in this town and is certainly welcome. Does Puffs need a drink of water?" He strolled toward the water dispenser without waiting for my response. "I have some paper bowls if needed."

"She's fine, but thanks." I cleared my throat. "I'm making an offer on the property."

"Really? I'm surprised." He swiveled slightly in his chair. "Okay, let me pull up the info on the computer. How about some water or hot chocolate while you wait?"

"No thanks."

He turned toward his computer and scrolled through the site. "Hmm...I see what you mean. The small print is pretty miniscule."

I bit my tongue. "Since the bed and breakfast isn't in great condition, or even close to great, I want an inspection before I give an offer. The inspector will probably tell me to demolish the place and start over. Maybe that's not a bad idea." I took a deep breath.

"So, you're saying you want the place if all clears with the inspector?"

I paused a moment and folded my hands on my lap. "I want the place regardless, but I'd like a fair price after the inspection. I'm offering earnest money to hold the property until inspection." I didn't waver.

"Rae, you know I have a couple coming by Tweeters shortly about the bed and breakfast."

Brittany filled her coffee mug as she eavesdropped on the conversation. "Mick, I forgot to tell you the couple interested in the B&B called while you were gone. They drove by the place last night and aren't interested."

Mick looked up from the computer. "What did they say?"

Brittany squirmed. "Do you really want to know?"

"Yes. They knew it needed repair before they saw it."

Jill attempted to whisper her response. "Their exact comment was, 'Anyone who buys this place is nuts.'"

My face felt warm again. "They're right. I'm nuts for even attempting this, but I do know I can't wait to tackle the bed and breakfast after the inspection, and you accept my offer."

Mick, Brittany, and Jamie stood speechless—for a few seconds anyway.

Mick pushed his chair away from his desk and walked to the printer. "I have all the paperwork you'll need to sign, and I know a great inspector."

"I have an inspector." I didn't mention the name Lauren Wyatt, Ph.D., Structural Engineer. Those qualifications and our lifelong friendship earned her the job. She would inspect every aspect of the property if I supplied rubber boots, gloves, and a slingshot. Lauren knew about the bed and breakfast and heard about the bear incident.

"I'll see if I can get you a better price. My parents nagged me to purchase it a couple years ago since I like to flip homes. But tackling that job—no offense."

"None taken. I'm glad my grandparents told me about it."

Mick set the deposit on his desk, we shook hands, and he walked Puffs and me to the door. "Rae, let me know when the inspector agrees to a date. This is an unconventional way to do business, but you're doing me a favor. It will get my parents off my back."

***

Puffs and I strolled to the car. We saw Penny and her Grandpa walking in the same direction a little ahead of us."

"Penny and Ike, it's so good to see you."

Penny dropped her Papa's hand and pivoted to Puffs. "Puffs, you're okay." She leaned down and gently wrapped her arms around Puffs' neck.

I smiled at Penny. "Look how happy Puffs is to see you. Her tail is twitching. She absolutely loved the doggy treats you left for her the other day. I'm so glad Puffs and I get to see you."

Penny gave me a hug and so did Ike. "It's good to see you, Rae, and it's wonderful seeing Puffs on the mend." He offered his hand for Penny to grab. "Come on Penelope, we need to get a snack before I walk you home."

Penny took her Papa's hand, waved to Puffs, and followed him inside Bitty's Buns. Ike opened the shop door and poked his head outside. "Rae, did you decide to buy the bed and breakfast?" He cupped his ear with his left hand while balancing the open door.

"You know it's in horrible shape." My answer floated into space as he nodded and stepped inside the bun shop at Penny's request. I don't know if he heard me or not. I smiled to myself. Mr. Ike Wood reminded me of my grandpa. A man of few words and much too vain to wear hearing aids. Sweet grandpa. Sweet Ike.

Someone called my name. I turned to see Molly. Her radiant face lit up like a sparkler as she walked quickly in my direction. "Dear, I know you're debating on whether or not to buy that junk heap of a place; however, please hear me out." She smoothed back her softly curled hair and clenched her pale blue sweater at the collar with the other hand. "Henry and I thought the place would always be vacant since Mick never did follow through with his parents' desires. Oops, sorry, I'm getting sidetracked. I'm offering, and I feel a little silly mentioning it, but . . ." She stopped mid-sentence.

"Molly, go ahead, please. I won't think it's silly. I promise."

She cleared her throat and stood straighter. "Henry and I thought maybe, just maybe, Molly's Restaurant might provide breakfast at the B&B. After all, it is a bed and breakfast, so you'll need food."

My smile broadened. "Your idea is fabulous, and of course, a nice wage will be offered." Puffs gave a slight tug on her leash. "We'll talk about the details at a later date if that works for you."

"Sounds great. I can't wait to tell Henry." She hugged me and turned to walk back to her restaurant. I'm sure I noticed a skip in her step.

With Puffs tucked in the back seat of the car, I called Joe and left a voicemail. "I signed the papers today and put down earnest money. Hope you're having a great day."

Tossing my phone in my purse, I turned to look at Puffs. "Let's head to Greenville. You game?" I peeked over my shoulder and handed her a doggy treat.

The Long and Winding Road played almost on cue as I maneuvered the winding roads to Greenville. The ultimate highlight of this glorious drive appeared just ahead at the next bend in the road. Burger King drive through.

The cheeseburger with extra ketchup, an order of fries, and a large chocolate milk shake—heavenly. My grandmother and I used every reason in the book to celebrate something with a milkshake. I thought about her live-life-as-if-there's-no-tomorrow attitude and that's just what I did. *I love you, Grandma. Wish we could share a shake together today.*

An old oak tree, with a few colored leaves still attached, provided a tad of shade. Reaching across the back of my seat, I gave Puffs a french fry. I know I shouldn't have. I settled back into my leather seat, popped a fry in my mouth, and looked up at the tree. I thought of all the beautiful possibilities it held in the spring. In some ways, it reminded me of the bed and breakfast's rough edges and emptiness at this season. *Someday, it might ultimately become my ray of hope.*

. . . If you have faith as small as a mustard seed . . .
Luke 17:6

Chapter Nine

My phone rang.

"Rae, congratulations. I'm really glad everything's working out." Joe took a breath.

I slurped the last of my milkshake. "I hated to call you while you're at work, but you're the first to know about the bed and breakfast. Know where I am?"

"I don't have a clue."

"Greenville. Eating fast food."

"Be careful driving home. Let's go out and celebrate your purchase."

"Let's celebrate after the inspection and the final paperwork is signed." I placed my empty cup in my food bag.

"I know you just ate lunch, but if you're hungry around 6:30 tonight, want to go to Molly's for fried chicken? Are you a fried chicken kinda gal?" He tried to muffle his laughter.

"I eat fried, boiled, baked, roasted—any kind of chicken. Molly's Restaurant have a special tonight?"

"Yep. Sound okay to you?"

"Absolutely. Six thirty is perfect."

"Mind if I pick you up?"

"Actually, why don't you drive over to my rental and let's walk to Molly's. This is my favorite time of year, and I love the fresh air. You game?"

"Sure, but I'll walk to your house and we can go from there."

"But that's out of your way. Isn't it?"

"No problem for me. See you later."

As soon as my conversation with Joe ended, my phone rang, again. "Hey, Joe? Anything new since we last talked?" Chuckle. Chuckle.

"This is Emily. Expecting a call from Joe? Sorry to disappoint you." She giggled.

"I just spoke to him, and when we hung up, the phone buzzed right away, so I naturally thought . . ."

Emily interrupted. "No worries. Want to join Blake and me for dinner at Molly's tonight for the fried chicken special? I'll check and see if Joe wants to meet us there." She finally took a breath.

"Joe already asked me. We're going at 6:30; I'm sure we'll see you and Blake there."

"Oh good. I can't wait to hear the details about the property. I heard you visited Tweeters today. Well, I'll see you tonight. Oh yeah, I don't know if Joe told you you're supposed to wear something red to celebrate Homecoming Week for the High School. Better run, I need to go to Greenville and purchase a new red sweater. I get so tired of wearing the same one year after year. This time I'm going to surprise Blake and get something new." The call ended.

Whew, if that girl has as much energy running as she does talking, she'd win a marathon without breaking a sweat.

***

I enjoyed the fall foliage on my drive back to Hope from Greenville. First task at hand: find something red in my closet. Maybe my old red coat and my threadbare corduroy slacks. Time to shop.

I left Puffs home and strolled down Beaufort Street. Pumpkin-lined steps greeted me as I stepped inside a small shop near the library.

The lady behind the counter welcomed me with a sparkly white smile. “Hi, welcome to Sweetness and Sweaters.” Her chestnut hair bounced on her shoulders as she spoke. “Are you looking for anything in particular?” She stepped in my direction. “By the way, my name is Sendy. Are you Rae?”

“It’s good to meet you, Sendy. How did you know my name?”

“Word travels fast in this small town, especially when you’re someone interested in the bed and breakfast.”

“I found out a little while ago I’m supposed to wear red tonight at dinner. I’m going to Molly’s for the fried chicken special.”

“Well, I think I have just what you need, and I’m sure Joe will like it, too.” Her eyes glistened.

Once again, warm cheeks. “Joe?”

Sendy smiled. “Small town.”

I quickly browsed through all the red items on the racks, then stepped into the dressing room. After trying on several things, I left the small boutique and headed home with a shopping bag in each hand. The idea of wearing something new tonight made me squiggle inside.

***

My red knee-length dress with the black leather belt fit me to a tee. I slipped into my black leather boots, put on quirky earrings, and brushed my hair back from my face. *Apple red lipstick — a must.*

Joe arrived and petted Puffs' head much to her tail-wagging delight. "Wow, you look great." He took my arm and helped me down the porch steps. "Your ankle must be feeling better," he whispered in my ear. "Those boots look awesome."

I caught a whiff of his aftershave—*me oh my*. "Oh, yes. Ankle is all better."

***

When we entered the restaurant, the students bellowed out a football cheer, then proceeded with another. Red streamers hung from the rotating ceiling fans.

"Joe, I love all the team spirit. I need to get some pompoms." I tried to speak over the cheering crowd to no avail.

He took my hand and guided me toward the back of the restaurant where Emily and Blake motioned to Joe and me. Blake sat at the booth as Emily scooted through the crowd and gave me a huge squeeze. "I'm really, really happy you came. By the way, I heard through the grapevine you're definitely buying the bed and breakfast." She shuffled into the booth and sat patiently with Blake as the two of them snuck in a kiss.

Emily didn't wait for my response; I don't think she really cared. She and Blake drank a milkshake and whispered sweet nothings to each other.

Joe gently whispered in my ear. "I didn't breathe a word about the bed and breakfast to her. Sometimes a small town can be detrimental to your health." He smirked.

"It's okay, Joe. I like this little 'detrimental to your health' town." I longed to tell him I liked a certain professor who lived in this miniscule place, but I didn't. Instead I placed my hand in his and gave a little squeeze.

The football team and cheerleaders led us in cheers to ready us for the big Friday night game. We savored each bite of melt in your mouth fried chicken, creamy mashed potatoes, and green beans. And, of course, macaroni and cheese pie—a staple in the south. This felt like family. I loved it. Really loved it.

Mick approached our booth. "Mind if I join you?" He pulled up a chair and added it to the end of our booth. "That red looks great on you, Rae. Glad you're here." He raked his fingers through his curls and adjusted his collar.

"Great?" Joe said under his breath as he moved closer to me. "Guess you're joining us, Mick?" Joe nibbled his last piece of chicken, took a long drink of sweet tea, then lowered his voice and leaned in my direction. "Better than great." His ears turned a light shade of red.

Mick cued our waitress. "Mandy, can you give me a tea, please?"

Mandy, Henry's oldest daughter, smiled and brought Mick a filled glass.

Mick took a gulp and awkwardly set his glass on the edge of the table, but it slipped and toppled into his lap. "Whew, that's cold." He quickly jumped out of his chair and grabbed a handful of napkins. "There's no way I'm sticking around. If you have time tomorrow, Rae, come by Tweeters. Better yet, I'll give you a call a little later." He zoomed out the restaurant door as the rest of us laughed.

After finishing their meals, the high schoolers left Molly's Restaurant. A few minutes later, the juke box music serenaded us all.

Blake smiled at Emily. "Wanna' dance?" He took her by the hand and assumed she would slide across the vinyl bench in his direction.

Emily stopped short. "Not so fast, Blakey. I'll come when I'm good and ready." She gave him a wink and pulled back.

I couldn't help myself. I smiled at the mention of Blake's new name.

Emily tapped on her temple as she pretended to contemplate if she wanted to dance with Blake, then she spoke rather abruptly. "I'm ready to dance now."

Blake didn't hesitate another second. The two of them twirled and dipped in no time at all.

Joe followed suit. "Want to dance, lovely Raey? I can't guarantee my feet won't step on yours, but I'll do my best to keep with the beat."

I giggled like a school girl and took his hand. "Sure, Joey."

We slow danced to some song I'd heard but the words and title slipped my mind. This professor cradled me gently in his arms and led me this way and that avoiding other couples and dining tables.

When the music stopped, I whispered in his ear. "I loved dancing with you." We returned to our booth and Mandy refilled our glasses with crushed ice and tea.

Joe smiled his curvy smile at me. Be still my heart.

I jokingly batted my eyelashes at him. My false eyelash stuck to my lower lid. My left eye remained shut, long enough for Emily and Blake to slip into the bench across from Joe and me, and for Joe to do a double take when he gazed into my eyes. Or should I say, eye?

Emily offered me her mirror and a clean tissue. She looked at Blake and then Joe. “Hey, fellas, I think Rae and I need to exit. Excuse us, please.”

Joe and Blake stepped aside and attempted to constrain their laughter. I’m sure when Emily and I got out of ear shot, they roared. At that thought, I began to laugh one of those uncontrollable laughs that’s contagious. Emily looked at me and started to giggle, Molly walked past us and started to laugh. We heard chuckles until we reached the restroom. I really don’t think anybody knew why they were laughing, but we did.

“Emily, thanks for your help. My fake lashes have never done that before.”

She giggled, “I’m so glad the lash surgery went well. Since we’ve accomplished that major undertaking, I must ask where you got your dress. It’s perfect.”

“I bought it today at Sweetness and Sweaters. It’s such a cute little shop and Sendy is adorable.”

“Sweetness and Sweaters? I can’t believe it. I drove to Greenville and couldn’t find a thing. I didn’t even think about Sendy’s place. Shame on me.” Emily pulled at her sweater, ran her brush through her hair, and followed me out of the bathroom.

No one mentioned the eyelash fiasco, but I did. "I'm never wearing fake eyelashes again."

We all had a good laugh and soon the subject changed to the high school football team, college football, and our favorite movies. Quite a diverse discussion. Loved it.

Several of us stayed at Molly's until it closed then went our separate ways. Except Joe and me. The chilly weather prompted us to shuffle briskly to my abode.

"Joe, let me get you some hot cocoa or at least a ride home."

"No thanks. I need the exercise." He hugged me quickly before I opened the front door, then waved as he trotted down the sidewalk toward his place.

***

My warm bath soothed every muscle, and a cup of herbal tea set the mood for a good night's sleep.

As I climbed into bed, I took one more peek at my convalescing dog. She snoozed in her comfy bed I had made for her on the floor right next to mine. My thoughts drifted easily into dreamland. *What an uplifting day.*

. . . He promises peace to His people. . .
Psalm 85:8

Chapter Ten

I got up early and decided to enjoy the fall temperatures. With hooded jacket and faux fur-lined boots warming me, I sauntered down Beaufort Street. The autumn colors displayed in most of the windows kept tempting me to enter. However, I moved on.

The day before, I'd noticed a few bikes for rent in front of Sweetness and Sweaters. It had been a long time since I'd ridden a bicycle. I swiped my card in the slot and pulled a pink bike from the rack. At first, I wobbled along trying to balance myself on the two-wheeled contraption. Then I took flight, so to speak. The cool breeze brought such a sense of freedom. I rode by a small home next to the library, passed Fenster Haus on my right, and slowly cycled through the residential homes directly across the street from the lake.

The historic homes on manicured lawns delighted my senses at every glance. I stopped in front of the largest home with white pillars and a small sign swaying in the breeze. Mayor and Mrs. Sounds.

I could see, in the distance, each of the homes on this stretch of road had small black and white signs displaying the names of the owners. Dean and Mrs. Byer's name caught my attention. *Dean and Mrs. Byer? Joe's mom and dad?* The Byers' wraparound porch, mum-lined stairway, and hanging baskets of ferns took my breath away.

I didn't dare stop in front of Grace and Lance's abode. Or should I say, Dean and Mrs. Byer's home? The gardener in the flower bed waved. She said something, so I stopped and stepped off the bike.

As she approached, I immediately recognized her voice. "Would you like a glass of wa . . ." She halted mid-sentence.

Grace Byer in gardening attire, complete with a big red floppy hat, paused, "Oh, it's you, Rae. I thought you were a tourist." She wiped a few drops of sweat from her forehead with the sleeve of her shirt and returned to her mum-laden flower bed. "Want a bottle of water?"

"I appreciate the offer. I've only been riding a little while. Thank you, though."

She kept plucking the brown flowers from her plants and never looked up again.

Is she relieved or offended? I certainly don't want to offend Joe's mom. "If it's not too much trouble, Mrs. Byer, a drink of water would be nice." I shielded the sun from my eyes and waited for her response.

Instead, she motioned for me to follow her. A wicker basket-type cooler filled with juice and water sat on the edge of her front porch, and a platter of cookies covered in plastic wrap sat on a large round wicker table. Lovely.

"Help yourself." She pulled off her hat. "Go ahead and take a few cookies, too."

"Thank you, Mrs. Byer. They look delicious."

"Emily brings the Rodriguez children here after school and they enjoy a little snack on the front porch. Today, they get out early because of Parent/Teacher conferences or some such thing." She sat on the swing at the opposite end of the porch.

An awkward pause made me realize I'd interrupted her daily routine. "Thanks so much for the water. The cookies are wonderful. I'd better scoot, or I guess I should say, ride." I smiled.

She offered no grace-filled smile in return. Instead, she got off the swing, covered the cookies with the plastic wrap, watched me exit the yard, and opened her front door. She didn't return inside until I left the area in front of her house. I realized that when I got on the bike and looked back, and saw Grace standing with hands on hips.

I didn't let that awkward moment stifle my bike riding adventure. The Tudor-style home with the colorful trees captured my attention immediately when I read the small sign by the sidewalk. Dr. and Mrs. Wood. *Oh, my goodness, it's Ike's home.*

I slowly approached the curve in the road and watched for cars. The ice cream shop, Peaches and Cream, huddled between a couple of trees. The bike veered, with my assistance, in front of the cute shop as if on auto-pilot. It fit nicely in the bike rack out front.

The pink, white, and peach colors on the exterior of the ice cream parlor lured me inside. Two young ladies behind the counter smiled and spoke in tandem. "Welcome to Peaches and Cream. Glad you're here."

"Thanks." Gazing into the glass-covered freezers at the counter, I chose two all-time favorites. "May I have a double dip waffle cone? One pralines and cream and one butter pecan, please."

"Of course." One of the girls carefully held the waffle cone. "Aren't you Rae Long?"

"Yes, I am. How did you know my name?" I pulled a few napkins from the dispenser.

"Everybody's talking about you and the bed and breakfast. You're a hot topic in Hope." She added a scoop to the cone. "Plus, everyone knows about Puffs and the bear incident. I'm Sidney, Molly and Henry's middle daughter." She pressed the second scoop of yumminess into the cone then handed it to me.

The other young lady interjected. "And I'm Natalie's daughter, Hannah. All of us are really glad you've moved here." Hannah proceeded to wipe down the counter.

"It's really great to meet you both. I love Hope and am adding your place to the top of my best things list." I took a lick of my ice cream. "It's scrumptious!"

I exited the cute shop, removed the bike from the rack, and pushed it across the street to the lake. It propped easily against a bench as I sat and enjoyed every morsel. Empty paddle boats bobbed up and down on the water as my thoughts drifted to the day the young man jumped from one of them and rescued Puffs. I met Professor Joe and Buddy that day. I'm so glad I did.

With ice cream devoured, I returned the bike to the rental rack near Sweetness and Sweaters and sauntered to Pecan Street.

Fran stood outside talking with her children. "Hi, Rae. Great seeing you the other day at the game. We heard you're buying the B&B and waiting for the inspection before you give your final bid for the property. We're so glad."

"You're right. Thanks so much for the encouragement."

We both waved goodbye and I walked a few doors down to the little house I temporarily occupied.

Puffs greeted me inside with her usual bark and whimper. I clipped her leash onto her collar and eased her down the front steps. The two of us took a short walk to the corner and as I turned around to return to 12 Pecan Street, I heard a loud bark.

"Rae, slow down. Buddy wants to visit his convalescing friend."

"Hi, Joe. Hi, Buddy." I stopped and waited for them to catch up. "What are you two doing in my neck of the woods?" I patted Buddy on the head.

"This is our usual walking route. Did we need a permission slip to enter your personal street?" He laughed out loud and leaned down to gently rub Puffs behind her ears.

"I'll cut you a little slack this time. Next time, you'll need permission." With hands on my hips and a smile on my lips, I looked at Puffs and Buddy. "Would you and Buddy mind if Puffs and I join you?"

"We'll slow down our pace to accommodate you ladies." Joe pretended to assist me by taking my elbow in his hand.

The two of us walked slowly in the direction of my home. Puffs' ears perked, and Buddy let out a billowing howl. Puffs didn't have the strength to tug at her leash; however, Buddy did. Neither Joe nor I saw why the two canines whimpered. As we walked a little farther down the sidewalk, we noticed my neighbor's black cat balanced on the picket fence just feet away from us. It shocked me how that cat kept from falling off the narrow fence slats. Her tail twitched as she teasingly meowed, hissed, and arched her back. The commotion started. Buddy's huge head slid from his collar and he plummeted toward the luring feline. Puffs mustered up her best bark. I believe she encouraged her Great Dane friend to 'get the beast.'

My neighbor pushed open her screen door. "You dogs get out of here. Don't hurt Midnight!" She picked up her broom and swung it at Buddy.

Joe grabbed Buddy and slid his collar back on his neck. "Miss Doris. Buddy's back on his leash. Please don't swing your broom again. I think Midnight ran under your front porch."

Miss Doris leaned her broom against the fence. "I'm sorry, Joe. I didn't know it was you." She opened the gate and proceeded to give Joe a huge hug. "Can I offer you and your friend a cup of hot cocoa?"

We both declined her offer, and Joe walked Doris to her front porch. "Take care, Miss Doris. Do you want me to try to get Midnight out from under your porch?"

"Heavens no. She'll scratch you to pieces. Let her stew a little and catch a couple mice, then she'll let me know she's ready to come in. Goodnight, dear." She opened her screen door. "Goodnight to you, Rae." Doris shut her door, and the porch light illuminated the area.

Joe walked me to my porch. "That cat incident offered a bit of craziness." He held open the screen door as I unlocked the inner door. "Sleep well, Rae."

"I'm calling my friend Lauren Wyatt when I get inside. She's the inspector. I'll let you know the details when I know them." I stepped inside with Puffs behind me. "Night, guys."

I felt refreshed after my bike ride this afternoon. I felt rejuvenated after the short walk with Joe. I felt renewed at the possibilities that lay ahead.

. . . for I have learned to be content whatever the circumstances.
Philippians 4:11

Chapter Eleven

I showered, put on my pjs, and called Lauren. Voicemail: "Hey Lauren. I hope you're doing alright. I put earnest money on the property; I'm buying it no matter what." I paused a second. "I need an inspector. Are you game? Give me a call when you get a chance. Love ya."

***

Slumber. Dreaming. Awakened by a strange sound outside my window. "What in the world?" Puffs' hackles went up when I cautiously opened the curtains and blinds. There she stood, the hissing cat with the arched back. *How did Midnight get in the flower box outside my second story window?*

The cat teetered precariously. *Sacrificing life and limb to rescue Midnight by letting her in my house—no way.*

Doris and I never exchanged phone numbers. I hated to do it, but I called my friend, Joe. I shuddered at the thought of bothering him. "Joe, I know it's almost 9:30; I'm sorry to call this late."

"Are you alright?"

"Yes, I'm fine. This sounds ridiculous, but do you have Miss Doris's phone number? Her cat is sitting in my upstairs window box. I can't imagine how she got up here."

"Miss Doris doesn't have a phone. I'll bet you have a tree limb close to your window. Look and see."

I glanced outside. "You're right. Midnight climbed that tree. Now I'm stuck with a howling cat."

"I'll come over with a kennel and try to lure the cat inside. Have any tuna?"

"Tuna? Will canned chicken work?"

"Yep. I'll be there in a few."

I slipped out of my pjs and into sweatpants and a sweatshirt. Capturing this relative to a mountain lion filled my every thought. I opened the can of chicken and left it on the kitchen table. Shortly afterwards, the doorbell rang, and Puffs bellowed.

"Come on in." I laughed.

Joe stood before me donning a catcher's mask, chest protector, and leather gloves. "I'm ready to tackle this mammoth feline." He tripped on my threshold and entered my miniscule entryway. Fortunately for him, my stairway post stood within grabbing distance.

Crazy guy. I noticed someone else behind him. "Emily, I can't believe you're here. Come on in."

Emily took off her cap. "Miss Doris, although a sweetheart, loves sharing every tidbit of news and believe me, if she saw Joe show up at your doorstep at this hour . . ." A loud bark from Puffs ended the conversation.

I carried the can of chicken upstairs with Emily and Joe trailing close behind. Joe immediately patted Puffs on the head. "It's okay, girl. Is there someplace you can put Puffs? When Midnight steps inside the kennel all heck is going to break loose."

I took Puffs by the collar, turned on the guest room light, and closed the door with her inside. Then I grabbed a coat, hat, and gloves from the closet.

Joe opened the small kennel and placed the can of chicken inside. Emily peered from outside the half-opened bedroom door. I stood next to Joe wearing my heavy coat, stocking cap, and old leather gardening gloves. *Ready to capture the enormous bobcat—I mean the house cat.*

My knight in shining baseball gear placed the kennel on the sill and carefully opened the window. Joe raised it a little higher, slid the kennel through the opening, and he spoke soothingly to Midnight. "Come on, sweet kitty. Come get some chicken." She cautiously crouched, whined, and moved inside the kennel. Joe immediately closed the metal door and carried the container downstairs.

I closed my bedroom window as Emily and I did a little cheer and trailed downstairs after Joe. "Go, Joe, go!"

Joe held the kennel in one hand and the catcher's mask in his other. The three of us walked to Miss Doris's home and Joe knocked on her front door. She peeked through her curtained window. "Who is it? Why are you at my house this time of night?"

Joe spoke first. "Miss Doris, it's Joe, Rae, and Emily."

"What are you three doing here? It's late."

"We found Midnight."

"I told you to let her stay outside, didn't I?" She finally opened her door and let out a gasp. "Why do you have my poor baby in a kennel? Get her out!"

This time I did the talking. "Miss Doris, Midnight was on the flower box at my second story bedroom window. She climbed a tree and got stuck in the box."

"Well, she's never done that before. Your dog lured her up there." She took the kennel from Joe and went inside her home. Soon after, her door opened, and Doris placed the kennel on the front porch. Minus Midnight. Doris turned off the porch light.

Emily wrapped her hot pink robe around her frame. She looked comical in her yellow rubber duck slippers. "I'm calling it a night. Come on, big brother, we've had enough fun for one evening." She grabbed Joe's arm and led him down the steps. "Rest well, Rae. Now I'll have something interesting to put in my diary tonight."

Joe stopped short. "Hold on, Em." He looked in my direction. "Rae, want to go out Thursday night?"

"I'd love to. Thank you both for helping me tonight." I heard yelping from upstairs while I stood on the sidewalk in front of my house. "Oh, no, I forgot about Puffs. Poor thing." I waved to Joe and Emily, turned, skipped up the steps, and closed the door.

I succumbed to sleep. No more cat meows outside my window, only Puffs' snoring at the foot of my bed. *Thank you, Lord, for this day. Thank you, Lord, for friends who arrive at a moment's notice. Good night.*

. . . for we have sworn friendship with each other in the name of the Lord . . .
1 Samuel 20:42

Chapter Twelve

Whirlwind. The perfect word to describe Lauren Wyatt. She agreed to inspect the grounds on Friday afternoon. Until she called again.

"Rae, my chances for a seat on the flight are better this evening instead of Friday morning. I'm flying standby; I need to take what I can get. I'll be in Hope tonight." Lauren took a deep breath.

"Tonight? What time?" My mind raced.

"My plane arrives at 5:00 p.m. I'll rent a car and be there around 7:00. Well, I gotta go."

My heart raced as I got things ready for Lauren's arrival. "Puffs, I want to go out with Joe tonight. I don't want to cancel." Puffs dutifully listened. "I'll give Joe a call in a little while and maybe catch him between classes." Puffs' tail wagged quickly as I kissed her head, put on my rubber gloves, and jogged upstairs to clean the bathroom. Fluffy yellow towels and pink tile reminded me of a birthday cake. Without the candles.

With gold flannel sheets on the twin bed and king-sized pillows propped against the wall as a makeshift headboard, the room oozed autumn.

A quick survey of the room triggered a note to myself: *Get fresh flowers. There must be a flower shop somewhere in Hope.*

I called Joe. Voicemail: "My friend Lauren Wyatt, the person who's doing the inspection, arrives tonight instead of Friday morning. Hate to cancel—rain check?"

Totally tuned out to anything other than dusting and vacuuming, I jumped at Puffs' bark. I turned off the vacuum and peeked through the peephole. Joe's smile. With a quick adjustment of my ponytail, I took a deep breath, and opened the door. "Hi Joe. I left a message for you a little while ago. I thought you'd be in class." I leaned against the door jam.

"I got your message. Exams are over for the day. Since your friend's coming tonight, how about lunch? Sorry for putting you on the spot."

"No worries. That's a great idea. I can be ready in a jiffy." I noticed him rubbing his hands together. "You must be freezing."

"I'll wait in the truck. Don't want any rumors to start. Miss Doris let her cat outside when I pulled into your driveway. Guess Midnight's on the prowl early." He grinned, turned around, and went back to his vehicle.

Another reason I like Joe. Respect.

Marathon transformation. Light cinnamon-colored sweater dress, knee-high boots, and hair left down. *Done.*

***

"I'm really glad you thought of lunch. This is perfect."

"How about Gill's Gourmet Grill?" Joe asked.

"I'd love to try it."

"Full confession—I eat there at least twice a week. If I call ahead, my burger is ready and waiting. But today I'm not in a rush." He grinned from ear-to-ear, gave a little cough, and pressed toward our destination.

The lunch crowd gathered outside the door for a seat at the famous burger spot in Hope. Joe put his name on the list and asked for a menu for me.

The colorful menu, in the shape of a burger, made me giggle. "Joe, I see why you like this place. I've never seen so many options in my life. Hmm—grilled pineapple burger, pizza burger, salsa burger, maybe I'll try one of those another time."

The tops of the colorful maple trees swayed as the wind took my breath away for a second. "Brrr, it's getting a little chilly." I buttoned my olive-colored flannel jacket, and Joe stepped a little closer to shield me from the breeze. I caught a slight whiff of his aftershave and almost forgot the burger discussion. However, I regained composure. "I've never tried a burger with avocado and bacon. Have you? I think I might give that a try."

"Honestly, no, and I don't think I ever will. Lettuce is the only green thing on my burger."

We both laughed as I shuffled from one foot to the other to keep warm. Joe placed his arm around my waist and did a little dance move to my shuffle step. Neither of us noticed Emily behind us until she let out a larger than life laugh and met us where we stood in line.

She rose up on tiptoe and kissed Joe on the cheek. "You're embarrassing yourself, big brother. Get a grip." She winked at me then strolled toward Blake.

Emily's comment didn't faze Joe in the least. He accentuated his dance steps a little more, then took my hand and twirled me. *Romantic.*

The hostess waved to Joe and me, and she led us inside the rustic restaurant. She motioned to the table near the window with a bird's eye view of the valley. "Hope you two enjoy your meal as much as you do dancing." She beamed and moved to another customer.

Joe and I grinned.

The waiter appeared, took our orders, and left to get our hot tea. I'd warmed up enough to remove my jacket and placed it next to me.

Joe smiled his crooked smile and offered me his hand. "Let's put some quarters in the jukebox. Come help me choose songs."

Music selected. A fast-paced country song blared loudly as a small group formed to line dance. A few of the guys moved tables aside. Emily, Blake, and several others formed the first line. Full dance floor. Shuffling, kicking, and turning in tandem to the familiar music, brought a trickle of perspiration from my forehead to the tip of my nose.

Joe just happened to notice, handed me his handkerchief, and pretended to tip his hat. "Hey beautiful lady, sure glad you decided to dance with me today." Standing next to me, he awkwardly bent down between dance steps, and placed his hand on my shoulder. His one misstep halted the entire line.

Several of the guys and gals lightly punched Joe's arm as we all left the dance floor. Emily glared at him. "Big brother, you have two left feet. Those lines flowed like a river until you decided to be a Casanova. Even Blake knew to keep his hands to himself." With that she gave a little kick in Joe's direction, blew him a kiss, and guided Blake to their booth.

Joe stood in the middle of the empty dance floor. "Everyone, I apologize for tripping y'all up with my professional dance moves." He bowed amidst the boos from onlookers.

The crowd clapped and dove into their meals. *No apology needed.*

The burger and fries smelled heavenly. Extra ketchup oozed from Joe's juicy burger as he tackled an enormous bite.

I tried to hold back a chuckle, but to no avail. "There's a glob of ketchup on your cheek." I broke into a silly laugh.

To make it even funnier, Joe pretended to wipe his cheek with the cuff of his green shirt sleeve.

"How did you get it on your cheek anyway?"

"I have no idea. Miss Rae, will you please assist me?" He leaned toward me, handed me his napkin, and I carefully wiped away the ketchup. *My goodness, handsome man.*

The burger ala avocado slice, chipotle sauce, and extra pickles melted in my mouth. The seasoned fries—delicious.

Although Gill's was packed to the gills, it afforded us a little privacy, until Mick walked over to our booth.

"Hi. Guess we dine in all the best places."

Joe nodded.

I smiled at Mick. "Hi, Mick, care to join us?" *Care to join us? What am I thinking? This guy who deceived me with online fancy-smancy pictures of the B&B in its prime?*

Joe looked confused when Mick slid into the booth next to me. *A little too next to me, I might add.*

My cheeks flushed as I attempted an innocent look at Joe. His face looked as red as mine felt.

Mick gave a toothy grin and spoke directly to me. “Sorry I didn’t call you. Did you get hold of your inspector?”

“Lauren arrives tonight, so the inspection can get underway. Is there a certain time we can schedule for Friday?”

He drew his fingers through his thick dark hair again. “Earlier the better. Eight thirty?”

My mind wandered to a funny visual of Mick running his fingers through his bald scalp years from now. *His thick hair obsession is so evident.*

“That works for me.”

“Want to meet me for breakfast at Molly’s. My treat?”

“I’ll pass on breakfast but will meet you at Tweeters.”

I glanced at Joe and noticed his jaw clenched a little.

Mick slid out of the booth. “Well, better get going. Look forward to seeing you and meeting your inspector.” He stepped a couple paces to the booth behind us where the other agents, Brittany and Jamie sat.

Joe spoke quietly. “Do you need any help tomorrow?”

“Don’t you have classes?”

“Nope. Exams are over for the week.”

“Please come.”

“You can count on it. Should I bring my boxing gloves in case Mr. Mick needs to be put in his place?” He punched at the air like a true pro.

"Hmm—boxing gloves, Professor Joe?" I chuckled. I didn't say it to him, but I really pictured him in full knight regale riding with sword in hand on a white steed to save me. *His maiden in distress.*

Joe gave a couple rapid punches at the air, again, like a boxer. The waiter approached. "Can I get you dessert?" He shuffled his feet back and forth like a boxer in the ring with Joe. He looked ridiculous, too.

I shook my head in disbelief at the two of them. "No, thank you. I'm stuffed." I squelched my desire to jokingly punch at the waiter and Joe. *Tempting, though.*

"I'll pass on the dessert, Lou. Great burger as usual." Joe patted his full stomach as Lou stepped away from the table and approached the booth with Mick, Brittany, and Jamie.

Within seconds, Lou returned to us. "Joe, Mick said to put your meal on his tab."

"Please tell him no thanks. Better yet, I'll tell him." Joe slid out of the booth, handed Lou a hefty tip and payment for our meal. "Sorry, Rae, are you ready to leave?"

"Absolutely." I grabbed my coat and stood next to him.

By this time, Mick stood near his booth. "Joe, you missed a free meal."

"Hey, Mick, next time I'll order something bigger, might even include an appetizer and dessert, then you pay."

The two fellas shook hands and let loose in tandem.

***

Joe and I left Gill's. His Ford sputtered along the winding road toward my rental. He slowed down before getting to Pecan Street. "Rae, if you'd like, we can get some dessert. There's an ice cream shop just past the turn off to Charleston Street."

I just told the waiter at Gill's I was stuffed, but a few extra minutes with Joe—heavenly. "Ice cream sounds great. Do you mind if we see the property since we're driving past Charleston Street? Might sound silly, but . . ."

"Doesn't sound silly to me at all." Joe smiled.

The truck tires crunched broken branches on the driveway and stopped in front of the dilapidated B&B.

"Joe, I know the big building looks awful, but I visualize it completed. Two stories, large front porch with several white rockers, porch swing, white shingles, and butter yellow shutters. I must sound crazy, but I'm so excited about buying this place."

He took my hand, kissed it. "Don't apologize. When I look at the building, all I see is a mess. You bring it all to life, Rae."

"Thanks. I appreciate you saying that. I just needed an extra little glimpse of the property and am more than ready for ice cream now."

With one hand on the wheel and the other on the back of the bench seat, Joe inched the truck out of "my" driveway and onto Beaufort Street.

***

Sidney smiled as we walked into Peaches and Cream. "Rae, it's good to see you again."

"It's good to see you, too," I said. "This place could be habit forming."

Joe looked bewildered. "I didn't know you'd been here before."

"Yep. It's only a hop, skip, and a jump from my soon-to-be locale." I turned to Sidney. "I'll have the usual." I laughed as she got a fresh waffle cone and did the double scoop order.

Joe chuckled. "So, you have a usual already? It took me at least two visits for Sidney to remember mine." He smiled and gave me a little wink.

Sidney mounded three scoops of chocolate ice cream into his cone and added a cherry on top.

Joe folded his arms across his chest. "Hey, Sidney, maybe I want something different."

"You've gotten the same thing for as long as I remember. Here you go." She carefully handed him his dessert. "Pay up big spender."

***

Before we arrived at my house, it dawned on me I needed flowers for Lauren's room. It might not have seemed important to some, but it did to me. "Joe, is there a flower shop around here?"

"Sure is, right near the sweater shop. I'm not sure of the name since I . . ." He stopped mid-sentence.

"Mind if we stop there before you take me home? I'm buying flowers for Lauren."

Joe parked in front of the bicycle rack where I'd rented the bike.

"I still don't see the flower shop."

"There it is." He pointed to a tiny building tucked almost directly behind Sweetness and Sweaters. The yellow flower shop glistened with white twinkle lights. The black iron sign in front of the shop swung on its hinges. Buds and Blooms.

"If you don't mind, I'll wait in the truck. The shop is hardly big enough to hold one customer."

As I pushed the French door open, a wind chime fluttered a welcoming tune. "Rae, it's good to see you again."

"Fran, I didn't know you worked here." I grinned from ear to ear. "I thought you were a stay-at-home mom."

"I am, but I work three days a week when the kiddos are in school. I absolutely love this little flower shop." She came from behind the counter. "Yesterday, my family and I talked about you opening the bed and breakfast. When George and I mentioned your name, little Olivia did a little curtsy and stated as a matter of fact, 'Miss Rae is a curtsy kind of lady.'"

I slowly brushed away a wisp of hair from my forehead. "Precious Olivia. Why did she say that?"

"Olivia told us you're like a princess."

"A princess? I'm anything but . . ."

Fran placed her hands gently on my shoulders and looked directly into my eyes. "That's exactly why you're a curtsy kind of girl, because you don't even realize what a princess you are to us all. Little Olivia just knew how to put actions to her words." Fran removed her hands gently from my shoulders. "When you see Olivia, please don't tell her I told you this, because I'm sure she'll want to surprise you with a curtsy all her own."

I felt tears welling in my eyes and reached into my purse for a tissue. Fran beat me to the punch as she grabbed one from the box on the counter and handed it to me. "Now, Rae, how can I help you?"

I regained my composure. Glancing around the shop my eyes darted from one colorful bucket filled with flowers to the next. “I need a cheery bouquet for my friend, Lauren. She’s arriving in town this evening.” I slowly did a 360-degree turn in the middle of the shop.

Fran arranged an assortment of flowers and intermingled baby’s breath for just the right touch. “Rae, I hope Lauren enjoys these.”

“She will. I guarantee I’ll be back.”

When I left the tiny shop and opened Joe’s truck door, I apologized profusely for making him wait. He reassured me he didn’t mind. *Ahh—Professor Joe, you are quite the gentleman.*

Joe’s truck chugged down the brick road and turned onto my street. In the distance, I spotted a blue car idling in my driveway. “Is that Lauren already? I’ll bet she got an earlier flight.”

Joe slowed his truck to a crawl. “Want to go out again after Lauren leaves?”

“I’d love to. I’m hoping the inspection is done so we can go to the Homecoming game Friday night.”

“Me, too.”

Joe parked in front of the house, and I jumped out.

Lauren stood next to the rental car. “Rae. I’ve been parked here for an hour; I’m freezing to death. Where have you been?” Her raven black hair was tucked loosely in her fur cap.

Her snarky attitude took me off guard. “You’re early. Why didn’t you call me?”

"I did. You must have been preoccupied with him." She pointed at Joe then took her hat off and let her hair flow. Lauren leaned down, gave me a quick hug, and extended her hand to Joe. She shook his hand vigorously as only a confident woman could do.

"So, this is Joe, the professor. It's so good to meet you."

"Good to meet you."

I watched as he spoke to Lauren. I trembled a little inside. For the first time in my life, I felt a twinge of jealousy toward her. She looked like a confident model. I didn't.

"Lauren these are for you." I handed her the bouquet as I unlocked the front door. "There's a vase in your room."

Puffs barked loudly and then her tail wagged easily when I pushed open the door. I turned to Joe. "I had a great time."

Lauren fidgeted. "Sorry to interrupt you two, but where is the restroom, Rae?"

I motioned toward the upstairs and she made a beeline for the steps.

Joe smiled easily. "Me too. I'd better get going." He turned and took the steps two at a time.

I entered the house and locked the front door. Opening the front window blinds, I noticed Joe turn and give a slight wave. I reciprocated and watched as he left in his clunky old truck. *I like that clunky old truck. I really like Professor Joe.*

The precepts of the Lord are right,
giving joy to the heart.
Psalm 19:8

Chapter Thirteen

Inspection day. Morning sunlight barely peeked through my bedroom window. I quickly went downstairs and returned to my room with a mug of freshly brewed coffee cradled in my hands. *Note to self: Someday, have a coffee nook in my bedroom.* Thoughts of the property raced through my mind. *Take a deep breath, girl. No matter the inspection results, you know you're buying it.*

I set my cup on the nightstand and dressed in layers. Grandpa's old sweater offered just the right amount of warmth. *I love you, Grandpa.*

The thought of the day before me made me almost hop down the stairs. I sat on the bench next to the front door and wiggled my toes, arched my foot, and struggled to pull on my gardening boots.

"Lauren, are you about ready up there?"

"Almost. Mind getting me a cup of coffee, please?"

"I'll bring it upstairs to you."

I poured her a cup, climbed the stairs, and tapped lightly on her door.

"Come on in."

Lauren peered over her shoulder to get a back view of herself in the mirror. "These doggone hips. Can't seem to lose the inches." Her jeans molded every curve, and her knee-high boots made her appear even taller than her five feet, ten inches. "Thanks for the coffee; it's just what I need." She sipped the java slowly. "From what you've told me and the pictures you've sent, Mick better be ready for a price reduction." Her head tilted as she slid her brush through her raven-colored hair. Lipstick. Flawless. "By the way, will Joe be at the inspection?"

"I'm not sure. He said he'd try. Why?" I attempted to roll up the sleeves on my sweater.

Lauren slipped into her coveralls. Her tool belt cinched at her waist. No way anyone might mistake her for anything but a young woman. With or without the belt. Another lipstick inspection, brush through her hair, and Lauren was the picture of perfection.

She turned toward me, gave a wink, and reached for the stair rail. "Joe's cute. Didn't want to say anything, but . . ." Lauren hurried downstairs with me trailing behind. She never finished her sentence as the two of us scurried out the door and into the car.

Maybe I should have chosen Mick's inspector instead of Lauren. I hate this jealous feeling. I don't like it one little bit.

***

The kudzu on the phone wires glittered with morning dew as my car crept down the driveway to the bed and breakfast. I kept expecting some comment from Lauren as we approached the cottages and main building, but she stayed silent until I parked.

I heard her mumble. "You've got to be kidding me."

No response from me.

Mick's car sat idling in front of the B&B. He exited his vehicle. "Good morning, Rae."

"Good morning." I plunged my hands into the sweater pockets.

Mick jogged to the passenger side to open Lauren's door. He cleared his throat and his smile practically covered his face as he helped her out. "My name's Mick Treavor. Great meeting you, Lauren." He stepped aside as she gracefully exited the vehicle. "I'm here to help."

"Thanks, Mick." She looked at him and returned the grin as she peered up at the main building. "I thought I'd have to climb up on the roof and check it out, but there's no way I'm even touching it. Let's get started." She put on her hard hat, grabbed her iPad, and motioned for us to follow. "By the way, Mick, I heard about your deceptive website."

Mick grinned sheepishly. "Small print."

Lauren snickered as she entered the front door to the main building. She gingerly stepped inside and attempted to open the pocket doors to the left of the entryway. Attempted was the operative word; they stuck closed. "Mick, take a picture of the doors and document they are in great shape but must be placed on track. Too many years of neglect." She entered the room to the right of the front door and tried to close the pocket doors leading into that room; they were stuck inside the wall. "Add this to the list."

She pointed to the staircase in the foyer. "There's no way I'm climbing those."

We followed her through the main floor until she pushed open the back door and it fell off its hinges into an overgrown yard. I thought I heard her mumble something not worth repeating.

Lauren continued. "The stairs back here off the kitchen look pretty stable. Did you know you have two sets of steps?" She didn't wait for my answer. "Years ago, servants probably used these since they're right off the kitchen." She began the ascent.

I chuckled to myself as Mick passed Lauren on the steps and started to assist her.

"No thanks, Mick, I'm perfectly capable. I don't need any physical help; however, I do need documentation and photos." With that, she carefully climbed the stairway. "Rae, please stay down there. I don't know what I'll encounter up here. I'll shout if I need anything."

I followed directions until I heard Lauren ask Mick a question. "Did you give Rae that info? She hasn't said a word to me."

At the mention of my name, I darted up the stairs. "What info are you talking about?" With hands on hips and tapping toe, I waited impatiently.

Mick shifted his gaze to me. "I didn't feel it needed to be listed online as a historical place. I thought anybody interested would do their own investigating. You didn't know?"

I gasped. "You're kidding right? I knew no such thing." Lines furrowed between my brows. "Lauren, what do you suggest?"

"Please come with me, Rae. Excuse us, Mick." She motioned for me to enter one of the rooms with her and shut the door. "Rae, you really want the place, right?"

"Sure." I almost quibbled.

"I've dealt with historical societies. Some members are close minded and demanding. On the other hand, I believe this society will be thankful someone is cleaning up the area. I say, take the plunge."

"You're right. I'll dive in. Good thing I can swim."

We exited the room and found Mick.

He didn't skip a beat. "The extra paperwork is ready to sign since I've been anticipating a buyer for about two years." He grimaced and raked his curls.

Lauren sidestepped in his direction. "Of course, it's ready to sign; however, Rae hasn't told you what she'll pay. So, that isn't on the contract. Make sure you have everything and everyone at the closing. Don't you have it scheduled for tomorrow?" She glanced at him and then at me.

I interjected. "Yes, tomorrow, but if you think I should wait, I'll wait."

Lauren straightened her tool belt and brushed a stray hair from her forehead. "Tomorrow's fine."

Lauren moved from space to space, with Mick at her side—close by her side—practically glued to her side. I noticed she didn't push Mick away. It looked like she enjoyed every ounce of attention he supplied.

As they explored each room, I browsed alone. I peered through the bay window in the largest bedroom and noticed the backyard view. Wow! It took my breath away as I saw the vast span of trees. This vision allowed my decorator's eyes to flit from yard to indoor space and mentally create my heart's desire.

Lauren summoned me. “How many rooms are you reserving up here or are you making this into a family suite?” She paused on the top step. Mick was right beside her. As a matter of fact, I laughed when I noticed the two of them trying to fit on the same step and bumping into each other. *Accidentally? I don’t think so.*

“Actually, I’m thinking the entire upstairs will be my domain.”

Mick sneered. “You’re kidding me. That’s prime footage for a family visiting Hope. Why don’t you build another home on the property or convert a couple of your cottages for yourself?”

I cringed inside. “Mick, it’s really none of your business what I do.” I slipped a bottled water from my sweater pocket and took a quick sip. *Stress—dry mouth.* “Maybe you’ll want to reserve a cottage someday, if there’s one available.” *Don’t count on it.*

Lauren tapped him on the shoulder. “If I were you, I’d keep my opinions to myself.”

We traipsed outside, and Lauren motioned toward the first cottage. “Okay, Rae, I’ve seen all I need of the main building. Cottages are next.”

“I’m right behind you.”

Lauren’s entourage followed. Mick readjusted his tool belt and removed his hard hat. Lauren did the same. I, on the other hand, placed my sweater on the hood of my car.

Lauren surveyed the first cottage then pivoted in my direction. “Rae, there’s very little that needs to be done. Are you keeping the wood burning fireplaces or converting them to gas or electric?”

I heard the putter of Joe's truck approaching, and Lauren's question zoomed in and out of my mind. My boots squeaked as I spun around when he beeped the horn. I could see Joe laugh at me; *oh—that oh-so-yummy smile peering out from under the brim of his baseball cap.*

As he parked the truck and jumped out, I slowly wadded up a piece of paper I had in my pants' pocket and threw it at him. The wind swept it up and landed the paper ball in front of Joe. A paper ball war ensued.

He leaned inside his truck, withdrew a newspaper, and quickly shaped pages into balls. "You're in trouble. Watch out! You didn't know I'm the champion paper wad thrower of Hope County." He lobbed the paper at me from the back end of his truck. "I'm gonna get you now."

Joe caught me in a baseball pickle situation, only there wasn't anyone on the other end of the pickle. He darted toward me, I fell, he leaned down, I grabbed his hand, and he easily tumbled next to me.

"I got you, Professor Joe Byer. Champion paper wad thrower of Hope County, meet the champion paper ball thrower of the world!" I barely caught my breath.

The two of us forgot all about Mick and Lauren until they laughed loudly.

Stunned, I heard Lauren's blatant comment. "It's about time you made a move, Rae. You're the slowest of the slow."

Lauren sauntered toward me and paused with her right hip cocked. "I've seen you and Joe together only twice, but you two have—oh, I can't think of the word—chemistry. He's cute, you're cute, and you're both a little wacky. Perfect match."

A giggle escaped me, and I felt the jealousy butterflies in my stomach softly flitter away. Lauren weaved between Joe and me and approached Mick. We followed Mick and Lauren to the last cottage and Joe took my hand in his. I wanted this moment to last forever; however, Lauren let out a blood curdling scream and zoomed out of the farthest cottage from the main building. Inside a family of five snarled—five raccoons that is. They made a clicking sound and flew out the door behind her. Mick grabbed Lauren and flung her in the opposite direction of the varmints, right into a nearby briar bush. The raccoons scurried up a tree, and Lauren's screeches and screams bounced off each branch. "Mick, get me out of here. This bush is killing me."

As Mick offered her a helping hand, he slipped on the oh-so-red clay and toppled beside Lauren. Joe and I offered the two of them a stick to hold so we could pull them out. Then we laughed like crazy.

Lauren's sticker-burr gloves and hair looked hideous; however, she appeared unscathed. On the other hand, sticker burrs stuck to Mick's jacket, his hands, and dappled throughout his curls.

Lauren picked the briars out of her hair and threw them at Mick. "Thanks for saving me from those ferocious beasts. But, no thanks for throwing me into a briar patch."

He followed her, apologizing the entire way and didn't know her well enough to realize she was luring him into her trap. I'd only seen her do that once, years ago, when she'd fallen head over heels for her high school sweetheart. Now, this déjà vu moment caught me by surprise. *Has she already fallen for Realtor Mick?*

I smiled at Joe. "Let's leave the two of them to briar pick. I want to show you the main building." We walked in tandem toward my someday home as Mick and Lauren laughed and flirted easily with each other. They never noticed Joe and I had gone inside.

I called Lauren's phone. "Joe and I are in the main building, in case you're wondering." I believe she couldn't care less.

"No problem, Rae. Mick is taking me to Greenville for dinner and a movie tonight. Do you mind?" Pause.

"Oh, I guess Mick isn't going to the game?" I smiled at the phone. "If you decide to go to my house to change before the date, the door's unlocked and Puffs will let you in since she knows you. Mick, on the other hand, better not enter since he probably smells like raccoons." Joe and I laughed loudly.

"Okay, miss smarty pants, Mick heard what you said. He's going back to Tweeters to change. Don't wait up; we're taking in a late movie." The phone clicked.

We stepped carefully up the back stairs to the second floor. "Joe, did you know the B&B is a historical landmark? I just found out."

"Of course, I knew. I thought you knew before you moved here." He stopped immediately.

My frazzled side emerged. "No, I didn't know until Mick told me in front of Lauren. I feel like such a fool."

"You shouldn't. If you don't mind adhering to the rules for historical buildings, all should go well."

"Lauren said the same thing." *Am I really that naïve?*

"I think we all did you a disservice. Even my mom and dad thought you knew the history. From what I understand, there used to be a little metal sign in front of the big building."

"What did the sign say?"

"The University of South Carolina at Hope."

"What? I'm buying a university?"

"Rae, it was the university before our time and later became a B&B." He pulled his phone from his pocket. "I assumed your grandparents knew."

"They never mentioned it to me."

Joe searched the Internet on his phone and found information about the historical university and Historical Society rules. We skimmed the website for a few minutes.

"Thanks, Joe. I feel better already. I'll check into it some more tonight. I don't want to look like an idiot tomorrow at closing."

"You won't. I'll be there if you'd like."

"Absolutely." I led Joe throughout the top floor, sharing my dreams with him. I got a catch in my throat when I thought about someday having a family to share the top floor. I didn't mention that to Joe; I didn't want to scare off this hunk of a man standing next to me, who patiently listened to my every word. My phone alarm buzzed indicating time to get ready for the game.

Joe snickered, "I can't believe you set an alarm."

"I knew I'd forget the time today. Especially this time with you." I teasingly tossed my last crunched paper at him.

Joe drove me to my rental then headed for his home. I ran up the front steps, and almost fell inside when the front door quickly opened. "Lauren, I thought you'd already left."

"I waited for you because I want you to know I'm miffed at Mick for duping you with the small print on the website. However, I do think it's to your advantage because you might not have come here if you'd read the miniscule disclaimer."

At that moment, Mick's car pulled into my driveway, and Lauren flew out the door.

Wow, I'd never thought of it that way. I mulled over Lauren's words as I showered then dried my hair, put it in a ponytail, and dressed in red flannel pants. Not pajama bottoms. I made sure Puffs was taken care of before I put my white faux fur hoodie over my red cable-knit sweater. I grabbed ear muffs, put on my furry boots, and sat on the porch to wait for the professor.

***

The bleachers overflowed on both the home team and visitor's sides. I never expected that many people at a football game in a tiny town. Many of the girls wore mum corsages and previous homecoming kings and queens were asked to stand on the field. Joe excused himself upon hearing his and Amber's names announced over the loudspeakers. The two of them jogged to the field as I sat in the bleachers and noticed Amber's beauty. The sniggle in my belly returned. *Jealousy. I detest that feeling. I wonder if Amber's boyfriend, Jack, feels the same way.*

Joe returned to sit by my side, and Amber rushed back to Jack. When Joe took my hand in his, the sniggle subsided.

The highlight of the evening wasn't the winning touchdown the Bulldogs managed to achieve in the last quarter. Holding hands with Joe, sharing a box of popcorn, and wearing his letter jacket trumped it all. I felt like a high schooler sharing this evening with my beau. I know he wasn't really my beau, but a girl could dream, couldn't she?

The evening ended too quickly. Joe kissed my cheek as we stood on my front porch. I returned his letter jacket. Reluctantly, I might add. Such a great day filled with wonder and surprise.

With front door unlocked so Lauren could come inside after her date, I inched under my covers, careful not to nudge Puffs since she claimed the foot of my bed.

Thank you, Lord, for this moment in time. I want to capture it forever in my mind.

Trust in the Lord with all your heart and lean not on your own understanding.
Proverbs 3:5

Chapter Fourteen

After closing, Mick shook my hand and gave me the keys to the bed and breakfast. "Congratulations, Rae. Everyone in town's glad I've sold the place to someone who'll cherish it." I detected a choke in Mick's voice.

"Thanks. I'll do everything I can to make Hope proud."

Joe gave me a gentle hug. "You did it, Rae. Leap of faith."

Lauren beamed and shook my hand in jest. "Nice doing business with you, Ms. Long, owner of the world-renowned bed and breakfast in Hope, South Carolina." She hugged me tightly.

***

Lauren flew to Maryland that afternoon. I wanted her to stay longer, but obligations called her home.

I entered my temporary home on Pecan Street as Joe walked to the football field to coach the young team. My phone buzzed after I tossed the guest room bedding down the steps to be washed.

Lauren. "Rae, I'm at my condo already. I had a terrific time seeing you, meeting Joe, and spending time with Mick. I forgot to tell you something. Has Mick called you?"

"No. Why?"

"When Mick and I went to lunch after the closing, he told me to let you know to expect a visit."

"From who?"

"The Historical Society. I can't remember what the specifics were, but he said they'd be at your home sometime today."

"He should have told me." I hesitated for a moment. "Thanks again for doing the inspection, Lauren, and giving me the message."

She kept talking. "I think I should thank you, Rae. I might have met the man of my dreams. Mick's black hair and deep blue eyes. What more could a girl ask for?" She chuckled and started talking again. "He invited me to come for a visit at Thanksgiving."

Puffs barked loudly. "Lauren, someone's at my door; Puffs is barking non-stop. I'm sure you hear her." I attempted to quiet my canine by patting her head. "Uh, Lauren, I need to go. Glad you and Mick had a great time."

I flew upstairs, looked out my bedroom window and saw cars lined in front of my home.

A red car, silver car, pink car, gold car, and cream-colored car lined the curb.

I pushed my glasses up on my nose and straightened my pony tail. As I descended the stairs, my sock feet slipped, and I fell backward just missing the edge of the step. *Note to self: buy non-skid slippers.*

Peeking out the peephole, my mouth went completely dry when I noticed Grace.

Lord, my house is a wreck, smelly dog bed in the living room, and laundry sorted on the kitchen floor. What will Grace think?

I smoothed back my hair and slowly opened the front door. “Hi ladies.” I froze.

“Oh, goodness, guess we should have called first, but Mick told me he’d give you a call, a heads up, as he referred to it.” Grace’s smile seemed timid at best. “He called you, didn’t he?”

“Come in, ladies.” I didn’t respond to her question. “Please forgive the mess.” I shoved Puffs’ bed out of the sitting area.

They sat on the doggy-haired sofa and worn chairs. As each of them settled in, introductions ensued. I found that Grace carried the title, President of the Historical Society. Lottie was the Secretary, Victoria, the Parliamentarian, Anna, the Second Vice, and Opal, the actual Historian.

Grace sat straight as an arrow and cleared her throat. “I have all of the paint colors approved for your business.”

Silly me, I never thought of it as a business.

“Lottie’s book shows some of the floor plans for the University.” Grace pushed aside Puffs’ doggy bone with her gloved hand, before she placed the paint colors and leather-bound book on my coffee table.

Lottie opened the photo book. “Here, let me show you the pictures and maybe one of you other girls can give Rae the history.”

Grace removed her gloves and pointed to each picture. “The main building at your bed and breakfast was the original University of South Carolina at Hope. The eight cottages were built later and used for classrooms and dorms." She flipped from page to page and cleared her throat with each page turn. "Rae, may I have a glass of water or something?"

Lord, please help me remember my manners and bite my tongue in the process.

"Anyone else want something to drink?" *Hostess mode.*

"That would be wonderful, dear." The other four women responded.

With the kitchen only a few steps away, I heard their every whisper.

"She seems so young."

"My goodness, I wonder if she'll even be able to run the place if she didn't do her homework before moving here."

I felt my face warm with every comment. Before I uttered a word, my phone rang. Tweeters Realty number showed up.

I immediately recognized Jamie's voice. "Rae, Mick just sent me a text saying the Historical Society ladies are supposed to visit you sometime today." Momentary silence. "Did he send you the same message?"

I whispered distinctly. "No, he didn't. Thank you for letting me know. They're here already, Jamie. Please tell Mick to block out some time for me this afternoon."

"Rae, just call his cell phone because he's gone for the day. Is there anything else I can do for you?"

"I'll call him a little later." I was livid at Mick. "You've already helped me, Jamie."

While sorting through the paint samples and refilling the ladies' cups, I eased into the moment.

Lottie patted my hand. "Rae, we'll leave you all the samples and the plans, so you can make a decision. Naturally, we don't need to know your choices today, since you haven't even started the rebuild process." Lottie's small frame scurried to the front door. "Ladies, I need to get back to the library. Story hour begins at two."

The rest of the women followed suit, put on their gloves, and buttoned up their coats. They left as quickly as they'd arrived.

I never divulged my plans to turn the upstairs into my own apartment. As each vehicle pulled from the curb, I gave an obligatory wave and turned to go back inside–until I saw Emily walking Buddy. She waved to me.

She trotted Buddy down the sidewalk toward my rental. "Wasn't that my mom's car?"

Emily's out of breath words sputtered at first, then I easily understood when she repeated herself. She and Buddy walked up my front steps.

"Come inside. Puffs will be thrilled to see Buddy. And yes, that was your mom." I quietly sighed as my thoughts raced back to calling Mick, and now Emily's visit put the call on hold. "Want something to drink or eat? I need to get some groceries, but I do have an apple if you want one? Come on into the kitchen."

"Sure." She plucked the apple from the glass bowl on my table and took a big bite. "By any chance was my mom here with her hysterical society group? I heard her talking to a couple of the ladies a few days ago about the main building being the old university. Funny thing is, I didn't know."

I laughed as I reflected on the hysterical society reference. "That's funny, Emily. I didn't say it out loud to the ladies, but it's what I wanted to call them."

"Don't panic about their suggestions, Rae. They, including my mom, love the prestige that goes with being the women in the know." She tossed the apple core in the trash can and grabbed Buddy's leash. "Since I've devoured your last shriveled apple, do you want to meet Blake, Joe, and me for dinner?" She giggled as she clasped the leash onto Buddy. "Besides, I know Joe would be thrilled if you joined us at his place."

His place? I'd never been inside his home. "I can't go to Joe's house. He didn't invite me, and I'd feel weird about just showing up for dinner."

"Well the invite stands. He'd love for you to come. I think he's just a little shy about asking." She opened the front door and exited with Buddy at her side. "Hope to see you tonight at six." Buddy pulled at the leash and Emily followed down the front steps.

Within minutes my cell buzzed. Joe's name and number appeared.

"Hi, Joe."

"Rae, Emily called and said she invited you for dinner. I'm glad she did. I hate to admit it, but I didn't have the guts to ask you to my place. You'll come, won't you?"

My heart did that flutter thing and took my breath away. "Are you sure?" I waited for his answer.

"Of course, I'm sure. Sometimes my sister can be a pain, but this time I've got to give her kudos. She helped her big brother more than she knows." He waited for my answer.

"I'd love to come. What can I bring?" *Be still my heart.*

"Just bring yourself. Hope you like lasagna."

I insisted on bringing garlic bread to Joe's. Date time 6:00. I felt giddy inside; my mind rushed to what I should wear.

Thoughts of calling Mick filtered out of my mind. I had more important things to do.

So do not fear, for I am with you; do not be dismayed,
for I am your God.
Isaiah 41:10

Chapter Fifteen

Hives. Yes, hives! Welts as big as quarters scattered over the sides of my neck; the intense itching which followed drove me crazy. Unfortunately, I inherited my mom's reaction to anxiety–itchy bumps. As gross as it sounded.

With half an antihistamine swallowed and lots of water to wash it down, I slipped into the shower and cringed as the cool water rippled across my body. I hate to admit it, but the idea of water conservation didn't enter my mind. Instead, I'd call this a 'my-body-is-itching-me-to-death-and-the-water-feels-wonderful' kind of shower. After quite some time, I hated to turn off the spigot, but I needed to get ready.

Slipping into my soft robe, I searched the sparse wardrobe in my closet for just the right outfit to wear to Professor Heartthrob's home. After pulling on my new jeans and chocolate brown pumps, I very carefully slipped a brown cotton sweater over my head. I didn't want to irritate my hives, since they'd almost completely disappeared. I straightened the sweater and added a bangle bracelet to my wrist. Puffs walked past the bedroom door and jumped upon the bed as my phone rang on the nightstand.

"Hi, Joe."

"Rae, why don't you bring Puffs with you? I didn't think to mention it earlier." I heard his slight breath.

At the sound of his voice, goose bumps formed on my skin. No hives. "Well, okay, if you're sure."

"Hey, our dogs helped us meet each other. They seem to get along well, just like us."

Heart palpitations. "Okay, see you in about fifteen minutes."

"Can't wait."

Little did he know, I couldn't wait to see him either.

The garlic bread fragrance permeated the entire tiny house as I removed two loaves from the oven and wrapped foil around each one. I placed them into a cloth bag along with a bread basket. As I guided Puffs to the car, my phone rang.

I tried to balance everything and take the call. Instead, the bag with the bread dropped next to the car. It was Puffs' lucky day. I don't know how she did it, but she managed to devour one loaf without eating the foil.

"Bad dog, Puffs. No bread. No bread." That's all I said before opening the VW door for her to jump inside. A smile appeared on those garlicky lips of hers.

I scooted myself and the one loaf of bread onto the front seat and looked at my phone. *Missed call from Lauren and voicemail.*

After fastening my seatbelt and starting the engine, I listened to her message. "Rae, give me a call when you get a chance. Not an emergency. Just need some girl talk time."

I called. "Lauren, I got your voicemail. You all right?"

"I'm fine. Or maybe I should say, great. I can't talk long because I'm at my folk's place straightening the guest room for guess who?"

She didn't give me a chance to guess.

"Mick's flying to Maryland tonight to attend a conference. Can you believe my parents offered him their guest room and he accepted? I'm all tingly inside at the thought of his visit." Pause—sigh. "Well, I'd better get going. I have a mani-pedi in ten minutes."

"Have a nice . . ." I looked at my phone. Call ended. I didn't even get a chance to tell her I'd be dining at Joe's place tonight and that I was annoyed, to say the least, with her new-found boyfriend.

The tiny welts on my neck began to itch slightly. *Lord, please help me stay calm.*

***

Joe didn't mention the shrinking hives on the side of my neck. He certainly knew how to boost my ego as he gave a little whistle when he opened the front door for Puffs and my entrance.

"Wow. You look great and smell good, too."

"Thanks, Joe, but the tantalizing smell is the garlic bread, not me." I laughed and unleashed Puffs. "I made two loaves, but Puffs decided she needed to eat one. She's such a helpful dog, as you know."

Buddy gave his I'm-guarding-the-house bark, then he and Puffs wagged their whip-like tails and trotted into Joe's kitchen. The open floor plan gave a direct view from the living room entryway into the gourmet kitchen at the back of his craftsman bungalow.

Emily waved from the kitchen island where she and Blake chopped vegetables. She stepped from behind the island, entered the living room, and gave me a quick hug. "Welcome, to the new B&B owner at Hope." She pretended to raise a glass to toast me but instead gave me another hug. "I'm glad you bought it." She cleared her throat. "Welcome, also, to her trusty canine, Puffs. Now even Buddy has a date." She winked at me, took the bread, and retreated into the kitchen. "We're just finishing the salad fixings, Rae. After Joe gives you a tour of his home, you can help set out the silverware." Emily opened the oven door and placed the bread inside to keep it warm.

I don't know if she was hinting to Joe to give me a tour of his place or if it's what he'd planned, but I liked the idea.

"Joe, the tour guide, at your service, Miss Rae." He bowed and pretended to tip his hat. "Right this way, young lady." We walked down the hallway. "To the right, you see an updated bath with craftsman-style fixtures and the latest in toilets," he said with a twinkle in his eyes, which made me laugh. Next, we entered the room across the hall from the bath. "This is my study. It started out with some color my mom chose. Something called Heather Blue. Now, as you can see, the paint color is hidden by the massive book shelves and all my school stuff."

He was right. I couldn't see a speck of paint color on the walls. However, I really loved the feel of the room. *Warm and homey.* "I like this room, Joe. It looks like you." I placed my hand on the corner of his wooden desk and felt the smooth ancient wood. "Wow. I'll bet if this desk could talk, it would have tons of stories to share. Has it been in your family a long time?"

He gave me that crooked grin of his. "Wait a minute. Before I answer the question about the desk, I need to get back to what you said originally. The room looks like me? So, you're saying I look worn out like those old books and my leather reading chair?"

"You know what I mean, silly guy." I turned away from his desk and approached one of the bookshelves. Placing a weathered book to my nose, I closed my eyes and allowed the old-book scent to tingle my nostrils. "This room feels like home, and you make me feel like . . ."

Emily surprised us both as she walked into the room. "Oops! Sorry you two, didn't mean to disturb you. Dinner is almost ready." She patted her brother on the shoulder and abruptly left the room. Within a few minutes, we heard Blake laughing with her.

Joe shook his head in jest as we both heard his sister and her beau in the kitchen. "Guess I'll have to fill you in on the history of the desk another time."

"I can't wait to hear all about the mystery of the antique desk in Joe Byer's office."

His rich green sweater deepened the green in his eyes as he took my hand in his. Just then, we heard a shout coming from the kitchen.

"Come and get it. Dinner's ready. Joe and Rae sitting in a tree . . ." They sounded so childish singing an old poem from the past. However, I laughed along with them.

"Rae, we'd better get moving. If Emily and Blake are hungry, they'll eat without us, and I want you to taste the lasagna before they devour it." We walked a few steps to the end of the hallway. Master bedroom. "This room is a work in progress."

At the sight of the massive gray-padded headboard, I gasped. "That's gorgeous, Joe." For the first time on the house tour, I became a little uneasy. The dime-sized welts on my neck were returning to quarter sized. I don't know what caused the itchiness to reappear except for the fact this was the place where Joe laid his head. "I really like your home." I stepped out of his room and into the hallway. "Dinner smells delicious, and I need to help Emily."

She'd arranged the plates on the table and looked in my direction. "Do you mind setting out the silverware and napkins?"

"I'd love to." I took the utensils from her and placed each piece carefully. I wasn't sure if the orange cloth napkins were Joe's or if Emily added the extra colorful touch. I stood back and examined the table.

"I need one more spoon, Emily."

"Silverware's in the middle drawer on the island."

I glanced into the kitchen and saw her hands covered in orange pot holders as she carried the steaming lasagna.

"My goodness, let me help you." I saw two trivets on the counter. "These for the lasagna?"

As she nodded, yes, I placed them in the center of the table next to a small vase of orange mums.

Soft music played in the background as I added the spoon to the place setting. Joe opened the fireplace screen and added a log to the fire, while Blake poured the water.

Joe pushed my chair in and sat next to me. His hand gently enveloped mine as he prayed.

"Lord, thank you for this meal, and thank you for bringing Puffs and Rae to Hope. In Your name I pray, Amen."

I gave his hand a gentle squeeze as I slipped my hand from his. "Thanks, Joe. I'm glad we came to Hope, too."

Blake tapped the edge of his water glass lightly while the salad and garlic bread were passed. "May I have your attention please? You'll notice the lovely display of vegetables mingled into the mixed greens. They've been carefully washed and cut precisely for your dining pleasure."

Emily punched him gently on his forearm. "I'm so proud of you, Blake. You are a genius salad maker. Just remember, Buster, you had help with this lovely display of greens." She took an enormous bite of her salad and tried hard not to giggle.

Blake leaned in and kissed her vinaigrette lips.

Joe offered to fill plates with lasagna instead of passing the heavy baking dish from person to person. He took mine and filled it with a large square of the Italian main course.

"Here, Rae, hope you like it."

Steam rose from the piping-hot lasagna. I blew on the hot pasta then took a mouthwatering taste. "It's to die for, and I want the recipe, unless it's a family secret." I took another bite.

Emily winked at Joe. "Joe made it. Do you think we should share our secret recipe, bro?"

Joe winked at her and got up from the table. "Hmm. I'm not sure, little sis. What do you think?"

"I really don't imagine Mom would mind if we give it to Rae, since Rae earned points for putting up with the hysterical society ladies. Go ahead, give her the recipe."

He left the table and hesitantly opened the pantry door. "Uh, hum. You must promise to never reveal this to anyone." He held up the lasagna noodle box and proceeded to read the recipe off the side of the container and returned to his seat.

I grabbed my napkin and swatted him with it. "Okay, Mr. and Miss Byer, you two got me on that one."

Blake joined in. "Hey, Rae. They got me, too." He leaned toward Emily and kissed her cheek.

Emily wiped the tomato sauce off her cheek and cleared her throat. "Okay, Rae. Spill the beans. Did Mom and the other ladies drive you crazy with all their ideas of colors, floor-plan designs, and rules and regulations for the bed and breakfast?" She cocked her head sarcastically.

"I hate to say it, but I have my own ideas about the floor plan and colors for the main building."

Joe leaned in a little closer to me. "What are they?" He sipped his drink.

"Well, first of all, I didn't tell them what I'm going to do with the second floor." I took a drink of my water. "I'm not telling any of you unless you swear to secrecy. I mean it." I folded my arms across my chest, stuck out my chin, and attempted to look serious. The serious expression lasted only a couple of seconds. I began to laugh, covered my mouth with the orange napkin, and couldn't stop.

Emily joined in my laughter and couldn't contain herself either. However, Joe and Blake watched us both, shook their heads, and devoured some of their lasagna.

About that time, the dogs trotted to the table. Buddy's huge snout caught a whiff of the garlic bread and lasagna on the edge of Joe's plate and within seconds, Buddy leaned in with ease, and snatched a bit of the divine meal.

Joe scolded the Great Dane, then started to laugh as he held Buddy's collar and wiped the sauce quickly from his muzzle. Puffs licked lasagna remnants off the wooden floor. I quickly got up from my chair, reached over the kitchen counter, and tore off a piece of paper towel.

Joe put his plate in the kitchen sink, while Emily grabbed a rag and helped me clean the floor. Blake called both dogs, guided them through the kitchen, and out the back door.

Joe chuckled. "Thanks for the help. Buddy's height and snout can be detrimental at times."

Emily and Blake didn't hear him. They'd already claimed a spot on the brown sectional in the living room. Soft music filtered throughout the area. Open floor-plan advantage.

Joe rolled his eyes at me in jest. "Guess we have kitchen duty, Rae. Hope you don't mind." He grabbed a dish rag and started wiping off the table.

"Since you shared the family recipe with me, cleaning the kitchen is the least I can do. Thanks so much for dinner, Joe. I've had such a fun time."

"Me, too." He dabbed some dishwater bubbles on my nose.

I giggled as I wiped them off with a paper towel. "I'll scrape the dishes if you load your dishwasher. I know some people can be picky on the loading process." I handed him the first dish. Then another, another, and another.

"We make a great team, Rae. We'll have to do this again if you're game?"

"I'd love it."

Emily came into the kitchen after we'd finished cleaning. "Ah, perfect timing." She grinned and proceeded to open the freezer door. "Pistachio ice cream for dessert, anyone?" She removed the carton and placed it on the counter. "Have you tried this, Rae? It's to die for!" She removed a cereal bowl from the cupboard, scooped three scoops of the rich dessert into the bowl, then opened the refrigerator and removed the can of whipped cream. She squirted a generous amount on top. "Thanks for cleaning up, you two." She grabbed a spoon and sauntered by her brother, nose in the air, cocky expression on her face. "Love you, Joe."

Emily and Blake sat on the cushy sofa and fed each other bites of ice cream. *Definitely love.*

"Rae, now that my annoying sister scooped almost the entire Pistachio ice cream in her and Blake's bowl, there's not much left for us. However, little does she know, I have Pecan Crunch in the freezer in the garage. Want some?"

"You had to ask?" My teasing grin, no doubt, said it all.

Joe soon returned with the carton and placed two bowls on his quartz countertop. He then handed me an ice cream scoop. "Thought you'd like to get your own since you know what you like."

"Thanks. I love ice cream. Guess you know that already." I drizzled chocolate and caramel sauce, then added a few slices of banana. A glob of whipped cream floated on top. "Heavenly." I swayed back and forth as if on cloud nine.

Joe filled his bowl in a jiffy and added pecans to his concoction. "Follow me, Rae."

He carried his ice cream to the sofa where Emily and Blake sat, and revealed his masterpiece. "Now, little sister, look what you and Blake missed."

Emily stuck out her tongue at her brother and proceeded to share with Blake. Never skipping a beat.

I loved their sense of humor. "Joe, you and Emily must have kept your mom hopping when you were little. The way you two irritate each other is hilarious. I must admit, I'm a little envious. Being an only child has its perks, but it can be lonely at times." I settled at the table where Joe and I ate our delicious banana split, Joseph William Byer style.

Time passed quickly as the two of us talked. We put words to the background music and twice Joe took my hand and danced me around the kitchen floor. With one last twirl he kissed the top of my head, spun me around, and reached down to turn on the dishwasher. *Whoa, the ultimate multitasker.*

I put my empty bowl in the sink. "This was wonderful."

With the open floor plan, it was easy to catch a glimpse of Emily and Blake sneaking a kiss or two. *I won't be surprised if an engagement ensues.* The two of them walked hand in hand into the kitchen.

I gave Joe a slight hug. "Thanks for so much fun and a delicious meal." I swiveled to face Emily and Blake. "I had a ball. Thanks for the invite, Emily." I gave her a wink.

"Glad I invited you, too, Rae."

Joe rubbed his jaw and smiled. "It's not very late, you're welcome to stay longer."

I picked up my purse from the fireplace hearth, and latched Puffs' leash to her collar. "Thanks, but I'd better go." I felt Joe's arm around my waist as we took the few steps to his front door.

"Rae, let me help you with your coat." He held my wrap as I slipped into it, then he kissed me lightly on the forehead. "Rest well tonight."

I looked back to say good night to Emily and Blake, but they enjoyed their own kisses.

Joe walked Puffs and me to my car. "Good night, Rae. You brought my house to life." His breath filled the cool evening air as he slowly closed my door.

My heart beat smoothly and easily as I thought about Joe and his home. I also realized–no more hives. *No stress in the least—peace. Thank you, Lord.*

Let everything that has breath praise the Lord.
Psalm 150:6

Chapter Sixteen

After dressing in gray slacks and a powder-blue sweater, I grabbed my purse, put on my coat, hat, and gloves, and kissed Puffs goodbye. *Brrr! It's colder than I thought it'd be!* The fall chill in the air invigorated me as I did a quick jog toward Molly's Restaurant.

As I turned the corner onto Beaufort Street, my phone beeped. Joe. I stopped under an awning a couple of shops from Molly's. The brick building shielded me from the blustery wind.

"Rae, you okay? You sound out of breath."

"I'm walking to Molly's for breakfast. Want to join me?"

"I'll be there in fifteen minutes. By the way, please don't wait for me outside. You've got to be freezing by now." He chuckled as the conversation ended.

My phone buzzed again. "Hi, Joe. Did something come up?"

"Rae, this is Mick." Bad connection. Every other word skipped over another.

"I can't understand you."

"Can't . . . you either. I'll call when I . . . to Hope. Still visiting Lauren."

Straining to hear this staccato-like conversation, I walked slowly to Molly's. I almost bumped into Grace as she entered the restaurant before me. Phone conversation over.

Mrs. Grace Byer held the French door for me and cleared her throat. "Excuse me, Rae, you'd better watch where you're going. A phone attached to one's ear is a dangerous thing." She looked up at me and forced a smile.

For the first time, I noticed tiny laugh lines and crow's feet. Seemed to be more crow's feet than laugh lines. *Shame on me.* "I'm so sorry, Mrs. Byer." I gave an uneasy smile.

"Well, Rae, the entire Historical Society is sitting at the long table at the back of Molly's." She motioned toward the far wall where twelve ladies waved and picked up their glasses as if to toast Grace and me. "Care to join us?"

"Thanks, but I'm meeting someone for breakfast." *She'll see soon enough Joe's dining with me.*

"Okay," she meandered to the long table.

I waved to those crazy ladies. Fortunately, Molly quickly approached and offered me the tiny table next to the front window. Table for one.

"Hi, Molly, I need a place for two. Joe's joining me." *Slight smile.*

Molly winked and pointed to the corner spot near the window. She handed me a breakfast menu. "Heard you went to Joe's for dinner."

Anxious giggle. "Are you kidding? How did you find out already?" I placed the menu on the table and smiled awkwardly. "Oh, yeah, small town."

"Well, I have my sources." Molly nodded toward the back of the restaurant where the ladies chattered away.

"Grace arrived when I did, so how did you find out?" I smiled.

"Grace got here when the other ladies did an hour ago. I think she just retrieved something from her car and returned when the two of you ran into each other." Molly smoothed her gingham apron. "Anyway, Grace told me about your meal with Joe. Want some coffee, honey?"

"Your coffee's always the best." I pointed to my mug. "Fill'er up, please." I gave her a silly grin as I tapped the edge of my cup with my finger like I'd been waiting all day. "I'll order my meal when Joe gets here."

"I can take your order because I already know what he wants. Joe never deviates. I'll have it ready when he walks in the door." She laughed and tapped the fold of the menu.

"All I want is the pumpkin bread, coffee, and a fruit cup."

"I'll be back in a jiffy." Molly filled another table's water glasses, and then headed to the kitchen to get our breakfast.

I shifted closer to the small table, opened my purse, and removed a tube of lipstick. As I applied it, I heard a tap on the window. Joe. His lips turned upward and caused me to grin. *Lord, please don't let me have Tango Tangier lipstick on my front teeth.* He opened the door to Molly's as I quickly attempted to wipe my front teeth with the paper napkin.

Joe sat down and smiled his crooked grin. "You look great."

"Thanks."

The tube rolled off the table and Joe snatched it up before it hit the floor. "Hmm, Tango Tangier." He chuckled as he handed me the lipstick. "Sounds good."

We both enjoyed this miniscule moment of silliness and didn't see the entourage approaching from the back of the restaurant.

Grace's sing-song voice filtered above the crowd. "Joseph William Byer, when did you get here?"

Joe stood. "Just now. I see you're with the Historical Society." He nodded in their direction. "Hi, ladies."

Lottie stood near the register and smiled. "Good to see you, Joe. Looks like you and Rae are getting ready to enjoy another date. We heard about the dinner at your home." She paid her bill then turned and winked at him.

Grace motioned for Joe to sit down. She kissed his cheek then spoke to me. "I didn't know your breakfast companion was my son." She shifted to the counter, then paid her bill.

Before she stepped outside with her friends, Grace approached our table again. "Joe, don't forget dinner Friday night after the game. I know it's a few days away, but just wanted to make sure you didn't forget." She looked at me out of the corner of her eye then focused on him. "You know, Amber will be there." Her eyes darted in my direction.

He didn't crack a smile. "I'm not sure I'll be there. I hoped Rae would go to the game with me and then out to dinner." Joe glanced in my direction. "As a matter of fact, I'm about to ask her." This time he turned and looked directly at me. "Would you like to go to the game and dinner Friday night?" Awkward.

Grace rolled her eyes when her Joseph William Byer put me on the spot.

I sipped my water. "I'll get back to you later this evening, Joe."

Grace patted Joe on the shoulder. "Well, if you want to bring Rae to dinner at the house after the game, go ahead." She put on her gloves and never asked me directly. "We're having chili." Grace wrapped her scarf around her neck, waved to Molly, and walked outside with the other ladies.

Joe looked at me and shook his head. "My mom never ceases to amaze me. I'm really sorry." He ran his fingers through his messy hair. "I'm not going to dinner at Mom and Dad's unless you go with me." He cocked his head awaiting my answer.

I fumbled with my silverware. "You put me on the spot, Professor. Your mom isn't comfortable around me, and I don't fit into her plan." I squirmed. "She'll never overlook the fact I'm a Yankee who just moved into the area, purchased a large property, and will probably live here for quite a while. Plus, I'm sure she doesn't like the fact I'm spending time with you." I lightened the mood with a slight smile.

Joe leaned toward me. "I'm sorry about putting you on the spot. That wasn't my intent. I don't care if you're a Yankee or from the moon. Want to go to the game with me Friday night? Afterwards, I'd like to take you to dinner." He wiped his chin.

Goosebumps. "I don't want to cause a problem with your family."

"You aren't the problem. My mom is. She thinks her job is to find the girl for me. I think she's shocked I already found . . ." His ears turned bright red. "Think you'd like to go out Friday?"

Whew! I felt my ears warm. "Hmm—give me time to think about it, please." I placed my napkin in my lap, pretended to yawn, did an exaggerated stretch, and sipped my water. "Okay, I've thought about it."

"You're killing me here, and the sad thing is, you love it."

"You're right. I do love keeping you guessing." *Ear to ear grin.* "Of course, I'm going." *Little grin with attitude.* "I can't miss seeing the Bulldogs beat the Hornets."

Molly discreetly slipped our food in front of us without skipping a beat. She poured us both a fresh cup of java, left us extra creams, and placed a basket of assorted jellies at the edge of the table for Joe's wheat toast.

He poured ketchup on his scrambled eggs, devoured his bacon, and slathered butter into his bowl of grits. "Would you like a bite of eggs?"

"You are a generous man, but I think I'll pass on the eggs with ketchup on them." I shuddered. "Mind if I try the grits?" I looked pleadingly at him and held up my spoon.

Oh my, this man has charm. He filled my spoon with buttery grits.

"Thank you, Joe, for this delicious taste of heaven."

"Glad you liked it. Guess I'd better finish this off and get back to work. This was a nice way to start the day." He set down his fork. "I don't mean to rush, Rae, but my class starts in fifteen minutes."

"I'm done too. I'm so glad we had breakfast together."

Joe pulled out my chair, helped me with my coat, and paid the bill. I suggested we go Dutch, but he paid anyway. *Stubborn man.*

He gave me a quick hug and a peck on the cheek then turned to the right as I headed to the left toward Charleston Street. I pulled my phone out of my pocket, took a picture of the street sign, meandered down the overgrown driveway, and took photos of one of the cottages and the main building. *For posterity, of course.*

I carefully wiped off the top step of the main building and sat down on the porch. With phone in hand, I perused a list of architects and noticed one was employed at the University. I'd give him a call tomorrow. I'd give him a call sometime today. I'd give him a call now.

I punched in the phone number. "Good morning, this is Rae Long. May I speak with Dr. Duntworth?"

"Class is in session right now. May I take a message?" His assistant paused.

"Yes, I've purchased the property on Charleston Street and am searching for an architect. Could you please have Dr. Duntworth call me?"

"Of course, I'll give him the message. Have a great day, Mrs. Long. Good bye."

I paused at the mention of the title, "Mrs." Long. Memories of Mom and Grandma.

Thank you, Lord, for giving me the courage to call an architect. Thank you, Lord, for breakfast with Joe.

Be strong and courageous. Do not be afraid or discouraged . . .
2 Chronicles 32:7

Chapter Seventeen

Breakfast with Joe and making an appointment with the architect warranted a cheery tune from my lips. I hadn't whistled in a long time. As I reached the front porch steps, my phone buzzed.

"Mrs. Long?"

I cleared my throat. "This is *Miss* Long." I removed my earring, so I could press the phone closer to my ear.

"Dr. Duntworth has an opening tomorrow morning at 9:00." Pause. "Will that work?"

"Yes. I look forward to meeting him." I wanted to do a hip-hip-hooray cheer but squelched my enthusiasm—until we ended the conversation.

Puffs' whip-like tail flung back and forth when I entered the house.

"Hey, Puffs, I got an appointment, I got an appointment, I got an appointment." Dancing and chanting from the living room to the kitchen and back again made Puffs start to howl. She eventually went to her empty water bowl, picked it up, and dropped it at my feet. She didn't care about an appointment. She craved water and a pat on the head.

I filled her bowl, let out another enthusiastic cheer, and then heard a knock at the front door. I hung my coat on a hook near the door and peeked out the peephole. On the other side stood Lauren Wyatt.

"Lauren, I can't believe you're here! Has something happened?"

"I can't wait to tell you, but first I want to know what all the cheering is about. I heard you when I stood at the front door."

"Gosh, I didn't realize I was that loud." I took her coat and hung it on a hook near mine. "I have an appointment with an architect tomorrow morning, and I'm a little excited."

"That's great! I sure hope it works out."

As we sat in the kitchen, Lauren's words flowed non-stop. "The university called me yesterday to lead a course here at the Hope extension. I couldn't believe it. I accepted the offer immediately, packed my bags, and hopped on Mick's flight. You've known me the longest of anyone outside my immediate family, Rae. I never do anything spur of the moment, but this just felt right for some reason."

"I can't believe it. How long will you be here? How did you get released so quickly from Maryland?" I sat on the edge of the kitchen chair eagerly awaiting her answers.

"This university exchange program has been in the making for a while. I knew about the possibility but didn't want to get my hopes up. When I got the call that they wanted an engineer to be part of the program at the extension in Hope, I couldn't refuse. I know I'll be here at least a semester. I just didn't know I'd have a one-day notice."

"Do you need a place to stay?"

"Mick already took care of that. You know he's a Realtor?" She chuckled and gave a little giggle. "He lined up a place for me."

"Where is it?"

"I'm swapping houses with Landy, the professor who's taking my slot temporarily in Maryland, and she'll be living in my condo. In all honesty, Mick didn't have to do a lot since Landy and I are switching places. He'll manage her property while she's in Maryland, and Mom and Dad will oversee my place. Landy's house is between Fenster Haus and the Hope Library and is across from the lake. From what she told me, it used to be the librarian's home back in the dark ages."

"It sounds fantastic. Okay, that takes care of your living arrangements." I tapped my fingers on the table top. "Are you and Mick getting a little serious?"

Lauren's phone rang. "It's Mick."

To avoid eavesdropping, I cleaned the countertops and rinsed out the sink. The conversation ended quickly.

"Mick has the keys to my soon-to-be rental; I'm going to walk over to Tweeters to pick them up. Want to come with me?"

We put on our coats and the two of us literally jogged to Beaufort Street. Lauren's long stride put her paces ahead of me. "Slow down girl. You're putting me to shame. I thought I was in pretty good shape until now."

She slowed to a walk and patted the top of my head. "Now that I'll be living here in Hope for a while, maybe we can go for morning jogs. I usually run at about 6:00."

Soft groan from me.

Mick stood in front of Tweeters with the house keys dangling from a chain. "Here they are, Lauren. Oh, hi, Rae." He handed Lauren the keys. "These open the front and back doors. The back door jams a little; I'll fix that later."

Lauren gave him a peck on the cheek. "Thanks, Mick."

We strutted toward the library and up the brick walkway that led to a charming home. Lauren made an abrupt stop. "It's a lot smaller than I thought it'd be."

"I can't believe you just said that. This place is adorable. Hey, if you don't like it, you can stay in my rental, and I'll stay here."

"No thanks." She laughed as we entered.

Lauren removed her shoes and stepped softly on the dark hardwood floors. The open concept flowed from the living/dining room area directly into the glistening kitchen. The shiny appliances and stone countertops drew her in. "Landy either hired a professional decorator or has a designer's eye." Lauren scanned the area. "Well, Rae, since I don't do any cooking, this place will always sparkle. As a matter of fact, it looks like Landy never cooked here either." She pointed to the label on the stove and one on the dishwasher.

We both laughed.

A king-sized bed, framed by floor-to-ceiling windows, enveloped much of the master bedroom. Lauren stopped abruptly when she opened the second bedroom door, which had been converted to a walk-in closet.

She sauntered to the living room and settled onto the cushy gray sectional. "This place is small, but ideal."

"I agree. Every square inch is put to maximum use. Especially the closet. I think you might have enough room for some of your shoes. You need a third bedroom for your clothes, though." *Chuckle, chuckle.*

"Ha, ha, Miss Long."

By the time we made a second sweep through the house, Mick showed up and Lauren walked through the house with him.

"Excuse me you two, I'm going to call Joe."

Lauren gave me a thumbs up.

I stepped out onto the front porch.

"Joe, do you have a minute?"

"I was going to call you."

"Mick and Lauren are here in Hope."

"Did you say Lauren?"

"Yes. She came on the flight with Mick. Long story. Mind if the four of us go to dinner?"

"I don't mind. Any place in particular?"

"Gill's is perfect. I'll ask them."

I lightly knocked on the front door to give a heads up to my entry, then peeked inside. "I spoke to Joe, and we'd like to invite you to dinner at Gill's." I cleared my throat. "Does that work for you?"

Lauren laughed. "Come in. You don't have to stand outside. The meal sounds good to me. What do you think, Mick?"

"Sure." He buttoned his jacket and slid on his gloves. "Lauren, why don't you and I walk to Tweeters and get my car? We can meet Joe and Rae at the restaurant."

Lauren cinched her coat belt. “I’m game if you are, but I’m not leaving Rae here. Come walk with us, Rae. Joe can pick you up at Tweeters. Okay?”

“Thanks. That’ll be great.”

Lauren and Mick ambled slowly toward Tweeters as I walked slightly ahead of them.

I called Joe. “It’s a go. Can you pick me up at Tweeters?”

“Sure. Be there asap.”

“I have an appointment with Dr. Duntworth tomorrow morning at nine. Lauren already knows, and I wanted to tell you.”

“Wow! That’s fantastic. I’m really glad for you, Rae.”

“See you soon.”

I turned and glanced at Lauren and Mick. “Joe will be here shortly.” They didn’t care, they were in their own little world.

***

Dining alfresco at Gill’s—brilliant. Twinkle-lights, umbrella picnic tables, soft background music, and scrumptious burgers delighted my senses. Outdoor heaters warmed the eating area to perfection. The conversation among the four of us never faltered. Sports, technology, restaurants, and great shopping areas dominated the dialogue.

The waiter offered us the dessert menu. Lauren and I declined. The two guys tortured themselves by scanning the choices.

Lauren tapped Mick on the shoulder. “With all the time you and Joe spend drooling, you could order and eat the largest chocolate concoction offered.” She easily reached across Mick and pointed to a share with four people chocolate, mammoth piece of luscious decadence. "How about it?" She batted her eyelashes at Mr. Treavor.

Joe glanced at Mick and back at his menu. "What do ya say, Mick? Wanna' go for the gold? I'll bet the girls help us eat it." He tapped the tip of my nose with his finger. "Are you game?"

Lauren and I agreed to a bite of the dessert.

Joe motioned to the waiter and ordered.

The chocolate dessert looked like a volcano. Four spoons—four mouths to devour the creation—humongous.

Lauren pretended to hold her stomach in discomfort. "I'll never be able to eat another bite of food." She reclined her head on Mick's shoulder.

I wiped chocolate off my lips. "Me either."

The fellas paid the bill, then Joe and I walked hand-in-hand to his truck; Mick and Lauren walked hand-in-hand to his sports car.

I called over my shoulder to Lauren. "Let me know if you need anything tonight. I'm so glad you're in town."

She waved, let go of Mick's hand, and trotted to me. "Rae, I'm praying all goes well tomorrow at your meeting. Let me know if you need anything."

"Thank you. I'm so ecstatic you're here!"

We hugged. Then proceeded to our fella's vehicles.

When Joe and I reached my rental, we sat on my front step and chatted a while. Of course, Puffs sat between us. No mosquitos to swat, no twinkling lightning bugs to catch. Only the stars and the moon enveloped us—mesmerized us.

No words needed on this spectacular evening until Joe spoke to Puffs.

"Puffs, you're a good dog, but you're cramping my style." He got up, walked in front of her, and sat on the other side of me. "Rae, Dr. Duntworth's an exceptional architect. Let's pray about your meeting." He held my hands in his, we bowed our heads, and prayed. A quick kiss ensued—trumping the moon and stars. *Heaven on earth.*

Every good and perfect gift is from above,
coming down from the Father of the heavenly lights...
James 1:17

Chapter Eighteen

Traditional white buildings and yellow shutters. My choice. Simple and timeless. I emailed an early morning message to the Historical Society ladies informing them I'd made my color decisions. However, I didn't reveal what I'd chosen. I invited them to lunch at Fenster Haus on Friday at noon.

My phone buzzed. Grace Byer.

"Rae, I just got your email. I'm an early riser, too. Can't you tell me the colors over the phone?" She was prodding.

My mind whirled. I didn't want to disappoint Grace. However, seeing and feeling colors and fabrics in person made it easier for many people to visualize the outcome. *Interior Design 101.*

I took a deep breath, in through the nose and out through the mouth, before answering her. "Mrs. Byer, I can't wait to show you the colors and want you to have the full experience when I bring the samples I've chosen. I'll fill you in on this piece of info, though, no one else will know this until Friday at noon." I cleared my throat. "By the way, will you be able to attend lunch?"

"Of course." She almost whispered her response. "Now please let me know that little speck of information."

I paused a second. "I'd love if you'd design the sign and logo for the bed and breakfast. Of course, I'll pay you." I waited for her response. It didn't come as quickly as I thought it might. "I know it's a lot to ask, but if you're willing, I'd be thrilled."

I heard her sniffle. "Rae, I don't know what to say." Silence. "I'm completely astonished you'd ask me. I've never done anything like that before."

"I've heard through the grapevine you're extremely creative. I don't need an answer right now and please don't feel obligated. This is our little secret. Is that a deal?"

"Absolutely. I won't tell Lance or anyone else." She coughed quietly.

"Of course, you can tell Lance."

Grace whispered. "Okay, Rae. Thank you for asking me to help in your endeavor."

"I'll see you Friday?"

"Yes, Friday."

Stress lifted from my shoulders after taking a *Grace-full* approach with Grace.

Lord, thank you for giving me the words to say to Mrs. Byer. I pray the anxiety between her and me subsides a little and that she realizes I'm not trying to steal her son. Although, I must admit, I'm falling for him. Thank You, God, for Your Amazing Grace.

Through Him we received grace . . .
Romans 1:5

Chapter Nineteen

Joe texted me shortly after I spoke with Grace.

Joe: Mom called. Said she had something to tell me that she couldn't tell me till Friday. Didn't make sense. Something to do with you. Do you have a clue what she's talking about?

Instead of returning his text, I called. "Yes, I know what she's talking about, but I can't tell you a thing." I loved keeping that fella guessing. "Actually, your mom can tell you on Friday." I giggled.

"Okay." He changed the subject. "Want to go to dinner tonight?"

Okay? Okay? Doggone Professor Joe isn't falling for my teasing. I gave no hint he ruffled my feathers. "Sure, dinner sounds great. Want to go to Gill's?" I asked.

"Gill's? We just ate there the other night with Lauren and Mick. You sure you want to go again?" He paused a minute then continued. "Let's get take-out and eat by the lake."

"Sounds great. Gill's has more than just burgers. Besides, you've got me addicted to the place. It's all your fault for introducing me to the gourmet burger spot of Hope." This time I paused. "Plus, I'd love to try one of their take-out meals and dine alfresco. This warmer weather doesn't feel like the end of October. Is 6:30 okay?"

I heard his clunky truck engine idling in the background. "That's fine. I'm praying about your meeting this morning. Please let me know the outcome."

"I definitely will."

***

My 9:00 meeting with Dr. Duntworth went smoothly and without a hitch.

He eased back in his chair and folded his arms across his ample middle. "I'm sure glad you want to renovate the old university. I'm a bit surprised the historical standards didn't require that of the people who converted the building years ago. I see a vision for the place."

"I'd like to hire you if you'll accept the agreement and my offer."

I handed him an envelope. He read it, stood, sealed the deal with his signature, and a firm handshake.

"Miss Long, I know a great contractor. Abel Dells. We've worked together on projects for years."

"Sir, your reputation is impeccable. If Mr. Dells agrees, he's hired."

Dr. Duntworth called Abel. Fortunately, he was on campus, met with us promptly, and agreed to be the contractor for the project.

I contained my excitement until I slid the paperwork into my new butter-yellow briefcase and drove to Pecan Street. With music blaring, I sang at the top of my lungs.

I texted Lauren to share the good news about the architect and contractor. She responded with three smiley face emojis.

On the other hand, I called Professor Joe Byer. "I know we'll see each other at dinner, but I couldn't wait to tell you I hired Dr. Duntworth and Mr. Dells today."

"Rae, they are the best of the best. You won't be disappointed. I'm proud of you."

"Thanks, Joe. See you in a few."

***

Gill's bustled, as usual. Joe and I stood at the take-out counter and chatted while we waited for our meal, until we heard a familiar voice in the background. Mrs. Byer's voice.

I heard Lance coaxing Grace to tell him the secret. He couldn't wait until Friday. Or so he said. It appeared Mrs. Grace Byer loved bantering with her hubby.

Joe grabbed the brown bag filled with our dinner then reached for my hand. "Let's leave out this door." He motioned to the door closest to us and farthest from his parents.

My first instinct was to follow him, but my heart felt differently. Hearing his mom and dad's laughter brought back tender memories of my parents. I yearned for family.

"Joe. I want to say hi to your folks." I tugged his hand in my direction. "Please."

Joe's thumb brushed a tear away from my cheek. His large hand gave mine a little squeeze.

Before I said a word, I saw Grace standing at the back table waving at me. Or was it at Joe? It didn't matter. We weaved her way.

Lance's voice greeted us. "Rae, it's good to see you again. Come and join us." He pulled two more chairs over to the long table which occupied four other couples. "I think you know everyone."

Joe lifted our bagged dinner for all to see. "Dad, we got take-out. We need a rain check."

I motioned for Joe to lean down so he could hear me. "Can't we just stay here for dinner? I'd like to for your father."

"Are you sure?" He set the bag on the table.

"I'm sure."

Joe's folks, Tilly and Gentry Wayne who were Blake's parents, and the others cheered when we sat down at the table with them and removed our dinner from the brown bag. I loved this moment.

Lou, the waiter, brought everyone's meal and noticed Joe and me. "Hey, I thought you two got take-out. I even put the candles in the bottom of your bag like you asked, Joe. Guess this won't be a romantic dinner for you and Rae." He walked back to the serving station to fill the water glasses.

Joe's ears turned beet red. His cheek color matched his ears. The taunting began.

Lance looked at Joe. "Son, if I'd known you had a romantic date night scheduled, I'd have kept my mouth shut."

Joe's face flamed with embarrassment and he surprised me when he pulled the candles and holders from the brown bag and placed them in front of us. He smiled that crooked grin of his, and I immediately noticed his ears and cheeks returned to their natural color.

Lou lit the candles.

Mrs. Byer never said a word about the romantic meal interruption. She did, however, ask Lance to pray. Such a sweet God moment as Joe and I held hands and bowed our heads with these more seasoned believers.

Joe placed my Gill's chicken burger and sweet potato fries in front of me and his double-decker cheeseburger and curly fries in front of him. Not the healthiest meal in town, but, oh, it tasted scrumptious.

Victoria washed down her burger with a drink of tea and turned toward me. "Rae, I heard you hired Dr. Duntworth. He'll never steer you wrong." She took another bite.

Molly chimed in. "One of his relatives from way back helped design the old university." She drank some of her tea.

Mrs. Byer didn't say a word about my choice. She did, however, let the ladies know she had a secret and would tell them on Friday at the Fenster Haus luncheon. From then on, the conversation focused on Mrs. Byer.

Joe and I finished our meal, he blew out the candles, and the two of us prepared to leave until Emily and Blake entered Gill's.

Breathless, Emily approached the long table. "Family and friends, Blake and I have a secret we want to share."

Lance whispered to Mrs. Byer. "It must be a night for secrets."

Emily kissed Blake on the cheek. "Everyone, Blake proposed to me by the lake." She kissed him again. "Blake said we should wait to tell you in private, but I knew you'd be busy tomorrow night with everybody at the house for chili after the football game, and I just couldn't wait any longer."

Lance spoke first. "Emily, take a breath. You're going to hyperventilate, girl." He stood up and wrapped his arms around his little girl. "Come over here, Blake. Sounds like you surprised my Em." Lance pulled Grace, Joe, Blake, Tilly, and Gentry into a sweet hug of all hugs.

Emily gently pulled away from the arms of everyone. "Dad, what did you mean when you said Blake surprised me? Blake and I surprised y'all." She patted her dad on his arm.

Joe stepped toward Blake. "Welcome to the family. I'm warning you, my sister is a handful, and you'd better treat her right." Then he looked at Emily. "You'd better treat him right, too, favorite sister of mine."

Emily looked stunned. "Dad, you didn't answer my question. You said Blake surprised me?"

The four parents stood in front of Blake and Emily with sheepish grins. Lance smiled. "Blake asked us for our blessing two weeks ago. So, we knew the surprise before you did, dear daughter."

Gentry added. "Emily, we've known for quite some time you captured Blake's heart. We knew about the proposal, too."

Joe chimed in. "Me, too. Blake asked how I'd feel about him marrying you."

Emily blushed. "You guys! I should have known Blake would ask dad's permission." She gave her dad a tender squeeze then turned to Blake. "Is that why you've been avoiding me?"

Blake took her hand. "Em, you can read me like a book. Remember last summer when you informed me my right eye twitches when I have a secret? I tried to surprise you with tickets to that concert, and you guessed it." He teasingly glared at Emily.

"I remember I loved the concert. Normally, I hate surprises, but this one is the best one ever." Emily snuggled closer to him. "I love you, Blakey."

Lou topped off all our cups of tea and poured more for himself.

Lance raised his glass. "I'd like to make an engagement toast to Blake and Emily."

We clinked our glasses in one accord and gave the proverbial, Hear! Hear!

The fellas moved to one end of the long table and the gals moved to the opposite. Chatter, giggles, and outright laughter dominated our end of the table.

Mrs. Byer took Emily's hands in hers. "Well, dear, any date decided for the wedding?"

"Of course not, I just found out about the engagement. Blake and I need to discuss it." Emily cried. "Mother, I'm overwhelmed." Tears flowed from Emily's eyes. "I can't stop crying."

Mrs. Byer gently hugged her daughter as we surrounded Emily.

The guys, on the other hand, looked bewildered. Blake got up and approached Emily, then wrapped her in his arms, and let her cry. Even if he didn't know why she was crying, he at least knew she needed his embrace. *Sweet couple.*

***

Joe drove slowly down Pecan Street toward the house. We barely said a word until he parked in my driveway.

"Rae, sorry our take-out dinner ended up being eat-in."

I sniffled. "Best dinner ever." I sniffled again and blew my nose into my tissue.

He wiped his nose with his gloved hand. "Guess I'm getting a cold." He gently patted my shoulder.

I looked into his eyes. "Want to know the best part of the evening for me?"

He chuckled. "The meal?" He gave a silly grin.

"No. The candles."

"The candles?"

"Yes. The fact you even thought of the candles meant so much to me." I dabbed my eyes.

Joe slid closer and kissed me twice on the forehead. Nothing more. Just enough kisses for this moment.

He walked me slowly to the door. "I've told you this already, but I have to say it again, I'm glad your meeting went well today."

"Thanks." I squeezed his gloved hand.

"Hope your luncheon goes well at Fenster Haus tomorrow. Pick you up at six for the game?"

"Thanks, Joe. Six works."

"I know we talked about going someplace other than my folks for chili tomorrow after the game. Want to go there anyway?"

I looked at him with watery eyes. "Will your mom be okay?"

"Yes." He reached for me, hugged my waist, and kissed me tenderly. "Good night, sweet Rae."

Thank You, Lord, for allowing this evening to go differently than Joe and I planned.

For I know the plans I have for you . . .
Jeremiah 29:11

Chapter Twenty

I slept like a baby and didn't wake until Puffs started barking at seven a.m. Midnight meowed loudly outside my bedroom window as she perched precariously on the flower box. Again. I wasn't going through the cat rescue antics I'd done previously with Joe and Emily. I pulled myself from beneath my comforter and stepped onto the cold floor.

"Brrrr. Where in the world are my slippers?" I bent down, found them under my bed, and slipped one on. Then I debated whether I should toss the remaining one at the window to scare that pesky cat.

I'm so thankful I paused before throwing my slipper, because in an instant, I heard Miss Doris calling her beloved *baby*. "Sweet Midnight. Come. Come to mommy."

I'd never seen a feline react so quickly to its *person*. Puffs barked again. Midnight leaped from the window box and onto a tree branch in a flash. I pressed my nose against the chilly window and saw the cat take a flying leap directly into Doris's arms. She gently hugged the kitty's neck and turned to shuffle back inside her home.

This incident was trivial in the scheme of living; however, I knew without any doubt I didn't want one single twig close to the cottages or the main building at the bed and breakfast. I couldn't stand the thought of a cat wake-up call or worse yet a raccoon staring in the window.

***

"Come on, Puffs, I need your opinion on what to wear today at the luncheon. After all, you do have exquisite taste." She looked at me, stretched, and laid down on the bedroom floor.

My melon-colored pencil skirt had a kick pleat at the back. I saw my mother wear it many times and loved it. The paisley top she wore with the skirt lost its beauty many years ago, but, oh, her skirt was another story. Frequently, she wore it to work and before changing into comfortable clothes at home, she would pick me up and place me on her knee. We occupied our time reading a book or two together while waiting for Daddy to arrive. Quite often when he came through the door, he leaned in to give my mother a kiss on the lips, and me a kiss on the forehead. My handsome prince daddy took Mother's hand and mine and danced with the two of us in the living room. No music—just laughter. The pencil skirt restored sweet memories.

I inched closer to the full-length mirror and applied the tangerine lipstick Joe liked. It matched the skirt perfectly. Not that I was the matchy-matchy type, but I absolutely loved the color. The tunic-length yellow top felt comfy even with the wide belt cinching it slightly. *Time to go. Time to get the ball rolling. Time to meet those hysterical ladies head on.*

I'm scared, Lord. Please guide me.

I sought the Lord, and he answered me;
he delivered me from all my fears.
Psalm 34:4

Chapter Twenty-One

I'll never get used to this red dirt! A downpour through the night caused that doggone red dirt to peek through the graveled parking lot at Fenster Haus. I entered the restaurant and made a beeline for the lady's room. There was no way I'd be able to wipe all the clingy red clay off my four-inch heels. I did the best I could to clean them with strips of toilet paper. This classy restaurant stacked pristine white-cloth hand towels near the sinks for hand drying. Not for red-mud shoe-cleaning. My winter-white heels had an orangey tint. *Autumnal. Quite appropriate for this fall day. Not!*

As I swiped lip gloss across my lips and dropped the tube into my leather bag, my phone beeped. I pilfered through my purse and finally located it.

Text from Joe: Prayin' all goes well.

Perfect timing. His message lowered my anxiety level and brought a smile to my lips. My "thank you" with a smiley face response zoomed to the professor. I felt peace knowing Joe was prayin.' Nothing else mattered.

I took a deep breath and walked to the back of the gorgeous window-laden restaurant. Fall-colored leaf branches decorated the center and length of the long harvest table. Shelly and her crew outdid themselves.

"Ladies, thank you so much for coming today. I know this was a last-minute invite." I picked up the crystal water goblet, took a couple swallows, then placed it gently on the table. "Order whatever you like and enjoy. We'll get down to the business of color choices after we eat." I sat in my chair and placed an orange napkin in my lap.

Opal clinked her water glass with her spoon. "Well, Rae, if you promise to treat us to a meal at Fenster Haus periodically, you can suggest any colors, and we'll go along with them." She closed her menu and nodded to the rest of the ladies.

My smile broadened. "It's a deal."

Victoria Sounds, the mayor's wife, stood. "Ladies, we've put up with that ugly eyesore of a university on Charleston Street long enough. We tried to talk Mick into keeping the property and fixing it up since he's a house flipper. He chickened out, but we're elated, because Rae bought it. Hey, girls, maybe our property values will tick upward when the B&B opens, and tourists stay in town instead of heading to Greenville. Anyway, I don't care what colors you choose. I'm in."

The conversation flowed from one lady to the next. Each one tried coaxing Grace to spill the beans on her secret. Grace kept silent.

The funny thing was, Grace never talked to me before the luncheon to accept or decline my offer. Guess she wanted to surprise me, too.

The waitress approached the table and took our orders.

The salmon melted in my mouth and the crunchy grilled asparagus tasted delicious. "Ladies, thanks for suggesting I get this. It's luscious." I flaked off another piece of salmon and savored the bite.

Everyone enjoyed easy conversation, wonderful food, and the glorious setting. I could tell because each one of them talked non-stop, took a bite of food, then talked some more. I glanced toward Victoria and Lottie and noticed they were laughing so hard tears streamed down their faces. These ladies who originally annoyed me were becoming my friends.

I hope they think of me the same way after seeing the colors I've chosen. Maybe I'd classify them as potential friends.

Butterflies fluttered their wings in my stomach as the reveal moment arrived. I sneaked a quick peek at my phone and re-read my text from Joe. *Prayin' all goes well.* I read it twice, tucked my phone in my purse, and breathed deeply. "I hope you like the choices I've made for the B&B." I took paint cards out of my large bag and gave two cards to each of them.

They didn't say a word. The silence seemed to last forever.

Victoria spoke first. "Well, I swanny."

I'd heard Grandma use that term many times. She'd explained ladies in the South didn't like using the expression, "I swear."

Lottie spoke. "Unbelievable."

Grace added. "Rae, I wish you'd shown us these colors sooner."

I became quite concerned. The ladies' serious expressions made my stomach flip-flop, until several of the women giggled. The giggles broke into all out laughter.

"What's so funny? Did I miss something?"

Lottie reached into her purse and pulled out paint samples. "Rae, here are the colors the ladies and I chose. We sure hope you won't be upset when we show them to you, but we did want to give our opinions."

Each lady put down her fork and watched as Lottie handed them to me. "Here they are, dear."

I gasped. "These are the colors you chose? I can't believe it."

The Historical Society got a little hysterical at that moment and slipped out of their chairs and surrounded me with hugs, kisses on the cheeks, and more laughter. I noticed other diners smiled and joined in the light applause.

I regained my composure. "I can't believe we chose the same colors!"

Victoria interjected, "We can't either. Out of all those choices, we agreed on the same thing. Now that's a miracle in itself," she sputtered.

Our waitresses stood nearby. One of them took the lead. "Ladies, this calls for a celebration. May we suggest chocolate cake a la mode all around and tea and coffee refills?"

I agreed with the rest of them. "Absolutely!"

I noticed Grace getting a little antsy. She tapped her fingers on the edge of the table, shifted in her seat, and gave me a quick glance. After all, she had some news to share.

I nodded in Grace's direction. "Grace, would you like to share a little something with the group?"

She popped out of her seat like popcorn in a popper, fluffed her hair a bit, and cleared her throat. "Ladies I hated to keep you in suspense about my little secret." Grace fiddled with her napkin. "First of all, Rae, I accept your offer." Her broad smile said it all. "Y'all, Rae asked me to help with something at the bed and breakfast."

Victoria spoke up. "Please tell us, Grace. We can't wait any longer."

The other women prodded her to spill the beans.

"Well, girls, Rae asked me to design the sign and logo for her bed and breakfast." She beamed.

Anna squirmed in her chair. "Grace that sounds wonderful. I'll be glad to help you. I'll have ideas to give you in a few days." She took a pen and paper from her purse and started drawing on the piece of paper. "You know I have an art degree."

Opal tapped Grace on the shoulder. "Dear, I have pictures of the old sign that was used in front of the university years ago. I'm sure you'll want to see it, so you can pattern your design after it." Opal smiled at each of us. "After all, we must remember the main building is an historical building."

Victoria almost choked on her water. "You've got to be kidding. We are the Historical Society. Don't you think we know the building is historical? Silly girl."

They all laughed in unison. I noticed the huge grin on Grace's face completely disappear. Her moment of grandeur nearly dissipated. At least in Grace's mind. Not in mine, though.

We all settled into our seats. Dessert arrived with an extra scoop of vanilla ice cream. A few of us added cream and sugar to our hot drinks.

Grace leaned over to me and whispered something. With all the ladies talking it was hard to hear her. "Rae, I don't think I can do the sign. It might be too stressful for me."

"Mrs. Byer, I know you can do it." I bent a tad closer to her. "I have faith in you."

"You might have faith in me, but I don't have it in myself. Anna is a gifted artist. She wants to help."

Grace's secret revealed. Grace's enthusiasm curtailed.

I stood slowly and cleared my throat. "Ladies, you've probably heard that I hired Dr. Duntworth and Mr. Abel Dells. I can't wait to get started on the B&B. You already know that Mrs. Byer will design the sign and logo for the bed and breakfast. I prayed about my decision in choosing her, and I truly believe God answered. I'm so glad she agreed." I smiled and nodded toward Grace then turned my focus toward the other ladies. "I'd like to incorporate each of you into some aspect of the reno. However, I must say, the sign design is of utmost importance. Do you ladies mind if I include you in some of the other decisions?" My Psychology 101 course came in handy with these ladies. *Forgive me Lord!*

Lottie beamed. "I'd love to help, Rae. What would you like me to do?"

Victoria piped in after Lottie. "I can't believe you're including all of us in the process. I'm at your service." She saluted, or I should say, attempted to salute me.

Anna and Opal looked bewildered until Anna spoke first. "I already thought we had the job of helping Grace with the sign. You know I have a degree in art." She slid her chair away from the table and offered me a piece of paper with a sketch on it. "See, I've already come up with a great idea."

Opal watched Anna and gave her a thumbs up. Both women looked completely assured Grace needed their help.

I glanced at the piece of paper Anna handed me. "Thanks, Anna. I've already hired Mrs. Byer, but I do have something for you and Opal to do." I gave a wink to Grace as a smile curved my lips upward. I handed the picture back to Anna, walked around the table, and gave her and Opal a little hug.

Victoria spoke up, "Rae, do you have any idea what you want me to do? Or do I need to wait?" She drummed her fingers on the table top.

I learned a little something about the mayor's wife in this quick process. Patience was *not* her virtue. I must admit, I slowed down the entire conversation a bit, just to aggravate Mrs. Victoria Sounds. *Forgive me, again, Lord.*

I drank my coffee slowly, then proceeded. "I do have a few things I can share with each of you, if you don't mind." I waited for a response.

This time they all spoke in unison. "Tell us!"

"Are you ladies sure?" By this time my teasing became annoying. *I better stop aggravating before they walk out.*

Anna wadded up the piece of paper with the picture and put it on her plate. Opal shifted back in her chair. Victoria leaned forward and scrolled her phone as Lottie sat straight as an arrow and folded her hands in her lap. Grace sat easily in her chair with a peaceful countenance.

My eyes turned to Victoria. "Would you mind printing small cards with sayings on them?"

She didn't give me a minute to explain. "Small cards with sayings on them? Why in the world do you want me to do that and what are they for?" She looked exasperated.

Patience.

I gave her a reassuring smile. "Victoria, what I'm asking you to do isn't trivial. I need a lot of cards printed. They'll have sweet sayings on them and be put on the bed pillows in the cottages. I'd love the logo to be placed at the top of each card, so you'll have to wait for Mrs. Byer to design the sign. That is, if you agree to do it." I paused. "I've seen the business cards you've printed for the Mayor and his staff and, I must say, I'm quite impressed."

Victoria's eased demeanor and smile appeared. "I'd be honored to make those sweet cards. I must admit, though, Sam isn't going to be happy about this."

"Why?"

"Because I guarantee I'll be lying awake every night muddling through precious little sayings in my mind. Come to think of it, I'd better keep my phone on the nightstand, so I can be ready if some brilliant idea emerges." She laughed. "Oh, I can see Sam's face when I tell him." She smiled and glanced at Grace. "Grace, you need to get busy with the logo, otherwise my project won't get done." The word *patience* came to mind. *Again.*

Everyone started talking to Victoria. Anna volunteered to help her create the cards. After all, Anna had an art degree.

I clinked the glass with my fork to grab everyone's attention then looked at Anna. "Anna, would you mind creating a small painting for each of the cottages? I'd like to place one on each mantel. If you accept this task, a 5 X 7 would be perfect." I tried to read her body language, but she glanced away from me. "Anna, I understand if you don't want to do the paintings."

She pulled a tissue from her purse and dabbed her nose. "I'm speechless, which as you know is rare. I'd love to, Rae. Please let me know the colors you'd like used." This time she attempted to discreetly blow her nose.

I chuckled as Grace confidently leaned toward Anna. "Would you like some help with the paintings?"

Before Anna responded, Grace got up from her seat, walked to the other side of the table, and gave Anna a hug.

"You know I'm just teasing you, Anna. You're such a gifted artist." Grace coasted back to her chair and added a lump of sugar to her hot cup of tea.

Ahh, God's grace.

I regrouped. "Ladies, before I move on, I want to tell you I will be paying you for helping me."

Instead of waiting for me to speak, Victoria shook her head no, Grace shook her head no, Anna shook her head no. I hadn't even asked Lottie and Opal to do anything, but they shook their heads no, too.

"You don't want to help?"

Grace added. "Of course, we do; however, we won't accept payment. Our projects will be our housewarming gifts to you. Right girls?"

"Yes!"

Lottie sat on the edge of her seat when I addressed her. "Lottie, could you please make an 11 X 14 printed copy of the original university?"

She looked surprised. "Is that all you need? Would you like it framed? I can even engrave the dates on it?" Lottie grinned from ear to ear. "I can't wait to get started." She gave me a wink.

"Yes, I'd be tickled pink. When Dr. Duntworth and Mr. Dells complete the project, the print will hang in the foyer of the main building."

Opal raised her hand like a schoolgirl. "What do you need me to do?"

"Would you be willing to design an advertisement about the bed and breakfast for the weekly Sunday paper? I'll set up a website on the computer, but in all honesty, I have no idea how to work with the paper."

Opal raised her eyebrows. "I'm not sure you girls know this, but I used to be the lead writer for the paper in Greenville. I'm honored and will do you proud, boss." She placed a straw over her ear mimicking a pencil, then removed her phone from her purse and sent multiple messages. I guess I awoke the reporter side of her.

I took a deep breath—and then I cried. This tender jubilant touch of heaven moment in time, cradled me. These hysterical society ladies, who literally drove me crazy, had now become a part of my bed and breakfast.

We enveloped each other in hugs and tenderly said our goodbyes.

The ladies exited the beautiful restaurant one by one. Grace and I remained.

"Mrs. Byer, thank you for agreeing to make the sign and logo. I'm sorry if all this has been stressful."

"Rae, I don't have the same expertise as Anna. Her college degree trumps my high school diploma." She glanced down at her coffee cup. "I'll try my best to copy the old sign."

"The old sign? I don't want anything like the old sign. I want something unique, something creative. That's why I hired you. The only requirement is that it's made of iron and larger than the old one which was much too tiny to catch anyone's attention. Maybe that's why half the people in this town never knew it was a university." I gave a little chuckle.

Grace sighed. "I can't wait to get started. Since you asked me to make the sign the other day, my mind has designed and redesigned it over and over. I already have some ideas, but I don't want to show you yet. I'll work over the weekend and present my diagrams to you next week if that's okay." She ate the last crumb of her chocolate cake.

"That's more than okay. I'm grateful."

The two of us exited the restaurant. *Peace.*

We have different gifts, according to the grace given to each of us.
Romans 12:6

Chapter Twenty-Two

Two hours later, my phone rang. Caller I.D. showed the name Grace Byer. I hesitated then answered.

"Rae, this is Grace . . ."

"And Lance." He cleared his throat. "Well, go on, Grace. Invite the girl."

"Lance suggested we invite you to dinner at our home after the game. Will you accept?"

Lance blurted out. "We'd love to have you."

I stifled a snarky remark. "I'd love to attend."

"See, Grace. That was easy," Lance said. "We look forward to seeing you. Bye, Rae."

***

Joe picked me up in his clunky old doggy-smelling truck with Buddy eagerly awaiting Puffs, who joined him in the back.

Red mums lined the Byers' front porch steps. My thoughts quickly flashed to the time I rode the bike past this beautiful home and thought Grace was the lawn keeper. I chuckled to myself as Joe opened the front door and the four of us stepped inside. The inviting smells of grilled hot dogs and burgers permeated the entire entryway. In addition, the spicy aroma of five alarm chili tempted my senses. I glanced at all the red decorations and the Bulldog rug in the family room as our canines made a beeline for the kitchen. Fortunately, we had leashed both pets and led them outside onto the deck.

Joe patted Buddy on the head and noticed a piece of hot dog dangling from his Great Dane's mouth. "Crazy dog. I can't believe you snatched that."

I patted Puffs' brown head. "Poor girl. You're just not tall enough to take anything off a counter." I leaned down to hug her neck and noticed something hanging from her muzzle. "How did you get a hot dog?" I grabbed a napkin to wipe the evidence off Puffs' doggy lips.

Joe chuckled. "Buddy must have shared his with Puffs. It's canine love."

As others arrived in the backyard, we all joined the team and cheerleaders in a Bulldogs' cheer.

Bulldogs, Bulldogs, Yes, Indeed

Bulldogs, Bulldogs, Keep the lead.

I'd seen this kind of enthusiasm for college football rallies, but never at a high school event.

Several of the students offered to take Puffs and Buddy and entertain them for a while. Built-in dog sitters. Joe and I meandered through the crowd in the backyard. He took my hand and my heart skipped several beats as we stepped onto the lush lawn.

A dinner bell clanged loudly when Dean Byer stood on the deck. "Bulldog fans, welcome to the fifteenth annual chili dinner fundraiser. We have plenty to eat, so chow down. Cheerleaders get served first, the team last."

The girls cheered, and the team groaned.

"Just kidding. We'll all get started after the blessing."

One of the pastors prayed about sportsmanship and remembering to keep God first. After everyone said amen, the lines formed along both sides of the lengthy tables.

I spotted Lauren, and we waved to each other. She motioned she was sitting toward the back of the yard near the fire pit. I saw Mick already heading in that direction with a cup in each hand.

"Joe, want to join Lauren and Mick? They're sitting at the fire pit. Okay with you?"

"Sounds great. I'm finished filling my plate, but I need to get a bowl of chili."

"Me, too. I can fit two bowls on my tray, so mind if I get yours for you?"

"That'll help. Thanks."

I filled the bowls and the two of us traipsed to the fire pit.

Joe grinned. "We'd better get seated and eat our chili while it's hot. Don't want our chili to get chilly." He laughed. "Chilly, get it? Like chili?"

"Yes, I get it." I rolled my eyes.

I noticed Grace socializing with her guests. As I passed by, I heard her telling them about making the sign for the bed and breakfast. Hearing her comments made me smile.

Lauren and Mick sat close together and shared a hot dog. Amber and Jack sat nearby, and we all enjoyed conversing.

Amber looked at Lauren and me. "If you girls think this Bulldog event is over the top, you won't believe how crazy it gets during Fall Festival. The volunteer fire department and shops put hay bales everywhere—pumpkins, mums, scarecrows, candy apples, you name it, they have it. It's really a touristy thing, but we all benefit from it." She stood up and stretched her long legs. "Come to think of it, next year we'll have a bed and breakfast for tourists to stay in during the festival. That'll be wonderful, Rae."

"Thanks so much for those encouraging words."

Amber's attention immediately turned to an older couple in the food line. "Excuse me, my parents just arrived, and I'll see if they need help balancing plates and bowls."

"I'll give you a hand," Jack offered.

Lauren glanced my way. "Rae, after you finish, mind if I talk with you?"

"I thought we were talking right now."

"I mean in private." She spoke quietly enough that Joe and Mick couldn't hear a word. As a matter of fact, they were so engrossed in their meals, it appeared they didn't care what we were talking about.

I took my last bite as Joe began eating his chocolate cake. "Joe, do you mind if I talk privately with Lauren? I hate to leave when you're not finished eating."

"Your friend needs you. There's no need to ask." He swallowed some of his tea.

"Okay. See you in a bit."

Lauren leaned in toward Mick and whispered something in his ear. He gave a half smile, nodded, and kept eating.

She walked slowly with me. "Rae, I don't know what's happening. Do you mind sitting in those Adirondack chairs?

There are heaters over there, too, so we should be comfortable.

"Perfect."

Lauren curled her legs under her as she situated herself in the wooden chair. "I'm falling in love with this town and a crazy Realtor I haven't known very long. You must think I'm losing my mind."

"I hope you won't be angry. I feel I need to say this." I paused a few seconds. "Remember how Mick posted deceptive pictures of the B&B on the website? I'm concerned about his honesty."

She looked at me and smiled. "Rae, I know you're worried about me. We're more like sisters than just friends; you can read me like a book. We've all made mistakes, and I'm thankful our God is the God of second chances. I feel Mick deserves a second chance to prove himself. As a matter of fact, I asked him directly about the pictures." She took both my hands in hers. "He feels terrible and at the same time, glad you're fixing up the place. Let's see what God has planned."

I didn't argue with her explanation. As a matter of fact, Lauren never shared her faith with me in such a direct way. God carried Lauren. *Footprints. Thank you, Lord.*

***

The evening ended much too quickly. Lauren and I learned the fundraiser money went toward Christmas gifts for needy families. Wonderful!

I offered to help clean up, but Joe informed me his mother hired the football team and cheerleaders to assist.

The money earned bought new uniforms. A win-win situation all around.

Joe drove me home, with our dogs dozing contentedly in the back seat. "Thanks for such a great time. I see why my grandparents enjoyed this place."

"I didn't thank you earlier for asking my mom to make the sign for the bed and breakfast. She stopped by the university after the luncheon to tell Dad and me."

"Your mom will do a great job." Before walking inside my door, I stopped short and moved a little closer to him.

His cool lips brushed my forehead tenderly. "Good night, Rae." Long strides carried him quickly to his Buddy-filled truck. He glanced back and gave me his crooked grin.

I waved to him from my living room window as he pulled out of sight, and then I closed the blinds.

Sleep well, Professor.

***

The cool night air flowed through my slightly opened bedroom window. Fortunately, the opening wasn't large enough for Miss Doris's cat. With my flannel pajamas and fluffy comforter, I snuggled into a restful sleep. Puffs snored lightly. *Contentment.*

Good night, Lord. Thank you for bringing Joe into my life. Thank you for being the God of second chances.

The Lord has done it this very day;
let us rejoice today and be glad.
Psalm 118:24

Chapter Twenty-Three

One morning shortly after the Bulldogs' fundraiser, I awoke with a tune Grandma used to sing floating through my mind. *Get up, get up, you lazy sleeper.* I jumped out of bed refreshed, dressed in split-second speed, and ate a granola bar.

I hugged my sweet dog, grabbed my coat and hat, and opened the front door. "What in the world is this?" My faithful companion stood beside me and sniffed at the manila envelope on the threshold. Puffs leaned to pick it up with her canines, but I snatched it before she did any damage.

The envelope had my name handwritten on the front and Grace's return-address sticker in the upper left-hand corner. *I'll take this with me.* I kissed Puffs' bubble gum, pink nose. "See you later, girl."

***

The envelope tucked easily under my arm as I pushed open the door to Bitty's Buns. "Good morning, Natalie."

"Good morning, Rae. Want your usual? The cinnamon buns are fresh from the oven." She washed her hands, wiped them on a paper towel, and straightened baked items in the glass display.

"Not this morning, Natalie. I already ate, but I'd like some coffee."

I set the package from Mrs. Byer on the counter and pulled napkins out of the dispenser. "Oh, those cinnamon buns smell heavenly." I tilted my head back and the aroma almost tempted me. *Almost.*

Natalie gave that precious laugh of hers. "Why don't you go out on a limb and let me add something extra to your java this morning?"

Although I'd only lived in Hope a short while, Natalie knew my likes and dislikes. She also realized I was a creature of habit.

"You know me, Natalie. I'm not the adventurous type."

"I'm sorry dear, but I beg to differ. You've taken the adventure of a lifetime buying the bed and breakfast. If you took a chance on that, you can certainly try something new in your coffee." She folded her arms and cocked her head. "What do ya say?"

Natalie's attitude made me laugh out loud. "You got me there, dear friend. Okay, I'll go for it. I'll take the coffee challenge. Don't get upset if I cringe when I drink it. You know my taste buds are extremely finicky." I flipped my hair with attitude and proceeded to cross my arms. "Coffee, please."

The two of us giggled as only friends do. Bantering back and forth brought such delight to my soul.

After picking up the unopened mailer, I peered into the display case. Within minutes, Natalie placed a tall Styrofoam cup in front of me.

"Rae, drum roll please." She added a dollop of whipped cream, chocolate shavings, and a hint of cinnamon. "Go for it!"

The other customers in Bitty's Buns began cheering me on. Mr. Ike Wood sat at a corner table and Sendy from Sweetness and Sweaters clapped. "Go, Rae! Go!"

Holding the cup with both hands, I sipped slowly and very cautiously. "Oh my, this is horribly hot. Terrible tasting. Icky, to say the least." I snickered and wiped my mouth with the napkins. "I can't drink another drop." With a disgusted look on my face, I put the half empty java on the counter.

Natalie slowly unfolded her arms and grasped the unwanted coffee. "I'm sorry Rae. I really thought this was the perfect blend for you. I wanted to name this Hope's Rae."

"I was just kidding!" I went around the counter and wrapped my arms around her. "There's no way you're throwing this out. It's absolutely deliciously delicious."

She slipped out of my embrace and looked up at me. "No, no, you didn't like it, so the coffee goes in the trash." She tried to look angry, but it didn't work. Instead, she winked at me, "I'm so glad you enjoyed this new creation, my adventurous friend. Success, ladies and gentlemen."

Mr. Wood and Sendy gave a standing ovation. The other two customers stood right along with the Bitty's Buns' cheering section.

I motioned for them to have a seat and curtsied in the process. Laughter. "What did you add to my favorite coffee?"

"A tad of almond flavoring. Just a tad, mind you." Natalie's hands floated through the air as she explained the process. "Notice the shavings are both dark and milk chocolate." Her smile was contagious.

"Now you know what my usual will be, Miss Natalie. No doubt about it."

"Rae, I'm not joking about naming the coffee after you. Kind of a signature drink." She swept a wisp of hair from her forehead. "It's Hope's Rae." Natalie's lips curved upward in a tender smile. "What do you think?"

"I'm speechless and honored." My eyes misted. "I've never had anything named after me."

"Come here, dear." Natalie gave me a motherly hug. "You've been an inspiration to everyone and showed us there's more to life than dreaming. There's doing."

"Thank you. Thank you."

More customers entered Bitty's, and Natalie stepped behind the counter to take their orders. We waved to each other as I exited with my manila envelope under my arm and my Hope's Rae coffee cradled in my hand.

***

The bench across the street called my name. I wiped colored leaves from its surface, sat, and savored my coffee. I took a deep breath and carefully opened the envelope. The drawing paper with black and white sketches revealed a rectangular-shaped sign. Simple. I noticed Grace added a few smaller illustrations of seasonal objects in the margins. Her written explanation: "The additional shapes might be hung on a small hook at the bottom of the iron sign according to the season. As you can see, I also included a larger sketch of Puffs."

Without any doubt, I'd chosen the right person to make the sign. I'd started this day in a hurry, had some heavenly coffee with Natalie, and now the sketches added a touch of delight to my heart. With my head tilted back and my eyes closed, I soaked in the sun's rays and the fragrance of Rae's Hope tickled my nostrils. This restorative moment brought delight to my senses.

I carefully put Grace's masterpiece into the mailer. The fragrance of my coffee lured me to take another sip. *Heavenly.*

I didn't notice the approach of a large canine, until he licked the back of my neck, and I jumped up off the bench. "What in the world?" Buddy ran around to stand in front of me. "You're a sneaky one, Mr. Great Dane." I kissed his big nose.

"Sorry we startled you. I didn't think this one-hundred-fifty-pound dog could sneak up on anyone. By the way, are you just reserving your kisses for dog noses or people noses, too?" Joe grinned that crooked grin of his.

I stepped back teasingly and placed my hands on my hips. "Hmm, Mr. Professor. I only kiss doggy noses." I giggled and plopped myself back onto the bench, then patted the space next to me. Buddy's tail wagged as he jumped and squinched in beside me. Joe sat precariously on the bench edge with Buddy between us.

He peered around his massive dog. "I see you have my mom's envelope. She ran out to the sidewalk this morning when I walked Buddy past her home. Mom spoke a mile a minute until I finally deciphered that she'd dropped her sketches by your house at zero dark thirty this morning. She's been driving all of us crazy. Emily finally convinced her to give them to you."

"I'm so glad she did. They look absolutely fabulous." I moved a little closer to Buddy hoping he'd jump off the bench. He didn't take the hint. "I sure hope it didn't stress your mom. I love the sketches."

Joe patted Buddy's head and motioned for him to move off the bench. He obliged as his long doggy-tongue took a swipe at my coffee cup and successfully slobbered on the lid.

Joe scolded him, slid closer to me, and put his arm over the back of the bench. "Rae, I'm sorry about your coffee. I'll buy you another cup."

He had no idea the lengths Natalie went to make it. "That's okay. I just don't want Buddy to get sick. Chocolate's in the cup, but I don't think he got much off the lid." I nuzzled my nose into Buddy's gray fur and hugged the mammoth canine. "By the way, did you see the illustrations your mom gave me?"

Joe shifted a little closer. "No, but I'd like to."

"Please be careful with them." I grinned sheepishly. "Of course, you know all the time your mom put into this."

Joe looked stunned as he examined the work. "I knew my mom could draw, but I never realized how well. She always drew stuff for Emily and me when we were kids. However, she's never felt qualified as an artist because she doesn't have a college degree. You've boosted her confidence." Joe gave me a kiss on the cheek, then stopped when Buddy stood, and licked him on the face. “Silly dog.” He glanced in my direction. “Now, where was I?” Joe inched closer and kissed my forehead, and then my nose.

“Joe, shall we check our calendars to see if this is National Kissing Day?” I threw my head back and absorbed myself in laughter. Until . . .

Joe cradled my face in his rough hands and tenderly kissed me on the mouth. *Pitter-patter, pitter-patter.* My heart skipped a few beats.

He smiled with ease. “I don’t care if this kissing day thing is on the calendar or not, because I’m declaring every day National Kissing Day.” Joe crossed his arms with a macho grin on his face.

“I like the way you think, Professor Joe. Shall I make us a calendar?” *Whoa, I let that slip out without thinking.* “Well, you know I’m just teasing. I didn’t mean you have to kiss me every day.” Awkward.

“Yes, I love the idea. Just so you know, I’m not teasing.” His arm set easily on the back of the bench again then slid gently onto my shoulders.

When I removed my crocheted hat, his smooth-shaven cheekbone rested against my static hair. Warmth from head to toe. My gloves and coat weren’t the culprits. I knew what warmed me. *Time to make our calendar.*

The God of peace be with you all.
Romans 15:33

Chapter Twenty-Four

Thoughts of Joe's kisses still lingered later that day. I could think of nothing else—until my phone buzzed. Dr. Duntworth.

"Rae, Abel and I are doing a little investigating and brought some of our team to your property. If you have time, come on by."

"I'm not far away. I'll be there in a minute."

I trotted to Charleston Street and trudged down the driveway as clumps of red dirt clung to my boots. I noticed the contractor and architect speaking to someone who wore a chartreuse hard hat. As I got closer, I read the black bold letters on the side of the hat, SHPO. State Historical Preservation Office. The state representative stood toe to toe with Dr. Duntworth and Mr. Dells. She wagged her finger at both men.

Even though I was within earshot of their conversation, they didn't notice me. The lady in the hard hat put her hands in her pockets and grimaced. "Dr. Duntworth, I told you this project is more complicated than plowing down that unsightly porch, throwing up a door that closes and locks, and re-doing a staircase." She pulled her hand out of her pocket, pushed her hard hat back a little, then brushed her bangs across her forehead. "I can't approve that building yet."

Dr. Duntworth noticed me standing nearby. "Rae, glad you got here quickly. Come join us. I didn't know Martha Ingles would be here today, or I'd have let you know."

I started to introduce myself to Mrs. Ingles but didn't get a chance.

Dr. Duntworth continued. "Martha, we already got approval for the cottages since they aren't historical, and we're not starting that doggone huge building for a couple weeks. I'm sure we'll get it all lined up just the way you like it." He touched the tip of his hard hat and smirked as he adjusted his jacket collar. "By the way, Mrs. D said you and Gabe are coming for dinner tomorrow night. She made me promise—no shop talk." Dr. Duntworth smiled as he and Abel Dells ambled toward the first cottage. Mr. Dells kept walking and Dr. Duntworth looked my way.

"Rae, everything's falling into place." He wiped his hands on his overalls. "When Martha, or I guess I should call her, Mrs. Ingles, reviews the proposal for the main building, we'll be moving fast." He paused and folded his arms across his substantial middle. "It's all going to be great."

"From what I just heard, it doesn't sound great."

"Things get a little tricky at the onset of a job. No worries."

I waved slightly and meandered toward Mrs. Ingles. She held her clipboard and used her pen to make notes. Her hat slipped down over her bangs and quickly covered her eyes. *You'd think she'd find a suitable hat size.*

"I'm Rae Long, the owner of the property." My crocheted cap slipped over my eyes, and I pushed it back. *Guess I need head gear that fits properly, too.*

Martha's staunch expression didn't waiver. "I must admit, I expected someone a little more seasoned." She balanced her clipboard in one hand, removed her hat, and swung it back and forth. "This is going to be quite the renovation. I hope you're up to the task. By the way, I'll be coming by each day to inspect. If you have any questions, you can give me a call." She pulled a chartreuse business card from her pocket. "Just so you know, I'm very persnickety. Please feel free to call me any time. Have a good day, Miss Long." She got into her official car with the SHPO logo and drove off.

Persnickety. Definitely. Mrs. Ingles is a lot younger than I thought she'd be, and I wonder if she can handle her job.

***

Dr. Duntworth stopped in his tracks as I edged closer to the nearest cottage. "Here, Rae, you have to wear this whether you want to or not. I know how you girls are with your hair and all." He handed me a beat-up hard hat. "Put this on. It's regulations. And by the way, everyone calls me Dr. D."

"Thank you, Dr. D." I wanted to tell him I didn't give a twit about my hair and he shouldn't stereotype women in that light, but I cut him some slack. He was certainly much older than I was, so instead of giving him a lecture in political correctness, I opted to show him respect. Maybe by my actions, he'd see that not all women were hair fanatics. *As a matter of fact, Mrs. Ingles wore her hat proudly. Why didn't he make comments to her? Come to think of it, maybe he did and that's why she wagged her finger at him earlier.*

***

The sound of horns startled me as cars turned into my driveway. It became a makeshift parking lot.

What in the world's going on?

Victoria Sounds waved vigorously at me and shouted. "Rae, Mr. Dells let us know you're here. It's lunch time; you and the workers need to eat. Come help us." She opened her trunk filled with multiple containers of food and several thermoses.

Joe's clunky old truck parked behind Victoria's SUV and out jumped Joe and Buddy. People removed tables from the bed of the truck then started unloading Victoria's vehicle. Molly and her helpers placed red paper items on the tables. I recognized them from the football party at the Byers' home a few nights earlier.

Joe jogged to where I stood then gave me a quick hug. "Looks like everything's underway."

I squeezed him gently. "You knew about this all along, Professor?" I stood on tiptoe and sneaked in a whisper of a kiss.

"Maybe." He laughed.

Lauren arrived and tapped me on the shoulder. "Stop the kissing you two and get busy. There's still a lot of food to unload." She patted the top of my hat.

"I'm shocked. How did everyone know I was here?"

Lauren snickered. "Small town. Remember?"

As we approached the vehicles, more cars parked, and popped open their food-laden trunks.

"I can't believe all this." I wiped a tear. "I don't know what to say."

Grace and the Historical Society ladies grinned and handed me a huge green bowl of potato salad, then transferred another to Lauren.

"Here, Joe." Grace put two huge bowls in his arms. "I guess it's pretty evident we society ladies brought the potato salad. We wanted to make sure there was enough."

Lance Byer appeared and stepped on the dilapidated porch. He cleared his throat then held a bullhorn to his mouth. "Ladies and gentlemen, please form a circle and grab hands. Let's thank the Lord for this feast, for the bed and breakfast, and for Rae." Lance removed his cap. "Dear heavenly Father, you created each person here and have allowed us to come together as one body of believers. Thank You for this food and all those who prepared it. In Jesus's name. Amen." He put on his cap, "Let's eat."

The lines formed on both sides of the tables and there was absolutely no shortage of potato salad or anything else.

Lauren manned the thermoses of water, lemonade, and iced tea. Of course, it was sweet tea, a Southern staple. I noticed a guy with a red baseball cap scooping ice into cups. I chuckled to myself when Lauren stooped down, removed the man's hat, and kissed his cheek. I knew right then and there the man was Mick Treavor. Instead of his usual perfectly combed wavy black hair, he had hat hair. After setting my plate on the top stoop of the closest cottage, I meandered toward my long-time friend who was sneaking another smooch.

I caught Mick and Lauren off guard. "Umm—Now it's your turn to get to work, Lauren. You too, Mick." Lauren's cheeks turned almost as red as Mick's cap. "Thank you, both." I picked up a cup of iced tea and saluted them.

Lauren came around the drink table and stepped toward me. "I didn't tell you earlier, but I can definitely see the vision you have for this property, and I didn't mention how easy it is to fall in love with Hope."

"Are you sure Hope is the only thing you're falling for?" I gave her a little wink.

"You got me there. Is it that evident?" Lauren attempted to wipe a spot of barbecue sauce from her sleeve. "I'm glad I moved here." She tried to avoid chunks of red clay as she tiptoed to the drink table. I noticed splotches of the destructive stuff matted against the calf of her jeans. If she only knew . . .

Joe sat next to me and scooped a spoon full of Jell-O fruit salad into his mouth. "This is my kind of salad. The only thing green is the Jell-O. Want a bite?"

"I'll pass. I see the coconut inside, and I'm not a fan. However, I'd love a nibble of pea salad. Somehow I overlooked it; it's one of my favorites." I looked longingly at Joe's plate. "Please?"

"He scooped as much as he could possibly put on his fork. "Here you go."

As I slid closer to him, I took a bite of the cheese-laden pea salad and ate every morsel. I wiped my chin and took a sip of tea. "Thank you, Professor Joe."

He bent in a little closer. "Rae, I need to fill my plate again. Want anything?" He gently kissed the tip of my nose.

"I can't eat another bite." Thank goodness I'd worn my sweat pants with an elastic waist. *Stretchy*. "I'm going to do a little mingling and thank everyone for coming then maybe get dessert."

"Hmm, would a kiss count as dessert?" He wiggled his eyebrows then weaved toward the food tables.

I sauntered to where Dr. D stood. "May I use the megaphone?"

He handed me the contraption. "Ladies and gentlemen of the best town in the world, may I have your attention please?" The bullhorn squealed loudly. "Sorry about that. This is my first time using one of these things. I can't thank you enough for this luscious meal. You are my family; I am blessed." I handed the megaphone back to Dr. D and couldn't contain a sniffle.

Natalie pressed through the crowd and stood in front of Dr. Duntworth. She looked hysterical. Miss Natalie, all 4'10" inches, looked up at Dr. Duntworth. "Dr. D, I need that speaker thing, please." She took it from his hand. The folks cheered as she raised the billowing bullhorn to her mouth. "We love you, Rae. I want y'all to know there's a new signature coffee at Bitty's Buns. It's called Hope's Rae. I expect a long line outside my place tomorrow morning to try this heavenly java. Also, dessert is on the five tables near the last cottage. The Rodriguez's of Fenster Haus helped me set up the entire sweet treat station. Please help yourselves." Natalie turned and gave 6'5" Dr. D his loud horn. The crowd erupted in laughter as he exaggerated a crouch to take the megaphone and Natalie stood on tip toes to give it to him.

Note to self: If Molly makes a meal for the bed and breakfast, ask Natalie to supply pastries and snacks. Just a thought.

Several ice chests were filled with leftovers for Dr. Duntworth and Mr. Dells' construction crew to take home after work. Joe's truck bed carried all the tables. With the tailgate closed firmly, he took my hands in his. "I'm glad we surprised you. I thought I'd slip and tell you about the meal when I saw you this morning, but fortunately we discussed a calendar instead." He raked his fingers through his hair and smiled his tempting smile. "After I return these tables to the church, I'll stop back by just in case you need help with anything. Okay?"

"I'd love that." I hugged him tightly. "Do you need me to help unload the tables?" It was the least I could do.

"No, I can manage, but thanks anyway. I'll see you in a few." He slid into his truck, kept the window down, and placed his elbow on the window frame.

I heard him singing loudly as he drove down the driveway. Very loudly, since his voice carried over his chugging truck motor. *My knight on a white horse—or rather—clunky truck.*

***

The construction workers loaned Joe and me well-used gloves, and Joe had brought new dust masks for each of us. We removed old carpet from three of the cabins and made sure the tiny nails were pulled up afterwards. The hardwood floors needed re-sanding and Dr. D assured me he'd consult me before re-staining.

I glanced at the time on my phone. "Joe, I'm pooped. Let's call it a night." I wiped my forehead with a paper towel and removed my face mask and gloves. "I feel grimy."

"I have a staff dinner and brainstorming session tonight at school, or I'd offer to take you to dinner. I know you're exhausted."

"Listen to me whining. Everyone got the meal ready and did all this magnificent stuff for me. I shouldn't complain." I dabbed my forehead again, stood on tiptoes, and placed a slight kiss on Joe's chin.

Megaphone Dr. D startled us. "Go home, Joe. Go home, Rae. You're distracting the workers. My crew is calling it a night, and I think you should, too. Remember the meeting at the university tonight, Joe. Dinner is provided, but I guess you've already had dessert," he said with a wink.

The workers applauded. Enough said.

***

Shower, pajamas, freshly changed sheets, flannel duvet, and Puffs at my feet. Warmth. Peaceful slumber. *Good night, Lord.*

Now I urge you to take some food.
You need it to survive.
Acts 27:34

Chapter Twenty-Five

Nightmares had zoomed in my mind throughout the night. I felt lousy. I sat on the bedside with my feet dangling and holding my achy head. My throat hurt so bad. I sheltered my eyes from the sunlight streaming between the slats in the blinds.

"My head is about to explode, Puffs." She looked at me with her I've-gotta-take-care-of-business look. "I know, girl. Let me put on my slippers." I pulled each slipper over my socks, and Puffs led the way downstairs toward the kitchen door. "There you go."

Scooping Puffs' dog food into her dish and filling her water bowl took every ounce of energy. She returned inside, and I dropped onto a kitchen chair. After my furry companion devoured her breakfast, she followed me upstairs into the bedroom.

"I need just a few more minutes of sleep, Puffs." I scrunched under the duvet cover and closed my eyes while Puffs nestled close to me and whimpered softly.

"I'll be okay, girl." I mumbled. Then fell into a deep sleep.

***

I awoke to the chime of my doorbell and the buzz of my phone. I propped myself up on my arm, shuffled through the items on my nightstand, then grabbed my phone. "Lauren. Are you okay?"

"Am I okay?" She paused. "What do you mean? I'm checking on you."

I pulled myself out of bed, and Puffs and I went downstairs. "Someone's at my door. I'll call you back."

I peeked through the peephole; Lauren stood on the other side. I immediately opened the door. "Why did you call if you were at the door?"

She didn't skip a beat. "Why are you still in your pajamas? It's 3:30 in the afternoon, and you look absolutely terrible."

"Thanks a lot. Just so you know, I felt worse earlier, but I'm feeling a little better now. I can't believe I slept so long. Come into the kitchen; I'll make us some hot tea."

Lauren pulled out a chair and pointed for me to sit down. "I'll make the tea. Do you have any cream? You know I don't want powder stuff."

"Yes, in the fridge. While you're at it, mind getting a couple scones out of the freezer? I'll warm them."

Lauren didn't get the scones. Instead, she walked toward the front door. "Heavens, I forgot something on the porch. When I called you and knocked, I set the box on the rocker. I think you'll opt for what I brought instead of a scone." She opened the door and brought in a pale blue pastry box tied shut with a blue tulle bow. "Natalie's cinnamon buns. Just the way you like them. She put extra pecans on both orders."

"I can't believe you went to all that trouble. I'm so happy you're here in Hope, even if it's just for a semester."

She heated two cups filled with water in the microwave, added tea bags, and set them on the table. I took a sip and waited while she removed two dessert plates from my cupboard and placed a cinnamon bun on each.

Lauren sat on a kitchen chair. "Let's bless this simple snack." She bowed her head. "Dear Lord, thank you for this time Rae and I can spend together. You know the plans for our lives. We praise You for our good friends, Joe and Mick. Thank you for this food, and please help Rae get well. Amen."

I took a bite of the mouth-watering cinnamon bun. "This is magnificent."

My dear friend added a little more cream to her tea. "I went to the bed and breakfast to see you, and Dr. Duntworth flagged me down. He asked where you were, and I told him I'd find out. So here I am." She picked up her napkin and wiped sticky frosting from her face. "I'll call him and let him know you're doing pretty well, or would you like to?"

"I will now."

My phone conversation with Dr. D eased his concerns and ended quickly. I liked his right-to-the-point attitude.

Lauren sipped her tea. "I hope Martha Ingles is cutting your architect and contractor some slack. These men and their crews are experienced, and she shouldn't hover over them."

"It's been several days since I've seen Mrs. Ingles, or as I refer to her, Mrs. Persnickety. She signed the permits, so that's encouraging." I patted my stomach. "I think I've had enough to eat. Thank you for my cinnamon roll."

Lauren got up from her chair, gathered our dishes, and placed them in the sink. "Care for any more tea?"

"I'm good. I can't believe I wasted an entire day sleeping." A yawn escaped me.

She smiled then changed the subject. "You and Joe make such a cute couple. I can visualize you two marrying and living on the second floor."

I tossed my paper napkin at her in jest. "We were talking about my illness, not Joe and me. Don't put the cart before the horse." I grabbed another napkin and wiped my nose. "What about you and Mick?"

"Talk about putting the cart before the horse. We haven't known each other very long at all, but I guess you and Joe haven't either." She fidgeted with her collar. "Mick and I get along quite well. I actually met his parents yesterday and they're really nice." She patted Puffs on the head. "And, by the way," she smiled, "there's something I wanted to tell you this morning at the bed and breakfast." Lauren sat up straighter and grinned. "I'm staying in Hope longer than a semester."

"What? I'm thrilled beyond thrilled! Give me the details!"

"The department heads of Engineering at the universities set up a conference call with Landy and me early this morning. The staff explained it would be beneficial for us to establish camaraderie with the students where we are now. Since we're enjoying the exchange program, we agreed to remain at our current locations indefinitely."

We jumped up and down like two young school girls.

"Lauren, what do your parents think? You've never lived far from them."

"I told them I met Mick's family, and this morning, after the conference call, I explained the opportunity for me to stay here. At first Dad sulked and then I invited him and Mom to visit Hope. They're coming in three weeks; I wondered if they could stay in one of your cottages."

"Of course. Three of them are almost ready for occupants now. I can't wait."

"Thank you so much. You've done a great job on the place, Rae. I'll bet that's why you're exhausted."

"I'm back to work tomorrow." A text message appeared on my phone. "Can you believe Dr. D just sent me pictures and updates? It's only been a day since I've been to the bed and breakfast. I miss one day, and everyone is concerned. I love these people."

Lauren gave me a gentle squeeze. "That's just part of the charm of this little town. Now get some rest and please let me know if you need anything at all. I'll let myself out."

I gave her a huge hug. "I'm so glad you're staying here. Love you, girl."

She smiled and slipped on her coat. "Love you, too, Sis."

***

I returned to my cozy bed and received e-mails from the hysterical ladies offering to bring a meal and do whatever I needed. After responding to their messages, and letting them know I was fine, I settled under my covers—until I heard a light knock at the front door. I sleepily slid out of bed, glanced in the mirror, and ran a brush through my tangled mane. Then I descended the steps.

When I opened the door, there was a plastic container on the banister with a note attached. A piece of plastic wrap lay beside the empty container. I'm sure it originally covered it. The note read, "Rae, I hope you enjoy the chicken soup. Doris." Midnight sat on my porch, licking her chops. Sneaky cat. I knew Doris's heart would break if she discovered I never tasted the soup. If I told Doris her beloved cat consumed it, she'd try to convince me Puffs ate the contents. After all, her sweet cat was perfection on four kitty legs. *Not!*

Before taking the container inside, I noticed a bouquet of assorted fall flowers on the wicker rocker. *Note attached. "I didn't want to disturb your rest. Prayin' you feel better soon. I'm there in a flash if you need me, Joe."*

I brought them inside and immediately called the professor. "I love the flowers."

"How are you feeling? And please be honest."

"Honestly, I'm feeling much better. Thanks for checking on me and for the bouquet."

"My phone is on 24/7 so don't hesitate to call or text if you need anything. Rest well, Rae."

I proceeded upstairs and stopped in my tracks when I heard a faint knock, again. I retraced my steps downstairs and checked my trusty peephole.

Emily stood on the other side of the door with a teapot in her hands.

I opened the door quickly, well as quickly as I could since the doggone thing stuck again. “Emily, it’s good to see you.”

“I thought you might need a pot of Chamomile tea to help you sleep. Mind if I put it in your kitchen?”

“Come in. That’s sure sweet of you.” She followed me. “Can you stay for a cup?”

Emily placed the teapot on the table. “Silly me. I didn’t even ask how you’re feeling.” She scooted out a kitchen chair and sat comfortably. “I have a few minutes to spare, so I’ll have some tea.”

“I’m doing so much better and I’ll definitely be at the bed and breakfast tomorrow morning.” I took some cookies out of a baggy and placed them on a plate.

“I didn’t want to disturb you.” Emily nibbled a cookie. “But I did want to tell you why Blake and I weren’t at the bed and breakfast meal yesterday.”

I put mugs on the table. “My goodness, I know you two are busy. Please don’t be concerned.”

Emily poured the steamy drink for us. She sipped carefully and removed a napkin from the holder. “I feel I can trust you with this information. I can’t tell my mother because it’ll throw her into a tizzy; Joe doesn’t know either.” She blew her nose and grabbed another napkin. “Blake and I haven’t exactly called it quits, but we’re on the verge. I couldn’t face him if he showed up at the meal yesterday.” She wadded up the napkins, got out of her seat, and threw them into the trash. “I’m sorry, Rae, here you are sick, and I’m whining.”

“I’m glad you shared with me. I won’t tell a soul.”

She pushed the chair under the table and patted me on the shoulder. "Thanks for the listening ears. You've helped me so much; I can't thank you enough." She gave me a quick hug. "I'll let myself out. Get well, dear friend." She opened the front door and looked back over her shoulder. "By the way, I'm so glad you and Joe are dating. You know he's fallen head over heels for you." She closed the door behind her.

***

I changed my sheets, showered, and raised my window just a bit. My gown warmed me as I crawled under the covers, then tapped the foot of my bed to signal Puffs to jump aboard. She did her usual circling, found a comfy spot, and quickly dozed. Rain played a tune on the tin roof as I prayed for my dear friend Emily and her fiancé Blake. She never revealed her angst with him, but the Lord knew, and that's all that mattered. I felt refreshed and blessed and thought only sweet thoughts of my Puffs and Joe. There was love in the air in this quaint South Carolina town.

. . . my body also will rest in hope.
Acts 2:26

Chapter Twenty-Six

Sometimes we have to squint our eyes just enough to block out the bad and see the sliver of hope. A treasured quote of Grandma's I tucked away nicely in my mind. Today, I squinted a little.

***

Dr. D approached me quickly as I walked up the driveway. "We have a little problem. Martha Ingles and her team came by as we got ready to start the engines and knock down the porch." He coughed in his gloved hand. "She told me and Abel the massive hole in the roof is a problem. Evidently, she got here early and saw it before I did. I swear she sleeps in her car, so she can catch everybody off guard. She's—well, guess I'd better stop complaining and show you what she's talking about. I see you're wearing your hard hat."

"Where's Mrs. Ingles?" I turned and did a 360-degree sweep. "I don't see her anywhere." My hard hat slipped below my eyebrows and I readjusted it. "Why does Martha need to be here anyway? I guess I don't understand the ins and outs of construction."

"Martha needs to inspect only when we've informed her that we've finished a project. I think the Historical Society ladies asked her to keep an eye on things. She's going overboard."

I followed him and saw the hole in the roof. Daylight streamed in from every angle and the wooden floors had warped. "This is unbelievable." I moaned.

Before I said more, Martha entered the main building, chartreuse hard hat teetering on her head and her legs balancing on stiletto heels. I almost did a double take, but instead, regained a little composure. Whether I wanted to hear it or not, Martha was determined to give me her two-cents' worth.

"Well, Miss Long, this massive hole in the roof will set you back a pretty penny. You'd better get that inspector back out here."

"Martha, there's no need for another inspection," Dr. D stated. "It's not our fault a tree fell on the doggone thing. We're already replacing the roof, and you've approved the next step in the process." Snicker.

Martha punched in additional items on her phone, then turned to him. "You know the Historical Society is adamant this is done right. I'm just doing my job." Slight grin. "I'd like the inspector to return. Let me know the date and time she'll be here." She rotated quickly and caught her spike heel between the damaged wood slats.

I squelched a giggle. "Martha, please let me help you."

She leaned down, removed her heels, then stood and placed them in one hand. Martha walked gingerly on the splintered boards and hesitated at the bottom porch step. She cautiously clumped through squishy red mud then pulled herself into the SUV. There she sat on the seat, dangled her feet out the door, and attempted to wipe them with a tissue.

Dr. Duntworth laughed. “Martha, I have a rag you can use.” His knee-high boots slogged through the muck to her vehicle.

“I don’t know how I avoided that puddle when I went inside the main building.” She wiped her feet and wadded up the rag.

“Don’t throw that thing away. I’ll take it home; Mrs. D will wash it.”

I sent Lauren a text message asking her to call when convenient. No emergency.

She called an hour later. “Rae, what’s happening? I heard something a little earlier from one of my students that your bed and breakfast got damaged.

“Mrs. Persnickety is salivating. I know it’s a terrible thing to say, but I believe it’s true. She wants you to inspect the roof of the main building and insists she attend.”

“I don’t need to check it again. You’ve made the purchase.” She sighed. “If it appeases Mrs. P and helps you, I’ll be there. Is this afternoon early enough?” She mumbled something.

“Were you talking to me, Lauren?”

“No, Mick is with me. I’ll be there at four, Rae. See you then.”

I walked home and let Puffs outside. While she did her usual sniffing in the backyard, I called Dr. D.

“Lauren will be at the site today at four. Do you want me to call Mrs. Ingles?”

“I’ll call.”

"Thanks."

Puffs came inside and retreated to the sofa in the living room while I ate my lunch.

Peanut butter and jelly. Nothing better.

***

Martha Ingles stood in front of the main building. She wore rain boots this time. Tablet in hand.

Lauren arrived. "Hello, Martha. Good to see you again. I hear there's a problem."

"Glad you came. Let's step inside the building."

I followed them.

Dr. Duntworth walked inside from the back of the structure. "Good to see you ladies." He took off his hat and wiped perspiration from his brow with his red dirt rag. Obviously, he hadn't put it in the laundry, yet.

Lauren didn't flinch when she saw the damage from the storm. "From what I see, my recommendations are still current. You're going to replace the roof anyway, Dr. Duntworth, aren't you?"

"That's what I told Martha." He looked pointedly at her and put his hard hat back on.

"You did, but it'll take a miracle to fix this mess."

I couldn't help but comment. "Hey, I'm all in for a miracle or two."

Lauren nodded at me. "Foundation looks great. You already knew this was a complete renovation. My recommendation is to go ahead full steam. Some floorboards need replacing, but I'm sure you figured that out already. Do you agree, Dr. Duntworth?"

"Yes. I'm getting back to work. I knew this was a waste of time." He tipped his hat at the three of us before exiting.

The two ladies finalized things and Martha drove her SHPO vehicle down my driveway.

Lauren stopped before entering her car. "Rae, Mrs. Ingles is quite a character. I'll bet she's new at her job and is afraid of making a mistake. When you find out she's coming to the property again, let me know, and I'll try to get over here."

"Thanks. I don't know what I'd do without you." I pulled on my gloves. "I really mean it."

"You're more knowledgeable than you think, Rae. Well, I'd better get going." Lauren zipped her leather jacket. "Mick and I are going to a meeting tonight. He's on a committee for the Fall Festival and says I'll enjoy it." She got into her car, turned it on, and opened the window. "The highlight for the evening will be dinner in Greenville after the meeting. Mick is taking me to Pallets."

"It sounds like fun. Let me know how it goes."

She waved as her car hummed down my driveway

I thanked Dr. D and told him I'd be back early the next day. He loaded his truck and offered me a ride, but I declined his offer and walked briskly to my rental house. I stood on the sidewalk and felt blessed to have a warm place to stay while waiting for my new historical home. *No squinting necessary. None whatsoever.*

***

Chicken pot pie, a small salad with dried cranberries—mmm. Puffs curled up at my feet as I savored every bite. A sweet movie played on TV, comfort food warmed my belly, and a sip of milk rejuvenated my body and soul.

I began to doze until the familiar jingle on my phone woke me. Joe. “Rae, hoping you’ll rest well tonight.”

“Thanks, I’m vegging right now and turning in early.” Yawn. “Hope you rest well, too.”

“I’m glad all is settled with your main building. I saw Dr. D tonight at the Fall Festival meeting. I was going to invite you, then figured you had enough going on already.”

“I’d like to help. Just let me know what I can do.” I yawned again. “Sorry, it’s not the company. I love talking with you.”

“I love talking to you, too. Sleep well.”

A person’s wisdom yields patience;
it is to one’s glory to overlook an offense.
Proverbs 19:11

Chapter Twenty-Seven

The fall breeze blew through the open car windows. Puffs snored on the back seat and I parked in front of a cottage. I left a car door open so she could get out if she wanted.

As I stepped into the main building, Abel greeted me.

"Rae, good to see you again this morning. What do you think?"

I quickly peeked inside each first-floor room. "Great job, Abel." I smiled then glanced at him over my shoulder. "Every room looks even better than I ever imagined."

"Glad it meets with your approval. I'll get back to work."

I proceeded outside and meandered toward my car to check on Puffs.

Dr. D emerged from inside a cottage. "Rae, come in. We've completed three cottages and should be done with the other five in the next month. Mind doing an unofficial inspection on the finished ones?" He removed his glasses and wiped them on his infamous rag. He pointed to the fourth cottage. "I'll be down there."

"I'd love to inspect them now, but Joe and Emily are meeting me at Molly's. Mind if they come here afterwards and help?" I paused a second. "I've ordered coffee for you, Abel, and the crew."

"Thanks. Coffee will be great. No problem if Joe and Emily come." He turned and entered the unfinished dwelling.

I awoke my sleeping Lab as my VW Bug puttered down Beaufort Street.

Joe and Emily showed up at Molly's the same time I did. I leashed Puffs and trotted her across the street to take care of business. Thankfully, no squirrels or ducks tempted her. She led me inside the restaurant and Molly had everything ready and waiting. We loaded our cars, carried enough java for the crew, then drove to the property.

Upon arrival, the aroma of the hot brew caught the attention of all.

"Please help yourselves. You're the best crew ever."

Without hesitation, the piping hot drink disappeared quickly.

The three of us stepped inside a sweet bungalow, while toting our Styrofoam cups.

Emily stopped abruptly. "Blake and I talked about reserving one of your cottages after we got married." She took a deep breath. "I don't know what we're going to do now. Blake wants to buy a place in downtown Greenville and that'd make both of us drive forever to get to work." She burst into tears.

Joe grimaced. "Okay, Sis, we can talk about that later. Remember, we're here to help Rae list anything that needs fixing. Not talk about you and Blake."

Emily blew into her tissue. "Joe, it's the most important thing in my life, and you're making light of it." She opened the front door and ran outside.

I followed close behind her. "Emily, come and sit in my car. I can check on the cottages later."

She stopped and cried even harder. "I guess I can do that." Sob. "Okay."

***

Joe walked outside and gave his little sister a hug before she entered my car. He stepped my way and mouthed the words "Thank you." He didn't linger. Instead, he returned inside.

I took a taste of my steamy coffee and glanced at Puffs. She slept soundly.

"Emily, how can I help?"

"I don't know. I think it might be over with Blake and me. We have way too many differences." She took the top off her cup and stirred the contents with her spoon.

"You're such a cute couple. I'd venture to say, you were made for each other."

"That's kind of what my mom said. Blake's mom, too." Emily took off her gloves and crocheted cap. "I've talked to Shelly Rodriguez, and she said the same thing." She looked my way and replaced the lid on her coffee. "I can't thank you enough for listening to me, Rae. I haven't spoken to Blake since I told you about our situation. He keeps leaving messages on my phone, but I'm not ready to talk."

"Maybe you should speak to him." *Yikes. Who am I to tell someone how to mend fences with a fiancé?* "I don't know a thing about romance, so I'm not the best person to ask for advice."

"Are you kidding me? You and Joe are a definite item. If you don't see that, then you're blind as a bat." Folded arms. "No offense, but everyone else sees how connected you two are even if you can't." She unfolded her arms.

"Hmm, I think we both have a little something in common."

"Yes, we both love Joe. Just in different ways." She smiled a toothy smile.

This time I turned toward her. "That's not what I meant."

"What did you mean?" Emily leaned over the seat and petted Puffs. "You're such a good girl. You and Buddy are so cute together."

"I meant . . ."

"Come to think of it, I guess you and Joe, Puffs and Buddy, and maybe Blake and I have quite a bit in common."

I noticed Joe exit the first cottage then walk toward the second. He didn't glance my way.

"Rae, I'm so grateful for you. Mom and Blakey's mom suggested we make a list of things we have in common. The two of them bought a gift card for us to use at Pallets when we finish our lists. Has Joe taken you there?"

"No, he hasn't, but Mick took Lauren."

"My brother is taking it slow. I think I'll nudge him to take you someplace other than Gill's. He gets stuck in a rut."

I shook my head and laughed. "Don't push your brother in any direction. I like moving slowly, too." I brushed my hair from my face. "Now, let's get back to discussing you and Blake."

Emily looked serious. "I heard through the grapevine Blakey's done with his list. I'll finish mine tonight and let you know how it all turns out." She grabbed my gloved hand and gave it a squeeze. "I hope you don't mind if I leave you and Joe to inspect the cottages. I need to go to the Rodriguez's before the kids get home."

"I thought they didn't get out of school until three."

"You're right, but I want some time to finish my list." She opened the car door, stepped from my car, and into hers.

I quickly waved to Emily. She didn't even notice.

***

Joe never mentioned Emily as the two of us checked the little buildings. The hardwood floors were gorgeous. He noticed a couple spots missing paint on the baseboards . . . six-inch baseboards, I might add. *Simple fixes.*

We walked together to give Dr. D and Mr. Dells our verdict.

My enthusiastic smile said it all. "The cottages are wonderful!" I moved a little closer and gave each a hug.

Dr. D grinned. "Glad the work paid off." He attempted to wipe mud off his overalls. "It won't be long before we tackle the historical stuff."

Abel Dells looked relieved. "Glad you like them, Rae. Hopefully you'll smile when we get done with the big building." He fumbled with his gloves.

"I'm giving you guys a thumbs up before you even get started."

***

The work day ended, and Joe and I stood toe-to-toe. "Professor, thank you for helping me."

"I had a great time and I'm really glad everything looks super."

I tiptoed to kiss his cheek. "I'm so thankful for you." Then, I slid into the driver's side of my car while Puffs positioned herself in the back seat. "Hope to see you soon."

"Tomorrow?"

"Sure."

He stooped toward my open window. "I have another meeting for the Fall Festival tomorrow evening at six. Want to come?"

"Perfect. It gives me time to get a few things done here beforehand." I loved looking at his crooked grin. "Want to get something to eat after the meeting?"

"Sounds like a date."

Blush. "See you then." I raised the window and waited for Joe to move away from my car. I watched as he climbed into his truck, started the engine, and paused so I could leave first.

Be still my fluttery heart. Guess I'll make a 'things we have in common' list just for the fun of it since Joe and I aren't officially boyfriend/girlfriend. Just sayin'.

The one who has knowledge uses words with restraint...
Proverbs 17:27

Chapter Twenty-Eight

Days skipped by, and before I knew it, the Fall Festival arrived. The cool breeze caught me off guard as I stepped outside on the front porch in jeans, knee high boots, and an oversized lime-green sweater.

I met Joe at the cotton candy machine and saw Emily and Blake in the distance dressed as scarecrows. *Looks like they're together again.* "Joe, I'm ready to help."

He turned around and smiled. "I'm glad. I need all the help I can get."

I laughed when I saw pink cotton candy stuck to his chin. "Here, Professor, let me help you there." I wiped off the sweet concoction and felt my cheeks flush in the process. His grin made my heart do flip-flops. I quickly picked up an apron and put it on. "Okay, I'm ready for some sugar."

"Some sugar?" Professor Joe angled down and kissed the top of my head. "How was that?"

A line formed before I could answer, and children waited eagerly. We became more coated in the sugary treat.

"Joe, I don't recognize half of the kiddos in their costumes."

He swept another paper cone along the inside of the machine and gave it to me. "I know what you mean."

After spinning the sugar mixture for what seemed like hours, I turned around and saw there was no line. "Where is everybody?"

"They're lining up for the hayride. Care to join me?"

"I'd love to, but first I'll make us some cotton candy." I failed to mention I'd never been on a hayride, even though I'd read about them in books, and had seen them in movies.

Joe took my free hand in his and led me toward the line.

Scarecrow Emily ran to where we stood. "The list worked, Rae. Blake's folks and mine were right." She caught her breath, "I need to get back to the hot dog stand with Blakey. Enjoy the hayride you two. Kissy, kissy." She gave me a hug and Joe a tight squeeze.

Joe laughed. "What was Emily saying?"

"Oh, nothing. Just girl talk." The sugary sweet treat made my teeth shiver.

"We'd better hurry up and finish these or we're going to have hay stuck to us." He reached in his pocket and removed a package of hand wipes. "Need one?"

"Isn't it obvious?" I dropped the last piece into my mouth and tapped my boot on the straw-covered ground. "Hand wipe, please."

***

Clydesdale horses pulled the enormous wagon in front of the long line of folks. White lights decorated the sides and hay spilled over the top.

A man dressed in a cowboy hat and heavy coat addressed all of us. "Ladies and gentlemen. Be careful stepping into the wagon and go to the front so everyone doesn't have to climb over you. All aboard!"

Joe and I sat in the center and other couples surrounded us. I didn't notice a child anywhere. "Where are all the little ones?"

"They have their own hayride with their parents." He wiggled his eyebrows, then moved a little closer to me as the crowd cozied in. *Togetherness.*

The wagon jolted as the driver shook the reigns. Music played, and we sang along.

Joe whispered in my ear. "So how do you like this?"

I laughed at him because he had a piece of straw stuck to his hat. "Feel the top of your head, then I'll tell you what I think about it."

"What is it?" He touched his hat. "I can't find anything. Can you help me?"

"Of course." I pulled off a long piece of straw. "This is what was sticking out of your head, well, I mean out of your hat."

He sneaked a kiss in. Two kisses to be exact. I snuggled into his arms until the ride ended. Then we jumped off the wagon.

"Joe, I love hayrides and can't wait till next year, so we can ride again." *If there is a Joe and me next year. Hopefully.*

"It's a date."

We helped clean the cotton candy machine and swept straggling pieces of hay off the street. Everyone pitched in so the work went quicker than I'd expected.

Joe walked me to my rental. The porch light shone on the two of us like a beacon.

"Good night, Joe. I had such a great time."

Joe gave a little chuckle.

"What are you laughing at?"

He moved a little closer and whispered in my ear. "Miss Doris is standing on her porch. She's spying on us, so let's give her something to talk about." He planted a kiss of all kisses on my lips, gently held my shoulders in his strong hands, and uttered, "Good night, Rae." He grinned and stepped off the porch.

I opened my front door but didn't miss his comment to my neighbor.

"Have a good night, Miss Doris."

"Good night, Joe. I see you had a little sugar tonight." She went inside.

Oh, yes, a sugary-sweet dessert-filled evening. One I'll never forget. Comfy bed. Puffs sleeping soundly. Midnight curled up in the window box outside my window. Rest. We were all dreaming—maybe of sugar and spice.

May your unfailing love be my comfort . . .
Psalm 119:76

Chapter Twenty-Nine

I parked in front of a shop on Beaufort Street. One I'd never seen before. The brass bell attached to the door jingled as I entered.

"Welcome to Angels to Zithers, and Everything in Between. I'm Sea." Her infectious smile welcomed me. "Feel free to browse and try some cinnamon buns courtesy of Bitty's Buns."

I paused a second. "I like your name. Is it short for anything?"

"No, it's just Sea. My mom put initials of her friends together when she was pregnant with me and that's what she came up with." She offered her warm smile again.

"Guess I can't say anything since my name is only three letters, too. I'm so glad your store is open. You have several items I need for my cottages."

"Cottages? Are you Rae Long? The owner of the bed and breakfast?"

"That's me." *Easy grin.*

"My sister told me about you. Since I live in Greenville, I don't hear all the latest gossip, or as the locals like to refer to it, daily information. However, I do know about the renovations. Everyone is thrilled." She sipped from her water bottle. “I’ve been inundated with remodeling this shop after the electrical fire and just reopened it the day before the Fall Festival. It’s sure good to meet you.”

“I’m sure glad you’re open.”

Sea continued. “Sweetness and Sweaters is my sister Sendy’s shop. She has the clothing and I have the do-dads and furniture. If you need any help, just let me know.”

“I will. I love your sister’s shop, too.”

Several silver mint julep cups found their way into the shopping basket. I knew the beauty they held underneath all that tarnish. Kind of like my bed and breakfast. *These will make gorgeous vases for all those flowers I’m ordering from Buds and Blooms.* Meandering through the shop took a little shifting this way and that to avoid knocking over all the lovely displayed items. However, my nostrils led me to a table at the back of the shop where tiny plates of cinnamon buns and cider-filled cups tempted me. I set my shopping basket against the table leg and enjoyed this delectable snack. My eyes bounced from furniture piece to furniture piece as I continued to meander through Sea’s shop. Luxurious table linens, china tea cups, and assorted silver candlesticks decorated nearby shelves. I almost heard them calling my name. *Buy me, buy me, Rae.* Okay, I might be exaggerating a tad, but I really did hear my name being called. Literally.

“Rae? Are you in here?” I looked over my shoulder and spotted Lauren on tiptoe. Not that she needed to be since she practically towered over the displays. “If you are, please jump up and down. I can’t see you.”

I stood still and captured this moment in time.

Sea smiled as she approached Lauren. “She’s here. Just in the back. Are you new in town, too?”

“Yes, I’m renting the little house near the library and teaching at the University.”

“Take your time looking and let me know if I can help.”

“Thank you.”

I didn’t say a word. Instead, I marveled at the fact Lauren acted rather goofy. Calling out my name in a store indicated a change in my long-time friend. She’d never stoop to my level, and I don’t mean height, to act a little wacky or draw silly attention to herself. Now don’t get me wrong, she drew attention at every turn— from male admirers.

Lauren found me. “You heard me acting like an idiot, didn’t you, Miss Long? I don’t know what came over me, because you’re the one who’s usually loony. No offense or anything. There’s just something about this little bitty town.”

“Oh, yes, this is not only a little bitty town, it’s a town with little Bitty’s Buns included.”

“See, that’s what I mean. You come up with crazy things to say.” She popped a piece of cinnamon bun in her mouth. *Another “not Lauren.”*

As Lauren and I perused the shop, I jotted down large items for the bed and breakfast that needed to be ordered. My list lengthened as I strolled through Angels to Zithers with Lauren at my side. My eye for design and hers for practicality made us a force to be reckoned with. I took my basket to the white French sideboard at the front of the store. Sea stood behind the counter sorting new items and putting them in a wooden box.

"Are you done, Rae?"

"I am. I have a huge order." I set the list in front of Sea.

"All of this?" She caught her breath.

"Absolutely. I didn't realize I needed so much stuff until Lauren and I put our heads together." I became uneasy. "Will you be able to accommodate the bed and breakfast?"

"Are you kidding?" She quickly slid up her sleeves. "I can more than accommodate your business and give you a ten percent discount to boot."

She scanned the numbered items, handed me my receipt, and assured me she'd have everything delivered within a week.

"Did I hear you right?" I questioned.

"Yes." Sea looked concerned. "Do you need everything sooner?"

"No, I'm shocked you can get it to me in a week. I'm thrilled."

Lauren and I left Sea and scurried in the downpour to Fenster Haus.

I slid my shoes off under the table and my tootsies began to dry from the warmth of the nearby fireplace. Lauren struggled to unzip her knee-high boots but somehow managed the feat with great finesse. Toasty tootsies. *What more could a girl want except a delicate croissant panini.*

"Lauren, I need to buy a desk for the reception room at the main building. I didn't notice one at Seas." I felt chilled and cradled my coffee cup in my hands. I don't think she heard a word about the desk.

"Rae, I'm falling in love." She sipped her coffee and took a bite of her chicken salad. "I'm beginning to think I left myself in Maryland; someone else is living in my body and using my name." Tears welled up in her eyes.

"Lauren, what do you mean? Are you falling in love with Hope?" I slowly chewed my cranberry and turkey panini. "Or are you falling in love with someone?" I knew the answer but didn't want to assume anything when it came to Lauren. I understood her confusion. She happened to be the most put-together, no-nonsense person I'd ever met.

"I don't know if it's this little town and the romance it oozes, or the fact that my biological clock is ticking. Or if Mick is the one." A tear fell down her cheek.

The waitress refilled our coffee cups. "May I get you anything, honey?" She pulled a small tissue packet from her pocket and placed it in front of Lauren. "Dessert?"

Lauren wiped her nose and shook her head. "Wait, I've changed my mind. Could I see the dessert menu, please?" She put the used tissue in her purse and situated herself more comfortably in the chair.

"I'll take one, too, please?" I grinned sheepishly.

Sweet confections ordered.

The noise at the front of the restaurant caught our attention. Historical ladies. I slouched into the chair as everyone in the group sauntered to the community table at the back of Fenster Haus—until Grace noticed me.

She removed a plastic scarf from her head, revealing a frizzy do, as she walked to our table. "Rae, we finally tracked you down. We've completed the tasks you assigned and left message after message on your phone today." She attempted to pat down her hair. "Oh, hi, Lauren. Are you okay?"

"I'm fine, Mrs. Byer. I'm just a little sentimental today. Guess I'm missing my place in Maryland. I'm not sure."

"Your hormones are raging, and your biological clock is zooming. I remember those days." She turned her attention back to me. "Rae, the girls and I set up a brunch to reveal our creations for the bed and breakfast. Of course, you know that already. Victoria made the invites, and Molly's restaurant is catering our meal. Natalie's supplying dessert from Bitty's Buns. Thursday morning. Be there or be square." She flung her wet scarf. "I know you've already received your snail-mail invitation, but you haven't responded." She turned to join the other ladies at the community table. Looking in my direction she added, "Of course, Amber received her invitation. She responded with a no. She's such a sweetie and will be missed. By the way, Lauren, you can come, too. We didn't send you an invite, so you're excused for not giving us a yay or nay. Make yourself a cup of hot tea tonight. It should soothe your nerves, Lauren."

We watched Joe's crinkly-haired mother pull out her chair. Lauren and I locked eyes for a long moment.

Then I spoke. "I'm speechless, Lauren; you know that's rare for me."

The waitress delivered our decadent desserts. We sat still—both in shock at the tornado named Grace Byer.

In slow motion, I scooped a spoonful of chocolate cake and ice cream into my mouth. "That woman drives me nuts one minute and is tolerable the next. I can't believe she mentioned your biological clock. Mrs. Byer's biological clock is a cuckoo clock." The giggle turned into a belly laugh. "Plus, I'm sick of her mentioning Amber. Nothing against Amber; she's a nice person."

Lauren started to chuckle, then laughed just as hard as I did. "Cuckoo clock is right." She cut a piece of carrot cake with her fork, closed her eyes, and allowed her taste buds time to savor the heavenly flavor. "I can't believe I've turned down desserts all these years. This is divine."

***

Outside, we hugged and went our separate ways. Her next stop—the university, and mine—the historical university and the cottages.

Have a blessed day, dear friend. So thankful you moved to Hope.

. . . so that I may come to you with joy, by God's will, and in your company be refreshed.
Romans 15:32

Chapter Thirty

The Historical Society's official invitation sat on my bedroom dresser. Today was the day of the great reveal. Grace and her entourage sent me text messages from 7:00 to 9:00 a.m. reminding me about their brunch. I couldn't forget it even if I tried.

With my satchel tucked easily under my arm and my new cream-colored coat covering my frame, I stepped outside onto the porch. Good thing Puffs didn't notice Miss Doris's feline on my rocking chair. I almost tripped over Midnight as she lurched in front of me. She hissed and headed for the tree. Yes, the tree next to my bedroom window. *Crazy cat.*

***

Lauren graciously declined the invite to the brunch. As I drove slowly along Beaufort Street, I saw her wave at me. I pulled my car to the nearby curb.

"Hey, Lauren, is everything all right?"

"Have a great time today, Rae. Wish I could attend the brunch, but you know I'm heading to work. I'm so proud of you." She flung her scarf around her neck with flair and strolled toward the University of South Carolina at Hope.

My eyes misted as I thought about our long friendship and the possibility of Lauren living permanently in town.

Brunch time. I pulled into the driveway with the sign, Mayor and Mrs. Sounds.

***

I gasped when I entered Victoria's home. It reminded me of a museum. Not in a stuffy sort of way, but in an I-can't-wait-to-see-what's-around-the-corner kind of way.

Victoria motioned me to follow her to the sun porch. "We've all been waiting for this momentous day, Rae. We certainly hope you enjoy our creations."

The ladies gave me a standing ovation as I stepped down onto the enclosed porch. Emily, who wasn't officially a member of the society, handed me a box of tissues and guided me to one of the cushy chairs. She sat next to me as Victoria rang a tiny silver bell for everyone to be seated.

"Ladies, welcome to my home. We'll eat first then take care of business."

Moans were heard all around until Grace tapped her gavel on a small piece of wood. "Order, Ladies. We'll do what the hostess says. Remember we are following the rules put in place. So, without further ado, Bon Appetit!" She started to sit down, but quickly popped up out of her seat. "Prayer first. Victoria, will you do the honors?"

After the prayer, Molly and her helpers served us as we passed through the buffet line. Made to order omelets and homemade waffles with strawberry sauce tempted our taste buds. The fruit bowls at the end of the table were as colorful as the leaves outside and beckoned a spoonful or two. I knew I'd chosen the right person to prepare the breakfast at my bed and breakfast.

Our conversations and sentences stumbled over each other as we enjoyed our mouthwatering meals and shared a morsel or two about our lives. Sweet fellowship and amazing food.

After Molly made sure all were served, she joined us for the meal. It was refreshing seeing her take a moment to enjoy herself. We continued eating as her staff refilled our drinks, and Grace called the meeting to order.

"Ladies, it's business time." She paused and nodded toward Opal. "Opal, please make sure you take minutes of the meeting. You know how picky Martha Ingles is when it comes to everything historical." She glanced in my direction. "You know exactly what I'm talking about, Rae. You deal with Mrs. Persnickety as much, if not more, than we do. By the way, Emily told me you call Martha Ingles 'Mrs. Persnickety' and I love it."

I turned toward Emily and grimaced. She giggled then took a sip of her coffee.

Grace smiled at Victoria. "Your turn, Victoria. May we see what you've created?"

"I must admit, I'm a little nervous." Victoria opened a small box. "Rae, here are a few of the pillow cards. I hope you like them." She handed me the little container. "Oh, yes, I still need to put the logo on top of each card." She tasted her coffee. "I know you haven't approved Grace's bed and breakfast logo on the sign yet."

The small rectangular shaped cards scattered in the box. "Victoria, I love the size of these and the butter-yellow color. After carefully picking up each one, I read them out loud. “May sugar-coated dreams abound.” Applause. “Sleep soundly.” I cleared my throat. “Rest and rejuvenate.” I smiled at Victoria. “When I awaken, I will rejoice.” They fit nicely back into the box; I returned it to Victoria. “Please let me give you a hug. These are magnificent.”

She sighed. “I wasn’t sure you’d like them. Sam told me you would.” She chuckled slightly. “As a matter of fact, Sam is thankful you asked me to take on this task, because I’m not pestering him as much during the football games on television.”

The ladies broke out in laughter and applause. Victoria sat down quickly, with a huge grin on her face.

Grace stood. “Thank you. Anna is next.”

Anna left her chair quickly and confidently. “This is for you, Rae. I hope you like it.”

She handed me an oil painting set securely in a cream-colored frame, then sat down humbly. Totally out of character for her. The picture took my breath away. I paused and turned it for everyone to see. Applause.

The lump in my throat almost prevented me from speaking. *Almost.* “Anna, this is even better than I envisioned. The sweeping view of Beaufort Street, Hope Lake, the pastel colors, beautiful. Will you please make one for each cottage?”

“Rae, I was wondering if I could do a different view of the lake and Beaufort Street on each picture. I’d use the same colors.”

“That’s absolutely okay with me. Thank you so much. Hug, please.”

We gave Anna a standing ovation, and she smiled in response.

Grace remained standing. "Whew, girls. The talent in this room is unprecedented. Do you agree?" Everyone clapped again. "Lottie, you are next, please."

Lottie nodded at each of the society ladies, then looked at me. "Victoria and Anna will be a tough act to follow. I only have one thing to present for the main building; I hope it meets your expectations, Rae." Lottie held up a beautifully framed picture of the original university."

"Lottie, this is spectacular. I can't believe you made such a great copy of the original."

"This isn't a copy. This is the original." Lottie paused. "If you don't like the mats or frame, I can redo it."

"I love it. It's perfectly perfect to say the least. Thank you, Lottie. It will hang proudly at the entryway to the main building."

Lottie blushed as all of us clapped. Then Grace called on Opal.

Opal smiled, "This is just a sample, Rae. Hope it reads all right for the paper." She handed me the typed page. "I didn't put the name of the bed and breakfast at the top because we don't know the official title yet."

"Thank you, Opal." I took a drink of water then read the paper article to all the ladies.

We all cheered. Opal's grin made her eyes sparkle as she added a slice of news. "If you don't mind, I'd like to take advantage of social media, too. We use devices regularly, and I hate to admit it, many people don't read papers as much. I'd like to go the techno route if you agree. I know you mentioned you'd take care of the website, Rae. However, I know you'll be very busy when the B&B opens, and I don't mind giving it a try. What do you think?"

"I agree one hundred percent. Thank you, Opal. Great plan." I hugged her gently.

Before Grace tapped the gavel, I remained standing. "Ladies, I have some very important information to share with you. I motioned for Molly to stand next to me. She hesitantly left her seat. "Molly, you and I chatted about this a while ago, and I'm making it official."

Her face beamed. "Is it what I think it is?"

"Molly is the Head Chef for the Inn at Hope."

Victoria grinned. "I was hoping you'd ask Molly." She sniffled. "But if she's working for you, how will Molly's Restaurant stay open?"

The other ladies looked as bewildered as Victoria.

Molly chimed in. "I'll still be at my restaurant for all the other meals. You know, Henry's the breakfast king at our place. I'm the waitress on duty." She straightened her glasses. "I'll train the girls and maybe they can take over as Chef at the Inn someday."

Everyone cheered and grinned from ear to ear.

Grace took her accustomed stance, gavel in hand. "Okay, ladies. This ends the business part of our time together."

The group booed. Victoria spoke first. "Oh, no, you don't, Mrs. Byer. You aren't leaving here without showing us the sign you made. Right, ladies?"

Everyone erupted in chanting, "Yes, yes, yes!"

Grace walked toward a large flat box leaning against the wall near the French doors. She picked it up and handed it to me.

"Grace, I expected this to be so heavy neither of us could hold it." I set it on the table.

"You know this is just a rendering, Rae. The real one will be metal, and we won't be able to carry it unless all the Historical Society ladies assist."

I laid the box on its side and slid out the sample. "Oh, my goodness, you read my mind. You actually improved my vision." I propped the plastic sign against the back of my chair. "Mrs. Byer, this is beautiful." My tight squeeze embraced her.

"Thank you, Rae." She sat down in her chair.

A couple ladies shouted. "We want to see the sign."

When I picked it up and showed them, they made a beeline toward Grace.

Anna's words to Grace were full of grace. "You certainly do have a gift, girl. Rae picked the right person for this job."

Grace blushed and said thank you. Enough said.

The rectangular sign read:

Inn at Hope
Today's Moments
Tomorrow's Memories

Simple and to the point. I loved it! Inside the box were the various seasonal items, and the silhouette of a dog. They weren't sketches; they were plastic.

No logo at the top of the sign, though. I hated to mention it in front of her peers, and I didn't need to.

Victoria spoke. "I need the logo, so I can finish the pillow cards."

Grace gave a slight grin. "Rae, look deeper into the box please."

I leaned over and reached inside. "What's this?"

"It's a plastic mold of the university main building. It's not fancy and I can add or delete anything you don't like." Her fingers intertwined as she looked at me.

These ladies are the most talented I've ever met. "This deserves another standing ovation. The only change I'd make is for you to go ahead with the final product and make it all in black iron instead of plastic." I laughed and raised the logo over my head.

Chatter filled the room until mid-afternoon. We all opted to go to Molly's for an early dinner. The line of cars, each a different color, pulled in front of the well-known restaurant.

I drove Emily and myself. "I remember seeing all those cars in front of my Pecan Street rental months ago. Mick neglected to tell me the Historical Society ladies were giving me a visit; I was a nervous wreck. Now I see these cars, and I'm so happy and feel so blessed. What a difference a few months can make." I parked, and Emily and I stepped out of the car.

"I remember. Thanks for giving these women a purpose other than nitpicking every detail about things." Emily paused a second. "Come to think of it, it might be good they are nitpickers. Otherwise, the items they made for the bed and breakfast wouldn't be nearly as nice as they are." Emily took my elbow. "Come on, Rae. I have a few details to give you about Blakey and me."

He has filled them with skill to do all kinds of work . . .
all of them skilled workers and designers.
Exodus 35:35

Chapter Thirty-One

Dr. D and Abel Dells finished most of the cottages in no time at all. However, they warned me several times the main building required all hands-on-deck.

When I parked my car, Dr. D exited a completed dwelling. "Need some help, Rae?" He lifted his nose to the air. "You know we appreciate this. I smelled those before you got here." Laughter.

I chuckled as I pulled the bagel-filled bags from my car. "This is the least I can do for you and the team."

A folded card table leaned against the porch rail of the first cottage. "Want me to set this up outside or in?"

"Outside, please. Oh, yes, here's a tablecloth."

"Let me help with that." He flung the plastic covering onto the top with ease—not grace. I avoided the temptation to straighten it before organizing the bagels, all the schmears, and jellies. "Dr. D, mind helping me get the thermoses? They're on the front floor board."

He eagerly opened the passenger door and handed thermoses to Abel and the rest of the crew. "Here, men and ladies, surely you can carry this if you can haul toilets." His laugh bellowed. The folks jeered right along with him.

Somehow the thought of comparing toilets and coffee didn't set well in my mind, but I guess the workers liked the visual.

I toured the cottages as the team enjoyed a break. The porches were large enough for two rocking chairs, small table between, and a porch swing at the opposite end. I entered the first cottage. A painted white-brick fireplace adorned the left wall, flanked by floor-to-ceiling windows. *Butter-yellow walls and creamy white baseboards . . . bliss.* The French doors on the back wall beckoned me to stroll outside onto the brick paver patio. *Serene.* I resisted the impulse to stay outside and re-entered the cottage. The space would easily accommodate a king-sized bed covered with pillows and comfy linens.

Abel knocked and looked inside. "Rae, I hate to disturb you. Mind if I come in?" He stood in the doorway. "I know we talked about combining a couple cottages for a family."

"Come in, Abel. Everything looks beautiful. Did you come up with any way we can do that?"

He carefully wiped his shoes on the makeshift mat and walked inside. "So, you're still game?"

"Yes. I can't wait to see the finalized plans when you get a chance to do them."

"Well, I took a risk and drew up some options. They're in here." He held up a long black tube. "Sorry, we don't have a comfortable place to sit."

I plopped down on the floor. "I'm stunned and thrilled at the same time. I can sit here if you can."

"Sure." He sat across from me, placed the blueprint on the floor, and removed his tablet from his jacket pocket. "Hope you like it."

We scanned the layout of the combined cottages, and he assured me it wouldn't be a problem to make it a two-bathroom place. "Rae, that'll be easy because we have a bath in each dwelling anyway."

"Great job, Abel. It looks spectacular."

We stood and shook hands.

"Hope you're not angry with Dr. D and me." His eyebrows arched. "We did something on our own. Have you looked in the bathroom of this finished cottage?"

I gave a quizzical glance. "No, I haven't. I was just about to when you came to the door." *Uneasiness.*

"Perfect timing. Glad I caught you before you did." He rolled up the blueprints and placed them in the cylinder.

I opened the door to the bathroom and glanced inside. "It looks wonderful."

"Rae, open the door on the right wall." He waited patiently.

I did. "How did you do this? A washer and dryer combination inside the dwelling?" I stood with mouth agape. "This is even better than using one of the buildings for a laundry unit. Will each cottage have its own?"

Mr. Dells smiled. "We easily converted the linen closet after doing a little finagling and rewiring. With a water source in the bathroom already, it was a cinch."

"Abel, you're absolutely brilliant."

He beamed. “I’m glad you’re happy with our decision. Now, I’d better get back to work.” He stepped into the living area, then out the door.

I sauntered back to the empty bagel bags and thermoses, cleared the area, and propped my folding table against the front porch wall. I peeked inside the first cottage again. My rental lease expired soon and moving temporarily into this abode seemed logical.

***

I hired a wonderful crew from the local elementary school custodial staff to clean and polish every square inch of all the cottages. Angels to Zithers delivered ordered items as promised. Time to decorate.

The soft butter-yellow pillows and cotton bedding enveloped the king-sized beds in each cottage. Yummy and inviting. I deliberately chose different creamy-white headboards for each place to give a touch of uniqueness.

I heard a light tap on the door. “Rae, open the door. My hands are full.”

I recognized Lauren’s voice and opened the door quickly. She stood with a coffee carrier from Bitty’s Buns in one hand and a Molly’s Restaurant bag in the other.

“Heavens. Come in. You’re a blessing, crazy girl.”

“I’m not sure I like being called crazy. As a matter of fact, maybe I should take my coffee and scones and go home.” She turned toward the door.

“Oh, no, you don’t. Get back here. I definitely need a coffee break and some girl talk.”

“Well, I guess if you put it that way, I can spare a minute or two.” Lauren grinned. She put the bag on the window sill next to the coffee. "All kidding aside, this cottage looks absolutely beautiful." She carefully walked around the boxes at the foot of the bed and peeked into the bathroom. "This is just lovely. You never know, maybe someday Mick and I will marry and maybe even . . ."

"I hope it all works out for you two. You really hit it off."

Lauren and I sat at our makeshift dining set, which consisted of two folding chairs with a cardboard box between.

My dear friend took a bite of her multi-berry scone and sipped her steamy coffee. "No pressure here, but . . ."

"But what?"

She wiped crumbs from her mouth. "Is it still okay if my parents reserve a cottage? They've definitely decided to come for Thanksgiving, so they can meet Mick's mom and dad."

"Absolutely. They'll be my first official reservation. I'm moving into the first cottage next week and five others are done except for the decorating. Will you help me get the fourth done for your parents? I love all of them, but that's my favorite. It's positioned just right to get a soft hint of the morning sun." I put down my scone and coffee, then gave Lauren a gentle hug. "Consider the Wyatts reserved. Or whatever you call it."

We enjoyed our visit until Puffs' bark startled us both. Familiar laughter came from outside the door. Emily and Amber.

Emily tapped on the door, opened it, and squealed. "Rae this is gorgeous. Gorgeous!" She grinned from ear to ear. "We can't stay long but want to help anyway we can."

For a second, Amber stood speechless. “I’m reserving a cottage for Jack and me someday, if he ever proposes.” She rolled her eyes. “This place is breathtaking.”

I snickered. “Amber, I knew you were casually dating Jack, but I thought you still might have a soft spot for Joe.”

She softly took my hand. “I love Joe, but as a brother. Grace tries to set Joe and me up every chance she gets, but that’s not happening. Joe and I both know it.” Amber dropped my hand and took Emily’s. “Emily, you know I love your mom . . .”

“No explanation necessary. My mom is so old-fashioned. She can’t stand the thought of the north and south combining forces. Hence, she shudders at the thought of her Southern baby, Joseph, marrying this Yankee.” She pointed at me.

“Me? Joe and I aren’t even classified as boyfriend and girlfriend. Your mom can’t be jumping to the thought of marriage already.”

Emily placed her hand on her hip and looked me straight in the eye. “My mother is a projectionist. If there is such a word. She likes you, Rae, and, I believe, hates to admit it. Don’t worry, she’ll come around.”

Emily and Amber left soon after they toured the cottage. Lauren and I broke out in laughter at the idea of me being an invading Yankee. Then we got to work.

We positioned furniture in all the right spots and accounted for linens and paper products stored in bathroom cabinets. My dear friend stayed with me that entire day and helped more than she’d ever know.

“Lauren, can I treat you to dinner?”

"Mind if I take a rain check? Mick and I are going to Pallets again for dinner tonight." She brushed a loose strand of hair from her face. "Have you and Joe gone there yet?"

"No, we haven't, and of course, you can take a rain check."

"Well, your Professor Prince better get his romance factor checked. He needs to take a few lessons from Mick." She swooned and leaned down to give me a hug. "You know I'm just kidding about the lessons. I'm the one who invited Mick to go to dinner there this time." With a wave of her hand, she stepped into her Prius. "Tootles, dear sister."

As I started to exit the driveway of the bed and breakfast, I stopped the vehicle, then turned around in my seat as best I could. "Goodnight, bed and breakfast. I'll be moving in soon."

When I opened the front door of the rental, Puffs whimpered and whined until I let her outside. *Note to self: Put a temporary fence in the backyard of the first cottage for Puffs.*

I looked at my phone while Puffs chased a few teasing squirrels up a tree.

Missed message from Joe: Wondering if you'd like to take a break tomorrow night. Emily told me she and Amber saw you today. Said you were hard at work. I didn't want to interrupt. Would you like to go to Pallets for dinner tomorrow?"

How about that? My Prince doesn't need any lessons from Mick. Far from it. Smile.

I called Joe after my bubble bath, comfy pajamas, and warm milk. "I'd love to dine with you tomorrow night, Professor."

"I'm glad. I've been wanting to take you there for a long time. Pick you up at six?"

"I'll be ready."

"Ready for a kiss or two? Shall we check our calendars?" He laughed so loudly I had to pull the phone away from my ear.

"I don't need to check my calendar." *Blush.* "Goodnight, Professor Joe."

Pallets. I couldn't wait. I sunk exhaustedly under my comforter, until thoughts of what to wear tomorrow evening kept my mind racing. I finally fell asleep after I decided Sweetness and Sweaters was on the agenda.

Good night.

. . . to make artistic designs for work in gold,
silver and bronze . . .
Exodus 31:4

Chapter Thirty-Two

The brisk November air chilled my nose as I jogged to Molly's Restaurant for a bagged breakfast, then walked a short distance to Bitty's Buns for my signature coffee, Hope's Rae.

Natalie brushed a wisp of hair from her forehead. "Rae, your coffee is a hit. You know a dollar from each sale goes toward the Children's Christmas Fund."

"I'm so glad the money is used to help families during the holidays."

"Me, too, but you know what? My hubby and I decided to keep the donations going year-round." She handed me my steamy java.

"I love that idea. I need to think of a way to give back to families when my B&B opens. You're an inspiration, Natalie." I gently hugged her neck, "Have a great day."

***

My stocking cap warmed my head while I sat on my favorite bench. A breeze blew across the lake and almost took my breath away as each bite of the ham and cheese croissant melted in my mouth. I tilted my head back and looked upward as I conversed with my Heavenly Daddy. *Exhilarating.*

***

Sendy smiled and greeted me when I opened the French door to Sweetness and Sweaters. “Good to see you this morning, Rae.” She hung a necklace on a nearby mannequin then continued. “I heard you and Joe are going to Pallets tonight for dinner.”

“I’ll never get used to the gossip.” I folded my arms and tapped my foot in jest.

“Gossip? I’ll have you know, we refer to it as sharing necessary news.” She grinned. “Bet you’re looking for something to wear.” Sendy pointed to a display at the back of the store. “The fancy dresses are over there.”

I oohed and aahed at the classy selection and quickly made my choice. “This one fits perfectly. I love it! Thanks for your help, Sendy.”

“You’re welcome. Let me know how everything goes tonight.”

I wanted to tell her I’d inform Grace. Then I’m sure Grace would disperse the info to everyone. *Shame on me.* Instead, I bit my tongue.

***

When Joe parked in front of Pallets, I let out a gasp. Enormous floor to ceiling windows and oil lanterns adorned the entryway and sent chills of delight through me. Joe squeezed my hand as he escorted me inside.

The *maître d’* greeted us. “Welcome to Pallets. May I have your name please?”

“Joseph Byer.”

He nodded. “Please follow me.”

We strolled slowly side by side to our white-clothed table lit only by a small silver lamp. I settled into my chair and then Joe into his.

"Enjoy your time with us. If you need anything at all, we are at your service." The *maître d'* departed and shortly afterwards the waiter took our water and iced tea order. I leaned toward the small vase with the vintage roses inside. *Glorious scent.*

"Rae, you look really, really beautiful." Joe gave my hand a gentle squeeze. "Did you know orange is my favorite color?"

I winked at him. "Well, sort of. When I went to your home for dinner, your napkins were orange, and so were your pot holders. I kinda guessed you might like the color." I grinned. "You look handsome. I've seen you in a sports coat but never a suit."

I noticed the waiter standing close by with our drinks. He waited for just the right moment to place them in front of us. He then took our orders and discreetly left our area.

I sat back in my cushioned chair. My eyes darted from one gorgeous object to the next. Fires crackled in two exquisite fireplaces in the dining area. One on the left wall and another near our cozy nook. Small tables were angled throughout the room to give each couple the right amount of privacy.

"Joe, thank you for bringing me here. I love it." The tea cooled my lips.

"I wanted to invite you sooner, contrary to what my sister would tell you. This wasn't her idea. I've had it in mind all along." Crooked grin. "I know we've been telling people we're friends, but would you mind if I start introducing you as my girlfriend? Or does that sound like something a junior high kid would ask?" He took a gulp of his water.

"I'd love it as long as I can introduce you as my boyfriend. Is that okay with you?"

"It's better than okay." He moved his chair closer to mine and kissed my cheek.

We chatted between our warm soup and crispy salad courses. The evening flowed easily. No rush. The attentive staff removed our plates and bowls, then brought the main course.

"Joe, this filet mignon melts in my mouth. It's the best I've ever had. The roasted asparagus is heavenly. Would you like a bite?"

"You bet I would." He wiped his mouth with his napkin.

I sliced a piece of the tender filet, placed it on my fork, and fed him the large bite. He chewed it slowly and closed his eyes in the process. I think he might have been exaggerating, but I didn't care. I loved that boyfriend of mine.

Joe gave me a bite of his chicken cordon bleu and we both agreed it rated five stars. Perfectly seasoned, moist, and mouth-watering. We finished each bite and talked about our dreams.

He listened intently as I shared my hopes for the bed and breakfast. "You know Dr. D and Abel are putting two cottages together to make a family dwelling? Or did I tell you that already?"

“Yes, you did tell me, but I’m glad to hear it again. Helps me visualize it better. When are you moving into the first cottage?”

“Next week. I need to get out of the rental and settle in before Thanksgiving.” I wiped my mouth and placed my knife and fork on the plate. “Lauren’s parents are staying in a cottage when they come to visit. Your mom rented one for someone in your family who is visiting for Thanksgiving, and Jack’s parents reserved a place. So, four little bungalows will be occupied, including the one I’ll be living in for a while. Two are still available and the family cottage is vacant.”

“I’ll bet they’re rented before Thanksgiving.”

The waiter appeared, refilled our drinks, and removed our plates. He returned with two tiny silver bowls of sherbet.

“Joe, tell me about some of your dreams.” My lips glided over the silver spoon and the sherbet melted in my mouth. *Refreshing.*

“It might sound boring, but I really want to take over my dad’s job someday. He knows it. It’s a goal for the distant future.” Joe wiped his mouth carefully with his cloth napkin. “Boring. Huh?”

“Not at all. It sounds exciting to me.”

“Rae, did you always want to be a designer?”

“Yes. I used to decorate shoe boxes with cloth, markers, and bling. I made my own little shoe box town.” *Silly grin.*

Joe moved even closer to me and chuckled. “I can visualize your shoe box villages because I see what you’ve done with the cottages. It’s really nice you’ve always known your life's goals." He sipped his water. "Anything else you want to do?"

"Of course. Someday, it'd be nice to have a family." My eyes diverted downward. "How 'bout you?"

We were distracted when the waiter removed our empty sherbet bowls and offered us the dessert menu. We chose to share *crème brûlée* and ordered two cups of coffee.

A violinist floated our way and serenaded the two of us. The minute he strolled to another table, the waiter brought our decadent dessert and refilled our coffee. *Such romantic bliss.*

"Joe, this restaurant is luscious and certainly relieves all the stresses of the world." I nestled further into the chair.

"I'm glad you like it. Let's try it again sometime." He smiled.

The waiter removed our dessert ramekin, then returned with the check. "Would you like me to take a picture? You two are a great example of a couple in love." He paused. "How long have you been married?"

Joe coughed into his hand. "A picture sounds great, but we're not married."

My face turned warm. "No, we're not."

Joe handed the waiter his phone for the picture, and we heard him mutter, "Don't know what you're waiting for."

The drive home was quieter than usual. Joe and I discussed the great meal and the ambiance but never mentioned what the waiter said.

My front porch goodnight kiss from Joe was a miss. A peck on my forehead, slight hug, and wave goodnight made my heart sink almost to my toes. The perfect night at Pallets ended in a perfectly heart-wrenching goodbye. *Did the waiter's word, marriage, bother Joe that much? If so, maybe Joe will never be more than a boyfriend.*

I slipped out of my princess dress, took the silver clips from my hair, and got into my flannel gown. Puffs sensed my sadness—doggy instinct—and curled next to me on my comfy bed. *Sweet dog.* Tears wet my pillow as I prayed.

The Lord bless you and keep you . . .
Numbers 6:24

Chapter Thirty-Three

I worked at the cottages for several days. Six decorated to completion and five of them reserved from Thanksgiving eve through the weekend. Joe and I only texted a few times since our evening at Pallets. *Better than nothing, I guess.* He assured me he'd help move my stuff from the house into the cottage. I wasn't sure I wanted him to, but I knew I needed muscle power, and he certainly did have muscle. Lauren, Mick, Emily, and Blake volunteered to assist, too.

***

Puffs slept on the back seat with Buddy as we stacked the boxes into the bed of Joe's truck. I deliberately placed a container of kitchen supplies on the passenger seat. I didn't want to ride with him. *Childish, I guess.*

Lauren rode with me to the B&B. She knew me all too well. "Fess up, Rae. What's going on? Did Joe take you to Pallets or not?" She took a deep breath. "I'm not getting out of this car until you tell me."

"Since we're almost at the B&B, let's talk later. Okay?"

"Now."

"Lauren, everyone's going to wonder where I am." I pulled to the curb and parked.

"No, they aren't. Emily knows I'm asking you about the date because she's been wondering what happened, too. She said Joe's acting like an idiot. Her words, not mine." Lauren turned in the seat to face me. "Emily will know where to put the boxes and she's agreed to watch Puffs. Mick and Blake will keep Joe occupied so we have all the time in the world. Emily and I agreed to a fast food restaurant in Greenville for dinner and you're going, too. So are the guys." She pushed up her sunglasses on her nose. "I'm all ears."

I squirmed in my seat and could feel my cheeks flush. After removing my gloves and hat I told my side of the story. "Joe and I had a wonderful time at Pallets. As a matter of fact, he asked me to be his girlfriend."

"What's wrong with that?"

"Nothing. I was thrilled, to say the least, and I told him yes." I fumbled with the heater vent. "The waiter asked if we'd like our picture taken because we looked like a cute couple, and he asked how long we'd been married." I took a deep breath after running my words together. My eyes misted. "The waiter commented under his breath. Joe and I heard him say, 'What are you waiting for'."

"Oh, did Joe get cold feet or something?"

"I guess so, because on our drive back to the house our conversation was sporadic and when he walked me to my door, he kissed my forehead. Not our usual goodnight kiss smack dab on the lips."

"Wow. I see why you're miffed with him." Lauren adjusted the seatbelt. "Yes. Cold feet."

“But why, when he just asked me to be his girlfriend? I thought he really cared about me.” I grabbed a tissue from the container.

“It sounds weird, but Mick did a similar thing. Mind you, we hadn’t dated as long as you and Joe, and he didn’t call me, girlfriend, but the girls in his office teased him and me.” Lauren shifted in the car seat. “We resigned ourselves not to see each other for a couple days, hoping they’d stop. They did.”

“That’s not the same thing. You and Mick agreed to stop seeing each other so people wouldn’t aggravate you. Joe and I didn’t.”

“I guess you’re right, dear friend, but I do believe it’ll all work out with you and Joe.” Lauren patted my shoulder. “Have you actually spoken to him other than today?”

“No, and I don’t plan to. Except, of course, to thank him for helping me move.”

“Well, I’m glad you explained all that to me. You know I’m here for you any time.”

We continued to Charleston Street. When I parked in front of the small buildings, I noticed Joe’s truck was gone. Mick’s car and Blake’s were gone too. Emily stood on my cottage porch with Puffs at her side.

I left the car in a hurry. “Emily, where is everybody?” I took a deep breath. “I didn’t think we were gone that long.”

“Rae, you didn’t have much of anything to unload.” She smiled broadly. “I supervised the guys.” She hugged me gently. “Check to make sure the boxes are where you want them.” She opened the front door. “Come on in, Miss Long and Miss Wyatt." She giggled as she motioned for Lauren and me to step inside my cozy cottage.

"Emily, thanks. I don't need to see where everything is because I'm humbled to say the least. Thanks for supervising those fellas. If you hadn't been here, no telling where all my stuff would be. Maybe on the front porch?"

Emily and Lauren laughed as they professed their love for their macho men. The corners of my mouth tilted upward with thoughts of Joe. *My knight in shining armor. Maybe?*

Emily took my hand in one of hers and Puffs' leash in the other. She guided the two of us to Lauren's car. "The guys decided they wanted a boy's night out. I didn't argue with them because I thought we needed a girl's night, too. Mom and Dad are watching Buddy tonight; they said they'd watch Puffs too. Leave your car here, Rae. You're in no condition to drive."

"What? I'm perfectly okay."

I sat in the back seat of Lauren's Prius with Puffs. "Lauren, I can't believe you're allowing my pup in your car."

Lauren looked in the rearview mirror. "I guess I'm softening since I moved to Hope." She chuckled.

Emily clipped her seatbelt quickly as Lauren revved her little engine and drove toward the Byers' home.

We dropped off Puffs, I thanked the Byers, and slid back into Lauren's vehicle. She drove around the lake and quickly pulled into her driveway. "This is where we're eating girls. I know we talked about going to Greenville for fast food, but I'm too tired to drive tonight. Plus, I ordered pizzas from Molly's while you were dropping off the dogs, and one of her daughters is delivering them when they're ready. Peaches and Cream is open till eleven tonight; we'll go there for dessert."

Both Emily and I curtsied to her when we exited the car.

Pizzas arrived along with non-stop laughter. Emily told us about her Blakey list and how she and Blake reconciled. They'd chosen January 1st for their wedding date.

Lauren almost choked on her pizza. "That's soon. Are you going to have time to get everything ready?"

Emily grinned. "Of course. You don't think I put the wedding planning on hold while Blakey and I had our little tiff? Plus, I've planned and scheduled things for months just in case he proposed." She took a bite of her third piece of pizza.

I roared. "Emily, you amaze me. You are such an optimist."

"Guess I am." She sipped her soda. "I miss my Blakey tonight, but I'm glad he's with Joe and Mick."

I put down my piece of pizza. "I hope Joe isn't spilling the beans about our evening at Pallets."

Lauren reached over to me and gently gave me a squeeze. "The guys aren't discussing you or Joe. They're bowling. You know Mick and Blake are decent guys and if something is said, they will encourage Joe."

I let a few tears fall then regained my composure. "I guess you're right. I never thought doing a renovation might lead to falling in love."

Emily kicked off her shoes and curled her feet under her. "Rae, Joe loves you too. He's just scared. He might have those macho muscles, but deep inside, I don't think he ever visualized falling in love. Then you came along." Emily reached for her soda. "He's glad you did, and so is everyone else. Even my mother, although, she hates to admit it."

Lauren cleared away the pizza boxes, grabbed her coat, and herded us into her car. Peaches and Cream time.

***

Sidney smiled as Emily, Lauren, and I entered the ice cream shop. "Hi, ladies. The usual?"

Lauren grinned. "I'm stuffed, so a kiddy-sized vanilla cone will do just fine."

Emily followed suit. "Same for me, Sidney." She stepped aside for me to order.

"Kiddy chocolate for me, please," I said.

Sidney completed our orders and the three of us ate our desserts in the Prius while Lauren drove to the Byers to drop off Emily and pick up Puffs.

I couldn't thank the Byers enough for caring for my canine. "I appreciate you both so very much."

Lance Byer grinned then handed me Puffs' leash. "She's easy to watch. No problem at all, Rae."

Grace nodded in agreement then stepped back inside their home.

Puffs jumped into Lauren's back seat, and I slid into the passenger side as we rode to Charleston Street. Two new street lamps lit the way down my driveway as the cottage lights peeked through the plantation shutter slats. We both gasped at the quaint sight.

Lauren dropped us off. Puffs led the way into our new home as I waved to Lauren. Her Prius zipped down my driveway and within minutes my phone vibrated in my hand.

I heard her voice on the phone. "Rae, I know this is your first night in your place. You think you'll be all right by yourself?"

"I'll be just fine. I'm only a few blocks from where you live." I chuckled and sat on the foot of my bed.

"Since I packed a bag, do you mind if I stay in the cottage next to yours for a couple of nights?" She paused.

"Silly girl, why didn't you ask me that before you dropped me off? Where are you?"

"I'm parked on Beaufort Street in front of Tweeters."

"Come on over." I fell back onto the bed and stunned Puffs with my laugh.

Within minutes, Lauren parked her Prius in front of cottage number two then pulled a massive suitcase and bag from the trunk. She rolled her luggage onto the front porch as I unlocked the cottage and wept on her shoulder. Uncontrollably.

She patted my back and spoke almost in a whisper. "Rae, I remember how scared you used to be about the dark and stuff. Thought an occupant in another bungalow might help. I'm just being neighborly."

"You know my trusty companion, Puffs, is always nearby, but having you here is even better."

Lauren turned on the fireplace and lit the lamp next to the chair. "Miss Bed and Breakfast Owner, I need to get my beauty rest and so do you." She started unpacking her suitcase and removed her shoes. "Now scoot."

I walked a few feet back to cottage number one, got ready for bed, and read until falling asleep in the comfy chair near the fireplace. Puffs nudged me with her nose and convinced me to crawl into my new bed. I slept contentedly knowing my dear friend rested close by. *Thank You, Lord.*

From the rising of the sun to the place where it sets,
the name of the Lord is to be praised.
Psalm 113:3

Chapter Thirty-Four

Days skipped by. Joe and I spoke on the phone a time or two and planned to go to dinner. I missed him. I hoped he missed me, too.

Dr. D's entire crew worked on the family cottage. I supplied them with breakfast, lunch, and dinner as they kept a pace beyond compare. Or I must admit, Molly's Restaurant, Bitty's Buns, and Fenster Haus made the meals.

Dr. Duntworth perused the bed and breakfast buffet line and his belly laugh caused the floor to quiver slightly. "Rae, you keep the food coming, and we'll keep working."

"It's a deal." I giggled.

***

I loved living in the cottage with the construction of the main building only a stone's throw away.

My skinny jeans, knee high leather boots, and creamy-white sweater felt so comfy. I French-braided my hair then heard Joe's truck come to a squeaky halt in front of my bungalow.

He didn't have time to get out of his truck before I jumped into the passenger side of the old Ford.

"Rae, you look really good." He grinned slightly. "Your hair is beautiful."

"Thanks." I sat quietly and didn't want to give him the satisfaction of knowing I'd cried myself to sleep a few times and missed him terribly. "Where are we going?"

"Mind if we eat at Gill's?"

"Fine with me."

At Gill's, we ordered our usual.

I remained rather somber as I watched Joe remove his stocking cap. His hair scattered in every direction; I squelched the tiniest chuckle.

"Rae, I owe you an apology."

I didn't say a word.

"I hope you can forgive me."

"Forgive you for what?" *I think I'll let him squirm a little.*

"You know what. I acted like a fool the other night at Pallets. When the waiter thought we were married, it freaked me out." He folded his hands on the table and his eyes shifted downward.

I cleared my throat and spoke softly. "You hurt my heart, Joe. You really did. You asked me to be your girlfriend, then you treated me like a stranger."

His eyes met mine. "When I heard the word married, it scared me." He sipped his water. "I'm sorry, Rae."

If his shoulders had dropped any more, he would have slumped under the table.

"Joe, I forgive you. That doesn't mean my heart is completely healed. Remember the waiter at Pallets said the word married to me, too. I felt a little embarrassed but not scared."

The fries and burgers cooled. Joe and I spoke cautiously at first then the words flowed.

"Rae, I'll be up front. I let Mick and Blake know what happened."

"Why? I thought that was between you and me."

"They're two men who are up front with me." He took the first bite of his burger and drank his watered-down soda. "I know Blake and my sister had some trouble along the way but mended fences. I also know Mick isn't the best example of sainthood, but he seems to really care for Lauren. I've never felt for anyone like I feel for you."

I swirled the ice in my glass then reached for Joe's hand. "You know what? I have no right to be concerned that you told Blake and Mick about us, because I told Emily and Lauren." I took a bite of my lukewarm burger. "You make my heart smile, Joe. I've never felt this way about anyone else either."

We devoured our burgers and drinks, then ordered a shake to go. With two straws.

A few minutes later, Joe and I sat on the porch swing and finished our shake together. No forehead kisses tonight. Lips worked just fine. We said our goodbyes and agreed to meet the next day after Joe's classes. I started to enter the cottage when he stopped me short on my porch.

"Rae, I didn't tell you the whole truth."

"You didn't?" My heart sank.

He moved a little closer. "The other night you asked about my goals and dreams for the future, and I told you I want to eventually have my father's job." He leaned down and whispered in my ear. "I want a family, too, someday." He softly kissed my lips, walked toward his truck, and sped down the driveway.

My heart soared.

***

With microwave-warmed mugs of milk in each hand and Puffs at my side, I walked to my neighborly neighbor's cottage, tapped on the door with my foot, and waited for Lauren to answer.

"Rae, is that you?"

I knew she could see me through the peephole. "Of course, it's me. Who else would be standing on your porch in a robe?"

She opened the door, and Puffs and I invaded her space. "I wanted to call you when I heard Joe's truck leave but thought you might be exhausted. After all, it's late . . . ten o'clock. Isn't it past your bedtime?" Her sarcasm filled the room as she grinned, took her warm mug, and sat on the foot of her bed. She raised her drink to me. "Thanks for this. Help yourself to cookies on the table over there." She sipped the white warmth. "This is perfect. Now, let's get down to the nitty gritty. Did you and Joe makeup?" Another sip of milk. "Curiosity almost got the best of me when I heard Joe's truck park outside. I tried to do a little spying to see if you got a forehead kiss or a dreamy kiss, but the sightlines between our cottages are lousy."

I nibbled a cookie. "Dreamy kiss." I swooned and pretended to faint. "He apologized."

"That's it? I want details. Where did you go for dinner? Someplace romantic?" She took a bite of her second cookie.

I filled Lauren in on the details. Well, most of them. I didn't share the last comment Joe whispered to me. I felt he said that for the two of us.

We said our goodbyes and I returned to my abode. *Time for rest. Complete rest. Sweet rest.*

Remember the wonders he has done . . .
1 Chronicles 16:12

Chapter Thirty-Five

The construction engines started early so I reached for my phone and called Dr. D. "Is everything okay?"

"We're taking advantage of the warmer weather. We know it won't last long. The crew wants to keep working as many days as they can. They need the money since Christmas is around the corner. Hope you don't mind the racket."

"Are you kidding? I'm thrilled you're willing to give so much time to this project. What can I do to help?"

"Mrs. Ingles is coming by today. I called her with a question, and she asked if we finished the staircases. I couldn't lie but . . . now she wants to see them when she inspects the roof and porch. I didn't argue with her, but I'll tell you this. The historical aspect of this building is the outside structure, not everything on the inside. I hate to say it, but she's being nosey." He paused for a second. "I want you to see the staircases before she does."

"I'll be there." The call ended.

A knock on my door startled me. Then I heard Lauren say, "Rae, are you awake?"

"Come in. If I wasn't awake, I'd need my hearing checked." Puffs greeted her with a lick on the hand.

"Why did they start working so early this morning?" She sat in the comfy chair.

"Mind if I talk to you through the bathroom door? I need to get dressed."

I repeated everything Dr. Duntworth told me, then added a request. "Would you be willing to inspect the roof and porch this morning?"

"Sure, I'll be glad to." She paused for a minute. "I hope you don't want me to crawl up on the roof, though. I'm not in my work clothes. By the way, want to go to breakfast afterwards?"

"Sure. Dr. D said Mrs. Persnickety wants to inspect the roof, porch, and see the staircases."

Lauren's voice rose a notch. "What? She really doesn't need to check all that."

"Dr. D said the same thing."

"He's right." She shifted in her seat. "Are you about ready in there? If I'm checking a roof, then going to eat, we'd better get started. I'm famished."

I twisted my hair into a braid, put on my knee-length wool sweater and leggings. "No, you aren't getting on the roof." *At least I don't think so.*

Lauren and I jogged to the main building and stopped before entering. She patted my shoulder. "Rae, you look like you're getting a root canal. All Martha Ingles can do is search for something out of code, but I'll bet she doesn't find anything." Lauren folded her arms and cocked her left hip. "Plus, Miss Worry Wart, where's all your faith? You tell me all the time I need to pray. I'm assuming you're following your own advice?"

"Okay, Miss Wyatt, you got me there." I folded my arms and cocked my hip just to mock my friend.

Upon inspection, Lauren shook Dr. D's hand and let him know everything looked great. We left before Mrs. Ingles arrived because Lauren suggested we give her space. *Much to my chagrin.*

***

We made a bee-line for Bitty's Buns. Natalie convinced Lauren to try my signature coffee along with a heavenly muffin.

I ordered the famous cinnamon bun I'd craved for several days, and carefully sipped my steamy hot coffee. *Delicious.*

Lauren's java/cream mustache made me giggle. "Miss Lauren, you need to use your napkin."

She took a compact from her purse, glanced at the mirror, then looked shocked. "I'm a complete mess. I can't believe I have more coffee on me than in me." She quickly swiped her lip and rolled her eyes. "This is so good." She fiddled with her earring while taking another taste. "Did you get an invite?"

"An invite?"

"To Fenster Haus for Thanksgiving dinner?"

"I did." The ooey-gooey cinnamon bun melted in my mouth. "By the way, I can't wait till your parents get here for Thanksgiving weekend. I miss them."

"They're giddy about staying at your B&B."

"I'm excited, too."

Lauren took the last bite of muffin. "Mom and Dad roared when I told them Bitty's Buns is a favorite place of mine. The name of the place made them laugh, but the fact I'd even order anything with carbs shocked them." She placed her napkin on her empty plate.

"Hope has so many sweet things to offer, my dear friend. We're so blessed."

We said goodbye to Natalie and her crew then went our separate ways. Lauren went to the university and I strolled to Angels to Zithers. The family cottage would open in time for Thanksgiving. I knew who I'd invite to stay in the large bungalow pro bono. I just needed to let them know soon.

Sing the praises of the Lord . . .
Psalm 30:4

Chapter Thirty-Six

Days scurried by and the Angels to Zithers delivery truck brought everything I ordered for the family cottage. Two sets of white bunk beds fit nicely in the children's area. One of the bathroom linen closets housed the washer/dryer combo. Great set-up. Small-paned windows flanked both sides of the breezeway that connected the two cottages. Carpenters built storage benches under the windows. Board games, blocks, and assorted coloring books tucked away nicely beneath one bench. The other one housed extra pillows and comforters. A wooden folding table stored easily in the breezeway.

My mind whirled as I took a break.

Text from Lauren: Mick and I are going for Chinese take-out. You and Joe want anything?

Me: I'll check with Joe. If it's a go, let's eat on the cottage porch.

Lauren: Sounds great. Let me know what he says.

I called Joe. "Want to come over for some Chinese food? Lauren and Mick are driving to a new place between here and Greenville and ordering food-to-go."

"Sure. What can I bring?"

Yourself . . . I couldn't ask for anything more. "Just yourself." Lauren and I are setting up a card table on the porch and we can dine alfresco. Thought we'd take advantage of the warmer November weather."

He chuckled. "So, you just assumed I'd say yes?"

I sniggled. "A girl can hope, can't she?"

"I love teasing you. What time?"

"In about an hour. By the way, what's your order?"

"Noodles, orange chicken, and two egg rolls. I'd like to bring something. How about a jug of iced tea from Molly's?"

"Yes. I hadn't thought of anything to drink. See you soon, Joe." *Be still my heart.*

I called Lauren with our order and showered quickly, slipped into my jeans and gray flannel shirt, and added orange dangly earrings.

***

The twinkle lights wrapped easily around the railing on my front porch. It only took me a few minutes to finish and add extra strands to Lauren's, too. I enjoyed referring to it as Lauren's porch. After all, she'd stayed a couple weeks in the cottage next to mine. She'd be moving out soon before guests arrived for Thanksgiving.

I heard Joe's truck sputtering down my driveway. He parked, slid out of the Ford, then stepped onto the porch.

"Thanks for bringing the tea." I kissed his cheek then tossed an autumnal-colored cloth on the table. I added four folding chairs. "Mind getting glasses off the shelf inside?"

"Not at all." He set the tea down then entered my tiny abode and returned with glasses. "Rae, you've created a home in the cottage. I really like it."

"Thanks, I never thought I'd love such a tiny space, but it's perfect."

Within minutes, Lauren and Mick drove down the driveway and parked in between both cottages.

Lauren hopped out of Mick's car. "Rae, I need your help. Mick went a little overboard with the food. He said he owed Joe a meal."

Joe scrambled down the steps. "Owed me a meal? What are you talking about, Mick?" Joe gave him a friendly punch on the arm.

"Remember that time at Gill's when you wouldn't let me pay?"

The guys bantered back and forth while Lauren and I removed the paper food boxes and lit a candle.

She swatted Mick with a cloth napkin and motioned for him to sit. I did the same to Joe and the four of us chatted with only a pause or two to nibble on our tangy and spicy cuisine.

After devouring an egg roll with spicy mustard, Mick gulped his iced tea. "This is really good, but I torched my insides."

Joe rolled his egg roll in spicy mustard. "Wimp. Mustard isn't for cowards." He took a huge bite. "See, nothing to it."

We all waited for Joe to grab his tea, but instead he chewed his food and added the rest of the egg roll to his mouth.

He finished the entire thing, took a sip of tea, and gave me a wink. "They don't call me hot lips for nothing."

I interjected. "They? Who calls you hot lips?"

Mick belly laughed. "Now you're in trouble, show off."

Lauren looked at Mick and grinned. "You're the one with hot lips, Mick." Lauren's face reddened. "Did I just say that out loud?"

Mick kissed her gently. "See, I don't have to impress a girl with mustard."

The teasing went back and forth as we cleared away the chop sticks and paper cartons. The guys took the trash to the dumpster, so Lauren and I had a couple minutes to talk.

"Rae, that was so much fun. I'm thankful our guys get along."

"Me, too. And I'm thrilled you've moved here."

"I never in a million years dreamed of living in a tiny town like this. I think my parents are going to be shocked when they see Hope. You know they aren't computer savvy so haven't seen pictures of the area."

The guys returned in time for all of us to see car lights approaching the cottages.

Emily popped out of Blake's Jeep even before he put it in park. "Hi everybody. I heard you were dining alfresco and figured you'd be done, so I convinced Blakey to get ice cream from Peaches and Cream. Thought we'd bring dessert."

Blake slowly closed his door. "We should have called first."

Emily scooped up the paper bag filled with six pints of ice cream. "Hannah gave me everybody's favorite flavor with spoons. We'll eat out of our paper pints."

Lauren and I laughed as Emily handed each of us our favorites. We girls sat on the porch swing savoring our ice cream while the guys sat around the card table devouring theirs.

I swallowed my Pralines and Cream slowly. “Thanks for bringing this, you two. It’s exactly what we needed. Maybe this will cool down Joe’s hot lips.” I winked at my handsome professor.

Lauren laughed and took another bite of her Chocolate Mumbo Jumbo, stopped the swing, and took a few steps to Mick. A kiss ensued, then she returned to the swing. The three of us giggled and enjoyed our cold delights while the guys talked and finished their dessert.

Emily and Blake left after goodbyes and thanks were said by the rest of us. Mick walked Lauren to her cottage and drove away shortly afterwards. Joe sat on the porch swing with me for a little longer. He hummed an old hymn in my ear. I knew the words and sang softly to his hum. Some might think singing an old hymn while sharing a moment as boyfriend/girlfriend might be silly. I loved it. *A perfect ending to a perfect evening.*

The two of us stopped the swing and approached my door.

“Good night, Joe. Thanks for coming over.”

“I’m glad you asked me. By the way, I’m off work till after Thanksgiving and will be glad to help with anything you need before your visitors arrive.”

“I just might take you up on that offer, hot lips.” I opened the screen door and giggled.

He raked his fingers through his hair, smiled his crooked grin, and placed those hot lips on mine. “Rest well, Rae.” He whistled and strolled to his truck.

I patted Puffs' head and ruffled her ears. "Time for sleep girl." I crawled under the covers as she settled onto the foot of my bed. "Good night, sweet pup."

. . . Go in peace, for we have sworn friendship with each other . . .
1 Samuel 20:42

Chapter Thirty-Seven

The Historical Society ladies' cars parked in front of the cottages. I remembered the first time they visited my rental on Pecan Street. What a change from our first meeting.

All of us crowded onto the front porch. "Ladies, thank you for coming today. This is a momentous occasion, and I'm honored you're here."

Opal interjected. "Girls, move together, because I want a current picture of all of you to place at the library. Plus, the newspaper article I'm writing will look more official if a photo is attached."

We all scooted closer together, then Opal placed her phone on a stick and took a selfie of us all. Then she snapped a photo of the Historical Society ladies only.

We meandered inside the first cottage and the "oohs" and "aahs" that flowed from these women of Hope sounded like a sweet melody to my ears. On the small round table were crackers, cheese, and various spreads. Small cups and a container of hot cider set nearby.

"Please help yourselves, ladies." I motioned for them to enjoy the snacks.

Victoria swallowed her cider carefully and set the paper cup on the mantel. "This cottage is so pretty. You've outdone yourself." She took a nibble of her cracker. "I can't wait for the first occupants to soak in the beauty."

"Thank you. I know you brought the little pillow cards. Will you put one on each pillow as we go inside every cottage?"

"Of course, dear. I have some in this envelope and more in the trunk of my car. They should last you quite a long time."

"That's perfect, Victoria. I can't wait to read all of them."

I turned toward Anna. "Did you bring the paintings with you?"

"I did." She opened a cloth bag, removed a picture, and handed it to me.

"It's absolutely fabulous. The colors are so soft and gorgeous. Thank you so much, Anna."

"You're welcome. The others are in my car."

"When you get a minute, please bring them inside. That way, you can put one on each mantel."

I blew on my cider to cool it just a little, took a small sip, and a bite of a cheese cracker.

Lottie cleared her throat. "I brought the matted and framed picture for the main building. It's in the car, but what should I do with it since the renovation isn't done?"

"Bring it inside, and I'll hang it in here temporarily. When the main building opens, I'd like you to place the picture in the entryway. Is that okay?"

"I'd love to."

I smiled as my eyes moved from one enthusiastic Historical Society lady to another. Each one grinned so much their eyes crinkled at the edges. Yes, they crinkled.

Grace tapped my shoulder. "What about me? Where are we going to put the sign? Joe is bringing it in a few minutes. As a matter of fact, he asked me to text him when you're ready. It's much too big to fit into my trunk. I sure hope you like it." She placed her hands on her hips. "Do you have a place to put the sign? With all the heavy trucks entering the driveway, I don't want it knocked down. You know I'm very protective of my baby."

"Of course, you are. Dr. D isn't doing construction after Monday. Everyone's arriving on Wednesday for Thanksgiving, and I'd love the sign permanently positioned on Tuesday. If it works for you, Mrs. Byer."

"Then maybe I should text Joe not to bring the iron work because I'm not leaving it leaning against the cottages. I don't want it snowed on or knocked down."

Victoria looked shocked. "Grace, dear, you know it's going to be out in the elements. It's not going to hurt the sign."

"I can't help it. I don't want it ruined." Grace mumbled something indecipherable. Maybe it's best I didn't hear her.

"Mrs. Byer, please ask Joe to bring the sign. I'd love for everyone to see it today."

"That sounds reasonable. I'll store it in my spare bedroom after the viewing. Lance told me to put it in the garage, but there's no way I'm taking a chance he'd park his truck near it and scrape it." She sent a message to Joe.

We by-passed Lauren's cottage then entered number three. Anna added a gorgeous oil painting on the mantel and received an applause. Victoria placed a note card on each pillow. One said, *Rest . . . Relax . . . Rejuvenate.* The card on the second pillow read, *Sweet . . . Soft . . . Slumber.*

We moved from dwelling to dwelling, each receiving a one-of-a-kind painting from Anna and pillow talk sayings from Victoria. After exiting the family cottage, we noticed Joe's truck parked in front.

Grace shouted and waved her hands in the air, "Joe, be careful! I don't want the sign to slip and slide in the bed of your truck before we use it."

He rolled his eyes and gently hugged her. "It's okay, Mom. Dad wrapped it in a million blankets. Don't you want to show the ladies the thing?"

"It's a sign, not a thing, and, of course, I want to show them. Come on, girls. You come first, Rae, because if you don't like it nobody else sees it."

Opal laughed uncontrollably and spoke a few words in-between laughs. "Rae, I think you've created a monster."

I walked with Joe and Grace to the back of the truck. Joe jumped into the bed and removed the blankets, so I could see.

I cheered, "It's even more beautiful than I anticipated. Come on girls. Please look."

Everyone crowded around in amazement. Joe propped the iron sign inside the bed of his truck.

I cried. Each lady offered me a tissue and Joe jumped from the truck and cradled me in his arms. He didn't flinch or try to stop me from crying. He let me weep for as long as I needed. Eventually I composed myself only to look up and see the rest of the ladies crying, too. Joe kissed my forehead and moved aside so I could share this moment with the Historical Society Ladies of Hope.

INN AT HOPE
Today's Moments
Tomorrow's Memories

The time spent together with these friends will certainly be one of today's moments and someday be yesterday's memories. I can't ask for anything more. I love Hope.

***

Before Joe left, he reassured his mom he'd put the sign in the extra bedroom. I got into my VW and the ladies trailed behind in their cars. We'd made some last-minute changes the night before, and, instead of dining at Molly's, her staff prepared child-sized Thanksgiving meals. We carefully placed the boxed lunches in our cars and delivered them to Hope Grade School. It was so much fun seeing the familiar little ones dressed in Pilgrim and Indian outfits. *Maybe someday I'll take cupcakes to my little . . .*

Shout for joy to God, all the earth!
Psalm 66:1

Chapter Thirty-Eight

I procrastinated long enough and finally called. "Val, hope you're doing well today."

"I am. How can I help you, Rae? Puffs okay?"

"She is. I'm not calling about Puffs. I wondered if you and yours would like to stay in my family cottage from Thanksgiving Eve through the Monday after?"

"A family cottage? That sounds wonderful. You know my husband and I never get to leave town because of my veterinary business. We'd love to stay. I'm so thankful you called."

"By the way, there's no charge. It's my way of giving back to families of Hope."

"We'll definitely pay. My hubby won't agree to stay for free and neither will I."

"I insist. My treat." Laughter. "See you Wednesday night."

I'd have cottage guests soon, so Lauren returned to her rental next to the library. I'd miss having her as a next-door neighbor. However, she lived only a hop, skip, and a jump away.

Mums of every color decorated the inside of Joe's truck. My professor boyfriend was true to his word and helped me every day before the arrival of my first occupants. Emily brought the Rodriguez children to help unload the mums and place them on the steps leading into each dwelling. I knew Shelly Rodriguez and her husband, Javier, needed time to get Fenster Haus ready for Thanksgiving. Another family I put on the list for an Inn at Hope getaway.

Autumnal wreaths hung on each cottage door, and white twinkle lights lit each porch. I knew without a doubt my grandparents would have loved the cottages.

***

Buds and Blooms delivered fall flower arrangements. "Fran, I didn't know you drove the shop van."

"I do about everything except grow the flowers. By the way, you inspired me to take the plunge." She gathered a box filled with vases and arrangements in her arms and shut the van door with her foot.

"What kind of plunge?"

"I'm buying the shop."

"You go, girl. I'm so proud of you." I had to quicken my pace to keep up with her.

I followed Fran from bungalow to bungalow. We placed a bouquet on each indoor table.

"It'll still be open only three days a week, so I can have family time."

We entered the combined cottage and Fran gasped. "I can't believe how beautiful this is, Rae." She set the flower vase on the table.

"Come take a tour."

"Rae, I'm stunned. Your vision for this place is spot on. Someday, hopefully, George and I'll make a reservation."

"I'm so glad you like it. Thanks for the beautiful flowers, dear friend."

"Well, I'm off and running. See you at Fenster Haus, Thursday?" Fran opened the van door and threw the empty box inside.

"I'll be there."

As I watched Fran's van putter down the driveway, I noticed Lauren's car driving in.

She parked and popped out of her car quickly. "Rae, we're here to help." She and Mick sauntered hand in hand onto the porch.

"You two are the best."

I put Lauren to work straightening comforters and fluffing pillows. Mick, on the other hand, helped Joe scrutinize the outdoors for sticks, low hanging limbs, and any other yard hazards.

Joe hauled branches to the dumpster and motioned he'd be in the main building.

***

I hugged Lauren tightly. "Thank you so much for all your help, dear friend. I couldn't have done all of this without you and Mick. Would you like some bottled water? I wish I had more to offer."

Lauren pulled her hair back in a clip. "The best thing you can do for us right now is to let us sit on your porch."

"That's easy enough. The swing's all yours." I giggled as I watched Lauren flop down and almost lose her balance.

She patted the slats next to her. "Come and have a seat, Mick."

He sat beside her and kissed Lauren on the cheek. "What do ya say we go to a movie in Greenville tonight? I'll be sharing you with your folks when they arrive tomorrow, and I'm not sure I like that thought." He sat with arms crossed.

"I'm not sure I like what you said." Lauren kept the swing in motion. "My mom and dad are looking forward to seeing you again." She folded her arms, too.

"Lauren, I want to see them. I'd like some one-on-one time with you because we'll be occupied with them and everyone else the entire weekend." He scooted closer.

Lauren bounced off the swing and walked to her car. "No movie for me tonight. I'm exhausted and want to get ready for my parents. I don't need you to go with me to the airport tomorrow to pick them up. Heaven forbid, you spend more time than necessary with Mr. and Mrs. Wyatt." She started her Prius and drove down the driveway.

Mick stood up from the swing. He just stood there for a moment before he walked down the driveway.

I watched silently.

Joe returned from the main building with hands in his pockets and a sheepish grin on his face. "Rae, what are your plans for the welcome area at the main building? Need anything?"

"I do. Why are you grinning?"

"I have an idea. Want something to eat?"

"What's your idea? Of course, I want something to eat."

"I'll tell you later."

"Let me put Puffs inside then you'd better tell me what you're thinking." I opened the door then glanced at Joe. "I'll be just a minute."

Puffs settled at the foot of my bed as I rushed into the bathroom to freshen up. Teeth brushed, hair clipped back, and apple-flavored lip gloss. Done. The door squeaked as I exited toward my beau.

"Sorry, Joe. Guess I took longer than a minute."

"It was worth it." He kissed my glossy lips. "Apple. I like it." His lips brushed mine again. "Just making sure I got the flavor right."

"Come on silly guy. Remember, I'm famished." I slid inside his truck. "Now you can tell me your idea."

"Sure." We puttered down the driveway then onto Beaufort Street.

Before Joe shared his thoughts, we spotted Mick walking toward Tweeters.

I put down my window. "Need a lift, Mick?" I couldn't help but laugh.

"Ha-ha. Very funny." His somber face looked almost pitiful.

Joe parked in front of Tweeters and shouted through the open window. "What's going on?"

"I don't know what I did wrong, but Lauren sure is mad at me."

I didn't say a word.

Joe, on the other hand, didn't hesitate to give advice. "Give her a call and work it out. Sometimes it can be as simple as that." He nodded in my direction. "Right, Rae?"

I gave him a silly grimace. “Easy to say now that you’re out of the hot seat, hot lips.”

Mick moaned. “Don’t start the hot lips thing again. I can’t stomach it.” He opened the door to Tweeters and went inside.

Joe disregarded Mick’s comments, put his arm over the back of the seat, and pulled me a little closer to him. “I don’t mind discussing the hot lips thing with you again.”

“Slow down, Professor. I need to check with Lauren and make sure she’s all right. Could you drop me off at her place?”

“Aren’t we still on for dinner and bowling tonight? If you don’t want to bowl, we can at least go eat.” He backed out of the parking spot and proceeded toward Lauren’s place.

“Can I take a rain check?”

“Are you sure? Tomorrow your guests arrive, and I know you’ll be busy with everyone. Just thought we could spend some time this evening together before the onslaught.”

“The onslaught? Is that how you feel about my bed and breakfast guests? Joe, I’m just beginning my new business, and you’re dreading it.”

“I didn’t mean it the way it sounded. I’m proud of you and am glad you’re opening the B&B. I love spending time with my girlfriend. That’s all.”

I pulled on my leather gloves and paused a second. “I know I’m being a little sensitive, and, I must admit, stressed about the grand opening.” I took his hand. “Thank you for all your help, Joseph William Byer.”

"You'll be the best innkeeper ever, Rae."

I kissed his cheek. "Thanks. Wish I had your confidence." I smiled easily. "Mind if I spend some time with Lauren tonight? I think she needs some girl talk." I winked at my green-eyed professor. "You and I will definitely sneak in a kiss or two before the onslaught." Kisses and more kisses. "Deal?"

He stopped in front of Lauren's abode. "You know you don't need my permission to see your friend, but thanks for asking." Crooked grin. "Deal."

"Night, Joe." I blew him a kiss. Then another.

***

Lauren was pleasantly surprised when she opened her door. "Rae, I'm so glad you came over. I know you must be exhausted."

"I'm never too tired to talk to you." Huge hug. "I'm withering and need dinner. Want to go to Molly's for carry-out?"

She agreed. We strolled to the restaurant, ordered a bagged meal, and took it back to her place. The chicken salad sandwiches, fruit salad, and peanut butter brownies hit the spot. We girls needed sustenance after a hard day's work.

Lauren bit into the heavenly brownie. "I got so mad at Mick today. He's such a baby and thinks he needs all the attention." She wiped a crumb from her chin.

"You know what? I thought the same thing about Joe because he referred to my occupants as an onslaught."

"What?"

"Sure enough. Then I took a moment and shared with him how I felt about the comment. I'm glad I did. It cleared the air for us both. He realized how he sounded, and I noticed I might have been a little sensitive. Could that be the case with you and Mick? Just askin'."

"Guess I hadn't thought of it that way. Honestly, I didn't give Mick a chance to explain anything. I'll give him a call later." She leaned back in her comfy living room chair. "Thanks. You put things in perspective."

Time slipped by. "Lauren, I didn't realize it was so late. I'd better get home. I didn't even leave a light on for Puffs, and I know she needs to be taken outside." I bundled up into my warm garb and reached for her front door.

"Let me take you home."

My life-long friend and former cottage neighbor drove me to my little abode.

Before I exited Lauren's car, she reminded me I needed to lock the door and close the blinds when I got inside. I chuckled at her mothering words.

I checked my phone and sent a message to Joe.

Me: You are important to me, Professor.

Listen to advice and accept discipline, and at the end you will be counted among the wise.
Proverbs 19:20

Chapter Thirty-Nine

My heart rejoiced. That's the easiest way I could describe what I felt as my guests arrived. The Inn at Hope occupants settled into their little bungalows. Inside each dwelling, a round table held flowers from Buds and Blooms and a small box of Bitty's Buns sweets.

Lauren's parents were the last to arrive. "Mom and Dad Wyatt, it's so good to see you." I hugged them gently. "You both look great."

"Rae, you've done a magnificent job. Lauren raved about your place, but I can honestly say, everything looks even more glorious than I expected." Mrs. Wyatt nudged Mr. Wyatt. "Right, Harrison?"

He nodded in agreement and placed a suitcase on the luggage rack in the closet. "Great job, Rae. I wish your mom and dad were here to see what you've accomplished. For what it's worth, Betty and I are very proud of you."

Lauren's dad felt like a warm teddy bear as I embraced him and kissed his cheek. "Thank you, Dad Wyatt."

When everyone had settled in, I strolled slowly back to the first cottage—my temporary home. I stood back and took in the row of cottages with lights twinkling on their porch railings, giving the entire property that extra holiday appeal. A light snow fell, as I leaned my head back, opened my mouth, and waited to catch a flake on the tip of my tongue. *Heavenly.*

I stepped onto my porch and caught a glimpse of a beautiful basket filled with fall-colored flowers on the porch swing. I opened the attached card which read: *I understand exactly why you were upset with me, and I'm sorry. I'm proud of you, Rae Long, and hope someday we can run the Inn at Hope together. Love, Your Professor Joe.*

Someday—the word played over and over in my mind. I loved that word and knew a call to my boyfriend was in order.

"Joe . . ."

"Are you all right?"

"The basket of flowers is stunning. I can't thank you enough."

"I'm so glad you like them. I meant every word I wrote."

I could hear him breathing quietly.

"Do you have time for dinner?" I paused. "I can't go far because my guests might need me. Is that okay with you?"

"More than okay. What time is good?"

"Give me an hour. I need to drop off little bags to each cottage. You know the ones Amber and Emily put together with all the info about the town. I also included a reminder that breakfast is provided for them anywhere in town—since this is a bed and breakfast. I can't wait till the main building opens so we can provide meals on the main floor." I finally came up for air.

"So, *we* can provide them with meals? I like the sound of that."

Nervous giggle. "It does sound good. Now I'd better get the information delivered." I took a deep breath. "See you soon."

I left a bag on each door handle, then put a tiny sign on my door informing occupants I'd be at Molly's Restaurant.

I had wrapped my fuzzy melon-colored scarf around my neck. Joe noticed it immediately. "You look fabulous, Miss Inn at Hope Owner. The only thing that might compete with you is the way the cottages looked when I drove down the driveway. They really look nice."

"Hmm, so now you're comparing the way I look to a cottage?" I giggled.

"You know what I mean." He held my hand. "Want to walk to Molly's?"

"I'd love to. I need to break in my new boots."

We walked down the driveway and enjoyed the short jaunt to Molly's. The snow started again. I tilted back my head, like I'd done earlier, and opened my mouth to catch a snowflake. When I glanced at Joe, he was doing the same thing. He looked at me, and we broke into laughter. *Laughter. Today's moment.*

For God is not a God of disorder but of peace . . .
1 Corinthians 14:33

Chapter Forty

Thanksgiving. Puffs and I woke early and walked to Bitty's Buns.

"I hope your guests like these muffins, Rae." Natalie handed me a cardboard box. "There are two in each bag. Do they look okay to you?"

I lifted the lid, then peeked inside. "They're fabulous, Natalie, and smell delicious. Thank you, tons. I love the way you tied each little bag with raffia." I closed the box. "See you later at Fenster Haus?"

"Of course, you will, dear. By the way, I threw in a couple muffins for you, too." She opened her shop door and motioned for me to exit. "Now skedaddle or your muffins will get cold." She closed the door then abruptly opened it. "Text me if your occupants want coffee. My aunt and uncle love a morning cup, and I don't want to call them this early in the morning. I know you have coffee makers in each cottage. But—now I'm holding you up, dear. See you later. Oh, yes, one more thing. My aunt texted me last night and said she loves the cottage."

***

My tea-length chiffon dress felt luxurious and feminine. The cloth buttons down my back added simple elegance. "I love this dress, Puffs. What do you think?" I twirled around the cottage. As usual, Puffs lifted her head at the mention of her name then went back to sleep. Earrings added. "I'm ready."

***

Comfortably seated at Fenster Haus, I whispered in Joe's ear. "Thank you for coming to get me. You know I could've driven myself."

"No way. I wanted to be the first to see you on this special day. Call it stingy. I don't care. By the way, if I haven't told you already, you look fabulous in green."

"Yes, you did tell me, Professor, but I don't mind hearing it again." I patted his hand. "By the way, just for the record, my dress isn't just green, it's hunter green."

"You sure don't look like a hunter to me." He gave my hand a gentle squeeze and added a little eyebrow wiggling.

Lance Byer cleared his throat and spoke rather loudly. "Would you two quit smooching and pass the mashed potatoes. We've been waiting for hours."

Grace jokingly hit him with her napkin. "Don't be silly, Lance. They're in love." She put her hand to her mouth. "I can't believe I said that out loud. Forgive me."

Did Mrs. Byer say "love"?

Joe gently patted her shoulder. "It's okay, Mom. We are in love." He picked up the mashed potatoes, put some on my plate, then on his, and passed the yellow bowl to his dad.

Emily spoke softly to me. "Rae, I can't believe my mother actually said that. The woman still won't let you call her by her first name. Plus, my brother should call you something other than girlfriend. Blakey and I skipped that part and went right for fiancé." She took a deep breath and turned toward Blake. "Right, sweetie?"

Blake finished chewing. "You'd think I'd get use to Emily's abruptness, but she never ceases to amaze me."

Emily kissed his cheek and offered him a bite of her stuffing. "Can you believe the wedding is just a little over a month away and the next Thanksgiving we share, we'll be married? And we might even have a baby on the way by then."

Blake coughed uncontrollably.

"Blakey, Blakey, are you all right, sweetie?"

"Emily, slow down, girl. We haven't even gotten married yet."

Emily's baby comment flowed from guest to guest until everyone in the restaurant heard. Someone began the little chant, "first comes love, then comes marriage . . ." Much to Blake's embarrassment and Emily's enthusiasm.

Grace's comment squelched the conversation. "Emily, I swanny. Don't even think of making me a grandma by next Thanksgiving. I'm much too young."

A few soft chuckles were heard here and there.

The succulent turkey practically melted in my mouth. Shelly's yeast rolls, smothered in butter, disappeared quickly from the bread baskets only to be refilled easily by her staff. The sweet potato casserole, deviled eggs, and homemade cranberry sauce tantalized my taste buds.

Victoria rang a tiny silver bell and stood next to her husband, Sam. "Ladies and gentlemen, let's give the Rodriguez family our thanks."

Everyone arose from their seats and gave a standing ovation. It continued until all the family and staff came from the kitchen area. More applause.

Victoria rang the small bell again. "Y'all will notice the little clear bag at each place setting. There are three corn kernels in each. We'd like you to share three things you're thankful for with everyone at your table. I know we really don't need things to help us converse, but we must remember what we are thankful for. Thankfully thankful."

Grace couldn't contain herself. "Victoria, thankfully thankful is something you could write on one of your pillow cards."

Everyone laughed and shared their blessings with each other. There was a constant hum around the tables and an occasional sniffle as tender thankfulness was shared by all.

Joe whispered in my ear. "The first thing I'm thankful for is you, Rae. The second is you. The third is you." He smiled his crooked smile.

I moved my chair closer to his. "You said what I was going to say, only change the name to Joe. Now it doesn't sound so special since you shared it first."

"I don't care who said it first. I'm glad we feel the same way about each other."

Lauren, Mick, and their parents sat at a different table than Joe and I did. When they got up to go through the dessert buffet line, I left my chair and moved in their direction.

Lauren introduced Mick's parents to me and let them go ahead of her in line. "I'll join you in a minute. I need to talk to Rae." Lauren smiled graciously at Mrs. Treavor then turned to me. "This is the best Thanksgiving I've ever had. The visit is going well and the Treavors are raving about the bed and breakfast. They want to book a cottage for Christmas, and you know my parents will too. I have so much to be thankful for."

Mick helped his mom carry her dessert plate to the table and then walked close to Lauren and me. "Rae, my mom and dad love the Inn at Hope and want a reservation for Christmas."

Lauren took his hand. "I just told Rae how much your parents love it."

He gave her hand a squeeze. "That's not all they love." He kissed Lauren's forehead and the two of them picked up a dessert plate to share.

Lauren's mom went through the line and instead of setting down with her plate, she motioned for me to follow her near the fireplace. "Rae, we love our bungalow, and you know, we love you. Harrison and I are so glad you moved to Hope because now we get to see you and Lauren. Plus, Lauren has met Mick. We love him and his family. Well, his parents seem a little quirky, but I guess Harrison and I are, too."

"I'm so thankful Lauren's here. She said you might return for Christmas."

"Yes, if you have any reservations available."

Mom Wyatt didn't wait for my answer. Instead she walked toward her table and proceeded to talk with Mick's mom. *Yes, she's a little quirky, too. Shame on me.*

Carrot cake and a piece of pumpkin pie topped with whipped cream delighted my senses.

Joe's plate practically overflowed. "Rae, want a bite?"

I crinkled my nose jokingly. "I can't decipher where the chocolate cake begins and the strudel, pound cake, and pie end." I took a quick glance at my food. "Guess I can't say anything; I have almost as much as you do.

We visited with everyone. The fireplace warmed the restaurant inside and the twinkle lights lit leafless tree branches outside. Truly a sight to behold. The evening ended much too quickly, and I hated to see my first Thanksgiving in Hope slip away.

Joe drove me to my cottage and kissed me goodnight. "Rest well, Rae. A quiet breakfast at Molly's tomorrow?"

"Yes, Professor, tomorrow. Sweet dreams." I tilted my head up hoping for another kiss.

He quickly obliged.

A thankful heart brought this Thanksgiving to a close. *Thankfully thankful.*

. . . let us be thankful . . .
Hebrews 12:28

Chapter Forty-One

I dressed very early and drove to Molly's to pick up pre-ordered goodies for the Inn at Hope occupants.

The restaurant lights shone, and when I entered, Henry greeted me. "Good morning, Rae. Everything's packed and ready to go. Let me help you put the individual bags in your car."

"Thanks so much."

"They all have the same selection of goodies, except the one for the family cottage. I added a generous amount of granola bars, trail mix, and apples to the larger container. Val and her family need extra since her four boys eat constantly." He situated everything inside my little car.

***

After delivering the bags to each bungalow, I regrouped and strolled back to Molly's for breakfast with Joe.

My phone buzzed. Emily. "Rae, I heard a little bit of news you might be interested in. Do you have time to talk?"

"Not much time. I'm meeting Joe for breakfast. I'm almost at Molly's"

"That's great because Blake and I are already there. We're in our usual booth if you and Joe care to join us. Amber and Jack were going, too, but she caught a silly head cold. Poor girl sounded horrible when she called to cancel this morning."

"Okay. See you in a couple minutes." *I wonder what earth-shattering thing that silly girl needs to tell me?*

My phone buzzed again. "Rae, it's Lauren. Mick and I need a break from our parents. They're getting along well, so we thought we'd go to breakfast at Molly's and leave them to fend for themselves. Do you and Joe want to come?"

"I'm only a few steps from Molly's. Joe and I are meeting there, and Emily called to see if we'd join her and Blake. Let's put some tables together so we can all visit. Emily said she has something to tell me."

Giggle. "As a matter of fact, I have something to tell you, too. I'll see you in a few."

Joe and I met outside the door to Molly's. "Good morning, Rae. Sleep well?"

"I slept great. Please don't open the door yet. Last night we talked about having a quiet breakfast this morning. Well, that's not happening. Emily called, and she and Blake are inside. She said she has some news to share. Then Lauren called, and she and Mick are joining us for breakfast, too. I suggested we pull tables together, so we can all visit."

"I should have known my sister had something up her sleeve. She called me very early this morning, but didn't say she was going to Molly's. I hope she doesn't talk your ear off." He opened the door to the restaurant. "Guess we'd better face the masses." He chuckled and winked.

We joined our friends. Molly and Henry filled coffee mugs and took our orders. All of us chatted while waiting for our meals and before we knew it, our piping hot breakfasts arrived.

Lauren took a bite of the egg white omelet she shared with Mick. “Rae, I haven’t even asked how you’re managing the bed and breakfast. I’ve only heard fabulous things from my folks.” She took a bite of her wheat toast and blew on her coffee before taking a drink.

Mick grabbed a piece of crispy bacon. “My mom and dad love the cottage.” He crunched and munched his protein then tasted his java.

“I’m so glad they’re enjoying themselves. It makes for an easy trial run for me.” My old-fashioned oatmeal warmed my throat. “Since everyone staying at the Inn is related to a resident of Hope, they’ve been more kind than strangers might be.”

“I think they’re being honest.” Lauren added cream to her coffee. “I have a little news to tell you.”

Emily quickly interjected. “Oh, no you don’t, Lauren. I wanted to tell her.”

I looked at them. “What are you two talking about?”

Lauren drummed her fingers on the table top and nodded to Emily. “How did you know?”

Emily sat up straighter. “Who told you?” She shifted in her seat.

I rolled my eyes then arched my brows. “Tell me, please.”

The bell to Molly’s Restaurant jingled and Lauren’s and Mick’s parents entered. The moms pulled up chairs, sat at our long line of tables, and the dads settled into a booth.

Lauren's mom beamed. "Rae, have you heard the news?"

"What news?"

She smiled. "Lauren hasn't told you?"

"Dear, Lauren and Mick haven't told you?" Mick's mom asked.

I jumped from my chair, quickly moved in Lauren's direction then gave her a huge squeeze. "I can't believe he actually proposed. Last night after Thanksgiving dinner?"

Mick rolled his eyes. "No."

Lauren looked uncomfortable. "You'd be one of the first to know if Mick did. That isn't what I've been trying to tell you." She took a small bite of fruit.

Mom Wyatt winced. "Guess I spoke out of turn. Let's give you youngsters time to visit." She glanced at Mick's mom and motioned for her to follow to where their husbands sat.

Lauren remained quiet while Mick finished his portion of the shared breakfast.

Emily took Blake's hand and sheepishly grinned. "Sorry I'm being such a baby about this. It's really not that important."

Joe looked at each couple, then at me. "Rae, what's going on? Is there some news I need to know?"

I'd had enough silliness. "I have no clue. Now spill the beans. This better be good."

Emily cleared her throat. "I heard my parents talking the other night and Dad said Dr. D and his crew are finishing the big building sooner than they thought." She slid closer to Blake. "I don't want to start any rumors."

I smiled. "I haven't spoken to Dr. D since before Thanksgiving, and I certainly hope the info is true."

Lauren laughed. "Emily, you and I are characters. We both wanted to tell Rae and had two different things to share. I heard from a close source that a local magazine wants to cover the Inn at Hope in their springtime edition. Since it's a small magazine, they can take pictures a month before publication. What do you think?"

"What do I think? I love it." I burst into tears.

Lauren handed me a tissue from her purse. "Here you go, dear sister. This has been a day of surprises. Sorry we kept you guessing."

Quiet breakfast? No way. Crazy breakfast filled with family and friends. The best.

Now, our God, we give you thanks, and praise your glorious name.
1 Chronicles 29:13

Chapter Forty-Two

After breakfast at Molly's, I took advantage of this Friday mid-morning lull and sipped a cup of hot tea. I received a text from Joe and another from Lauren reminding me of the Christmas tree lighting. The festivities were to begin with a parade circling the lake and ending near my favorite tree. I couldn't wait. But first things first. I needed to talk to Dr. D to find out if Emily's news was right. I finished my tea and meandered to the main building with Puffs.

"Dr. D, I heard through the grapevine the university building is ahead of schedule. Is that true?"

He cleared his throat. "Sure is."

I jumped up and down like a schoolgirl. A kindergartner to be exact.

"Rae, I can't promise you anything, but since the roof and porch are done, we don't need good weather to finish the inside." He pulled his rag from his pocket and wiped his forehead. "If you'll let us work inside 24/7, we can get this place up and running by Christmas or at least by New Year's. That's the plan at this point."

"Yes! There'll be a Christmas bonus for everyone, too, Dr. D."

***

I worked with the team the entire day until Mr. Dells announced everyone needed to stop and get ready for the parade. The men and women scrambled to put away items, grabbed their coats, and sped out the door. I took my time, wiped down the banisters, and strolled dreamily throughout the upstairs. I glanced out the second-floor window and saw Joe's truck parked at my cottage. He must have thought I was inside. I giggled. He knocked a couple times, shifted from foot to foot, and pulled his stocking cap over his ears.

"Come on, Puffs." The two of us flew down the stairs and out the front door of the main building.

Joe's expression switched from bewildered to a smile. "Rae, I thought you were in there." He pointed to my dwelling.

"We saw you from the second floor," I said, breathlessly. "Maybe someday you'll park in front of the big building and come home to me." I gasped. "I said that out loud, didn't I?" *Embarrassed—just a tad.*

Joe took me in his arms and gave me a tight squeeze. "I love that thought."

My trusty four-legged companion squinched her stout body between us and ended the embrace.

I opened the door to the cottage. "Do I have a couple minutes to freshen up?"

"You look great already, but I can wait." He sat on the porch swing and whistled a familiar tune.

Quick change artist. I washed my face, applied mascara, blush, and lipstick. My hair was a tangled mess, but my cap hid all the imperfections. Shirt changed to sweater,

Grandpa's coat thrown on, and I flew out the door. Lickety-split.

***

The crowds lined the perimeter of the lake as the color guard brought us all to attention. *The red, white, and blue. Nothing better.*

We spotted Mick and Lauren at the curve in the lake and waved. Emily, Blake, Amber, and Jack rode horses in the parade. I caught a glimpse of Penny riding on a float with other members of her Brownie troop. It seemed like ages since I'd last seen her. She waved and smiled a toothless grin. *Precious.*

Joe bought two cups of hot cocoa from Bitty's Buns and we savored the steamy liquid. Twinkling lights, Christmas music, and Santa engulfed the evening. But the best part of all—I realized I had fallen head over heels hopelessly in love with a certain stocking-capped professor who made my heart go pitter-patter.

After the parade, we visited a while with friends, then Joe and I strolled to the cottage. We ended our evening on the porch swing. My toes grew numb and fingertips tingled, but one thing I could say, this smiling fella made sure my lips were toasty warm.

The Lord Almighty is with us . . .
Psalm 46:11

Chapter Forty-Three

The Inn at Hope occupants left the Monday after Thanksgiving. I hired a few local teenagers to help clean and prep for the next group of visitors. Although cottages were reserved for Christmas and New Year's week, I needed to be prepared for sightseers who moseyed into Hope for a shopping spree and a romantic weekend.

I splurged. Winter bedding. Flannel sheets. Heavier comforters. Sea's, Angels to Zithers, supplied me with everything the cottages needed. Everything.

***

Dressed in hard hat, and paint-stained overalls for the next few days, I worked side by side with some of Dr. D's crew.

Joe entered the historical work scene each day after teaching and helped with some of the heavier stuff. *My muscle-man professor.*

With Dr. D's consent, we painted the railing on the front and back stairs. "The two of you need to stay focused. Not on each other, I might add. You've pretty much mastered that, but you're dripping paint on the wood floors. If you need a clean-up rag, you can use this." He pulled his tattered, dirt-stained rag from his pocket. "Here you go."

I remembered that rag and there was no way I'd use that dirty thing. "No thanks, Dr. D, I have something else I can use."

Joe started to take the rag from him. However, I quickly maneuvered between them, thus stopping the grimy rag transfer.

Dr. D put the cloth back in his pocket. "Guess you two will figure it out, but you'd better hurry and clean the mess before it dries. I'll be working in the kitchen."

Joe put his hands in his pockets and gave me a confused look, "What was that all about? I appreciated him offering me a cloth because I didn't bring anything with me."

"Oh, Joe, someday when we have a little time, I'll explain, but right now we need to wipe up the paint drops. I'll run to my cottage and get some old rags."

Joe and I cleaned the splatters and continued painting until we finished the first coat on both staircases. We worked easily together and didn't stop until Dr. D and Mr. Dells announced it was dinner time. Everyone skedaddled. Joe drove home to wash up, and I walked a few paces to my cottage. No driving necessary. I could gladly get used to this locale.

***

Chili—Joe and I wanted chili for dinner. No substitutions whatsoever. Molly's chili.

Christmas decorations covered almost every square inch of the restaurant. Some might classify it as gaudy, but this designer's eye called it tradition. Paper chains and stars hung from the ceiling.

I practically fell onto the booth bench. "I'm exhausted, Joe. I want a piping hot bowl of chili." I jokingly placed my head on the table.

"Hang in there, Rae." He smiled and sat back on the bench. "Did you say you're chilly?" Toothy grin.

I lifted my head. "Oh Professor, you need to get your hearing checked." Wink. Wink.

Molly set a basket of hot cornbread and butter on the table. "You two look tired. Shall I assume you need something hearty and want the special tonight?"

Joe and I nodded in unison.

Henry delivered our meal, and I spooned a heaping portion of deliciousness into my mouth. "The best chili I've ever tasted. Hands down." My eyes closed—no exaggeration—as I savored every bite. "This cornbread rivals my grandma's." I gazed upward. "Please forgive me, Grandma."

Joe nearly choked on his enormous bite of the meaty concoction. "I don't think you majored in Interior Design. I think you majored in Drama. Drama Queen." He leaned across the table and wiped chili off my chin. "I hate to admit it. This is better than my mom's. The woman would die a million deaths if she heard me say that."

He paid no attention to my wide eyes and somewhat discreet motion to glance behind him. Until . . .

Grace tapped him on the shoulder. "Well, son, don't ever ask me to make you chili or cornbread again." She swatted his shoulder with her purse. "You're in trouble now." She joined Lance and another couple at one of the tables.

Crimson. The color of Joe's ears. "Why didn't you warn me?"

"I tried, but you didn't notice my bulging eyes. I hope you didn't hurt her feelings."

Joe tried to look stern and the next minute burst into laughter. "My mom's cooking is pitiful, and she'll admit it. We were joking around."

"Joking? At my expense? I won't stand for it." I slid across the bench, stood, and stepped toward Joe. "Here you go, prof." I gently hit his arm with my napkin.

Joe gave me a puzzled look. "Are you really mad?"

This time I tried to look serious but burst into laughter. "Gotcha."

***

Our "chili" night wasn't chilly at all. Joe's embrace warmed me while we sat on my porch swing humming Christmas carols.

"Girlfriend, thanks for another great evening. I love you." He drew me closer in his arms.

His kiss warmed me from head to toe. "I love you, too, boyfriend. See you tomorrow?"

"You bet." He stopped the swing and walked me a few steps to my door. "Rest well."

"Sleep tight." I opened the cottage door, stepped inside, and kept it ajar as I watched Joe enter his truck and start the engine. He waved to me and I waved back. *See you tomorrow, Joseph Byer. I can't wait.*

***

Puffs slept peacefully at the end of my bed while I slid under the comforter and turned off the silver lamp on the nightstand. After talking to my Heavenly Father, I drifted into a deep sleep. *Sweet sleep. Sweet, sweet dreams.*

They broke bread in their homes and ate together with glad and sincere hearts . . .
Acts 2:46

Chapter Forty-Four

Lauren called me early the first Saturday in December. "Rae, did I wake you?"

I mumbled and took a sip from the water bottle next to my bed. "I'm awake." *Sort of.*

"The director of the university called and asked if I'd like a permanent position in Hope. Landy, who took my place temporarily in Maryland, wants to stay there if I accept. It's a win-win for us both. I won't keep renting her place, and she won't be leasing my condo."

I immediately pulled from under the comforter and sat on the edge of my bed, "I hope you said yes."

"Of course, I did. I'm going to buy her place, and she's buying mine. It'll still take time to get the paperwork done." She took a deep breath.

My head spun as I tried to grasp every word. "I'm so excited, Lauren!"

"Me, too. Mick said eventually it'll be a nice rental investment."

"What are you saying? Has he proposed?"

Lauren sighed, "No, we were just talking about the future."

"Sounds pretty serious."

"Okay, Rae, you can't tell me you and your boyfriend haven't discussed the future." She gave a slight giggle.

"Well, girl, we have. You're right." A yawn escaped as I stretched. "What are you doing now?"

"I'm sitting in my car in front of your cottage and waiting for you to get your fanny out here, so we can go to Greenville to do some Christmas shopping."

I opened the front shutters. "I can't believe you're out there. Come in."

"Nope. I know if I stay out here, you'll hurry. Bye."

***

We opted for breakfast at a well-known place in Greenville. Maple Street Biscuit Company. The hot chocolate swathed my throat in comfort. "What can I do to help you with the transition here?"

"I'm flying to Maryland the week before Christmas and filling a trailer with all my stored stuff. Mick offered to go and drive back with my parents and me." She sipped her latte. "I thought it was sweet, but I really want one-on-one time with my parents. He understood."

"Isn't it wonderful how you and I are starting a new beginning again? Only this time we're grown-ups?" I plopped a strawberry in my mouth. "Are your folks okay with all this?"

"They are. You know my mom. She hinted that she wants a vacation home in Hope. Dad and I think she's contemplating a permanent move here. Since he's completely retired, he's just as game as she is."

"What do you think?"

"I think it can work. Mick's parents and mine really get along well." Lauren bit into her flakey biscuit. "Enough of all this Mick and me discussion. Any new updates on you and Joe?"

"I don't like being Joe's girlfriend, and I almost despise calling him boyfriend." I drank my hot chocolate.

"I know."

"You know? How?"

"Well, Miss Rae, the last time I heard you say you wanted a boyfriend was in high school. Never since." She wiped her mouth and put her utensils on the empty plate. "I'd almost bet Joe wants to be more than a boyfriend, but he's chicken." Lauren pulled a mirror from her purse and applied lip gloss. "Ready to get our shopping done?"

"Yes, Miss Lauren, I believe I'm ready to shop. However, I don't think you're right about Professor Joe being a chicken. I think we're both being cautious." I picked up my purse, paid the bill, and we were off to meander through the cute shops in downtown Greenville.

Lauren and I never mentioned another word about Joe or Mick. We were power shopping and accomplished our task before lunch. With piled purchases in the back seat, Lauren drove to a drive-through in Greenville, and we ate a snack on the trip back to Hope. As she pulled into my driveway, I pointed at three familiar vehicles parked in front of the completed cottages. "What are the guys doing here?"

"I don't know. Mick didn't mention anything to me. I sure hope nothing's wrong." She parked her car next to his.

"Me, too." I opened the car door and jogged to the main building.

Lauren followed closely behind.

***

I quickly pushed open the front doors. "Joe, is everything okay?" I stopped dead in my tracks.

He stood near the top of the ladder with a light fixture in one hand. "I wanted to surprise you." Crooked grin.

"You did." I stood and looked up at my sweet boyfriend and tears started streaming down my cheeks.

"Isn't this where you wanted it hung?" Joe began to descend the ladder.

"It's perfect." When his feet touched the floor, I hugged his neck.

Lauren called out for Mick. "Where are you?" She waited for an answer.

"Up here on the second floor. Care to join me, lovely lady?" Mick appeared at the top of the stairs. "You don't think I trusted Joe to hang that mammoth light by himself, do you?"

Lauren immediately raced up the stairs and into his arms. "What are you doing here besides supervising Joe?"

Blake entered from the backyard. "Emily's helping out back. She's a work horse."

Emily scooted inside behind him. "Did you call me a horse? Hmm, Blakey, you're in trouble now." She swiveled and pretended to return outside.

"Oh, no you don't, Em. You're—oh well, I guess I can't get out of this one." He jokingly followed close behind her and the two of them went outside. Hand in hand.

We all assisted each other. Teamwork. The time flew by. We took a break just as Joe's phone rang.

"Mom," Joe said to us as he answered. He listened a moment then put his phone on speaker mode. "Chili?"

"Of course, son. You know I make the best chili and cornbread." She bantered. "By the way, Amber is coming, too."

"Mom, please quit mentioning Amber. You know she and Jack are dating."

"I guess I failed to mention, I invited Jack, too." She sighed. "I'm not as naïve as you think."

"Love you, Mom."

"See you tonight, son. You can bring Rae, if you want to."

"She's right here, Mom. You can ask her."

I squirmed. Nothing like putting Mrs. Byer and me on the spot.

"Rae, you're invited."

"Thanks, Mrs. Byer. I'd love to come."

Lengthy pause. "Rae, I guess by now, I should ask you to call me Grace. After all, you've requested my talents for the Inn at Hope sign and you are dating Joe." Another sigh. "Guess I'd better get over the fact you're a Yankee."

Grace's comments caught me by surprise, and I shushed Joe and Emily as the two of them started to say something to their mom. "Thank you, Grace." The sniggle inside my belly caused me to cough.

Conversation ended.

Emily chortled. "You are so gracious with my obstinate mother. She's been given a lot of grace in her lifetime, and I do believe you've given her an over-abundance." She slung her purse over her shoulder and zipped her jacket. "By the way, I don't know what all the chili conversation was about, but we aren't having chili. Mom's grilling chicken and we're also having Molly's famous baked beans and all the other trimmings."

Joe and I laughed at the comment. Only the two of us knew the conversation we'd shared with his mom at Molly's Restaurant.

***

Everyone gathered in the Byers' home for dinner. We all took our seats at the dining room table. Amber and Jack snuggled closely and fed each other chicken bites. Emily and Blake teased each other as they enjoyed their meal. Joe and I sat near Lance and Grace and refrained from sharing food with each other. I tread softly because I wanted Grace to be comfortable. Joe, on the other hand, felt differently.

"Come a little closer, Rae. You're all the way over there; I'm all the way over here."

Lance heard Joe, then chuckled. Mr. Byer eagerly shoveled a spoonful of beans in his mouth and winked at Grace.

Joe slid nearer and I blushed. Funny thing was, Mrs. Byer blushed, too, when her hubby grinned at her. *I guess I should refer to her as Grace.*

The evening chatter ended when Emily announced. "As selfish as this sounds, I'm glad the Inn opened because guests at our wedding will need a few cottages. Don't forget, the wedding is January first."

Joe moaned. "You won't let us forget." He rolled his eyes and smiled at his little sister.

After the laughter subsided, Jack and Amber stood. Amber made an announcement. "Rae, just so you know. We'll need reservations for family sometime in late spring. We're engaged! We've already told our families!"

Emily grabbed Amber's left hand. "Where's your ring?"

"Here it is." She removed it from her pocket, gave it to Jack, and he placed it on her finger. "I took it off before we came tonight because we wanted to surprise y'all!"

Joe shook Jack's hand. "Congratulations." He turned to Amber and gave her a gentle hug. "So happy for you both."

We complimented and congratulated the newly engaged couple. Emily and Amber showed off their rings and included me in the excitement.

Such a fabulous night. I love this family.

***

I rested peacefully in my bed while watching a cozy mystery and sent a message to Joe. Our texts crossed which meant we thought of each other at the same time. *Be still my heart.*

Joe: I love you, Rae.

Me: I love you, Joe. Good night.

Good night, Lord. I love You the most.

By all this we are encouraged.
2 Corinthians 7:13

Chapter Forty-Five

Slacker. Every night I flopped into bed by eleven and fell asleep in minutes while Dr. D and Abel's crew worked hard. Today I made a slight upgrade from the slacker status. Puffs stretched as I got out of bed. I slid into my overalls, pulled on my steel-toed boots, and donned my hard hat. I clipped Puffs' leash to her collar, and we strolled to the historical building.

Several of the workers halted in their tracks. One of the older gentlemen spoke first. "Miss Long, what are you doing here this early?" He removed his hard hat. "Sorry we woke you."

"Mr. Martinez, it's about time I do a little late-night, or I guess I should say, early morning work." I put on my goggles. "Please tell me what to do."

Hearing the men and women singing as they worked, inspired me to relish my 4:30 wakeup. Mr. Martinez appointed me the task of painting the small guest bath under the back staircase. It should have been a breeze. However, it turned into a blizzard. Literally. When I opened the small window to ventilate the miniscule room, a sweeping snow-filled wind blew inside, knocked the paint tray off the sink, and onto the floor. Unfortunately, the light turquoise splattered everywhere. Such a simple task became a gargantuan one. I knew if Dr. D were here, he'd offer his rag for clean-up. Whew. I dodged that.

One of the crew members stopped her work and came to my rescue. "Miss Long, let me help you with this." She crouched down to clean up my mess.

"Miss Clare, please call me Rae. Thanks for offering to help, but I can get this. The snow popped up from nowhere."

She smiled and left a pile of clean rags. "I'll be in the dining area if you need anything."

I wiped every drop off the floor and anywhere else the spill landed. Then proceeded with the task at hand.

***

The guest bath looked sensational. The smallest room in the building presented an enormous impact at every miniscule angle. Joe had helped pick the paint color. He said it reminded him of the color of my eyes. I loved his exaggeration, because my eyes were devoid of even the slightest hint of turquoise. But as they say, "love is blind."

As I swept my hand across the smooth, cool marble vanity top, I heard a familiar voice. "Rae, are you alright?"

I turned around at the sound of his voice and threw my arms around his neck. "Why are you here this early, Prof. Joe?"

"Why am I here this early? It's 6:45 a.m. Almost afternoon." He raised his eyebrows a tad. "Aren't you usually asleep at this time?" Crooked grin.

"I couldn't sleep and felt I needed to help." I dropped my arms from around his neck and smoothed my scraggly hair.

Mr. Martinez joined the conversation. "Rae, Joe's worked every night with us. He told us not to say anything but guess the cat's out of the bag now." He nodded to Joe, walked toward the back of the building, then turned in our direction. "You two make a great team."

Joe beamed. "Yes, we do. Thanks, Mr. Martinez."

***

We strolled hand in hand to the front porch.

"Joe, I can't believe you've been helping each night." I laid my head on his chest and squeezed him gently.

"I wanted to help. It's the least I could do."

"The least you could do? I've done absolutely nothing for you, except be your girlfriend."

He brushed a whisper of a kiss across my lips and placed his hands on my shoulders. His green eyes met my "turquoise" eyes. "You've brought life back to Hope and you've brought . . ." He stopped speaking and cleared his throat. "You've brought me happiness."

He walked closely by my side as we slowly meandered to my cottage. "Rae, I'd rather be spending the day and evening with you, but classes call, and I'm giving a lecture tonight in Greenville. Still want to tree shop tomorrow?"

My heart—tickled pink at the thought of Christmas tree shopping. "You bet I'll go. I can't wait, boyfriend." I wrapped my arms around his waist, tilted my head upward, and kissed his chin. "Have a great day, Professor. I can't wait until tomorrow."

Carry each other's burdens; and in this way you will fulfill the law of Christ.
Galatians 6:2

Chapter Forty-Six

The anticipation of Christmas tree hunting kept me awake most of the night. The Byers invited me, little old me, to go with them.

My phone buzzed as I let Puffs outside. Emily. “Rae, did Joe tell you to bundle up?”

“He told me to be ready to pick a tree. I’m wearing jeans, a sweater, and will pull on my leather boots when we quit talking.” *Hint, hint.*

“You’d better dress warmer.”

“Why? Tuttle’s Trees is set up next to the library. I’ll be fine, even if we walk there.”

“Well, I guess my big brother only told you the basics.” She cleared her throat. “Good thing I called you.”

I heard a shuffling sound in the background. “What are you doing?”

“I’m pulling on my wool-lined boots, wearing flannel-lined jeans, flannel shirt, and multiple layers beneath.” She hesitated for a second. “You need to dress for a hiking expedition. We don’t buy our main Christmas tree from Tuttles, we forage through the woodland outside town in pursuit of the perfect evergreen. Tradition.”

“Thanks for letting me know. I’m changing my wardrobe.”

"We'll be there in a few minutes to pick you up."

***

Joe apologized for not filling me in on what to wear. "I wanted it to be a surprise, Rae, but guess it's a good thing Emily called you. Otherwise you might've frozen to death." He wrapped his arm around my shoulder.

"It's okay. I'm plenty warm now." I snuggled into his embrace.

Joe, me, Emily, and Blake, in that order, crammed into the back seat of the big Ford.

Grace slid across the bench seat next to Lance and kissed him on the cheek. "If you kids can snuggle up in the back seat, dad and I can certainly do the same."

The tree farm sat quite a distance north and covered a massive area. Snow crunched under the tires of Lance's truck. He purchased a ticket and the owner told us which area to search.

Blake and Joe pulled sleds from a fenced area.

"Emily, jump on board." Blake pretended to struggle as he pulled Emily on the long wooden sled. "Em, are you sure you're going to fit into your wedding dress?" Within a nanosecond, he realized that wasn't the smartest thing to say since it was Emily's worst nightmare. "You know I'm just pulling your leg, honey. You're as light as a feather."

"You don't have to patronize me, Blakey. I haven't even purchased a dress and who knows if I will." She pretended to pout for only a second or two. "I love you Blakey."

Joe and I pulled our wooden contraption and followed Blake and Emily until Lance stopped us. "Hey, you two, I purchased this so Rae can have a tree." Lance waved the ticket in the air. "You heard me, Rae. Choose any tree in that area of the forest." He pointed straight ahead. "Joe, Mom and I are going into the coffee shop and will see y'all when you return."

"Thank you, Mr. Byer," I said.

"Call me Lance, please."

"Joe, the ticket was sure sweet of your dad. Plus, I get to call him by his first name."

He grinned, "Get on, Miss Long. This one's reserved for you."

Without hesitation, I positioned myself on the sled and held on for dear life. "This is so fantabulous, Joe." I clinched the sides tightly. "I've never bought a tree from a Christmas tree farm. Woohoo!"

Joe wove back and forth on the snow. *Crazy guy.* I loved every minute of his teasing and the verbal bantering between us.

He stopped pulling the sled and sat down next to me. "What do you think?" He blew his warm breath onto his gloved hands. "Shall we do this again sometime?"

"It's even more wonderful than I imagined." I moved a little closer to this southern gentleman. "I don't think I'll have time to come back, and I don't need more than one big tree."

"I didn't mean this year." Crooked grin. "In the future?"

"Of course. That would be nice."

***

We trudged through the snow until I found the perfect tree. Or so I thought.

Joe laughed loudly when I pointed to the chosen evergreen. "Rae, if you think that's going to fit in the main building, you'll have to double the ceiling height."

"Is it really too big?"

He nodded.

I picked up snow, molded it into a ball, and threw it at him. "Here you go, smarty pants. So, what if I can't visualize the height of a tree in the forest. Cut me some slack, please. Remember, I'm a city slicker."

My snowball landed in front of Joe. "Nope." He scooped up snow, shaped it, then threw it underhand in my direction.

"You call that a throw? Watch out buddy." The icy ball landed smack-dab on top of his winter hat. "That's how you do it."

"By the way, I'm not Buddy. That's my dog's name." He shuffled in my direction then stopped in front of me.

His embrace warmed my heart and almost melted the handful of fluff I'd gathered in preparation for another toss.

Joe's phone rang. *Lousy timing.* "Hi, Dad. Yes, we're almost done." He ended the call and put his phone back in his pocket. "Dad says Emily and Blake returned with their tree. Guess we'd better hurry up."

We strolled hand in hand until I stopped short. "That's the one." I pointed to a blue spruce tucked between two Douglas firs. "I've never seen a more beautiful tree in my life. I love it, Joe."

"Perfect." Joe was looking at me, not the tree.

He cut down the tree, and the two of us quietly pulled the sled together. No words needed. Tradition. I love it.

The guys laid the trees in the back of the truck. Emily and Blake picked a Douglas fir, so it was easy to decipher which tree belonged to which couple. We stopped at a quaint restaurant near the farm and devoured our comfort food. Cheesy mac and cheese, meatloaf, mashed potatoes, fresh green beans, and yeast rolls to die for. Everything was served family style, but the best part—being with family.

Grace offered me another spoonful of mashed potatoes. "Here, Rae. You need some meat on your bones."

Joe dropped his fork and looked at me. "She looks great just the way she is."

I caved and opted to take another portion of potatoes although my stomach was about to pop. "Thanks, Grace," I said as I glanced at Joe with appreciation.

Lance dabbed more potatoes on his plate and Grace nearly swatted his hand. "Now, Lance Byer, you know better. The doctor said you need to watch your cholesterol or some such thing." She added more to her plate. "You know I only scold you because I love you."

Everyone at the table heard Lance's comment. "Wish you didn't love me so much."

"Well, bless your heart, Lance Byer, you are the love of my life." Grace smeared butter on a yeast roll, turned her gaze to Lance, and gave him a flirty wink.

They were the craziest couple I'd ever seen, but it seemed to work for the two of them. *Maybe someday I'll be an official part of this crazy couple's family. Maybe. Someday.*

***

After Joe pulled the tree through the front door of the historical main building, I knew exactly where it should be placed. In the foyer.

"Rae, are you sure you want it there? With everyone still working on the house, don't you think it'll be knocked over?"

"You're right. For now, let's place it in the living room area. I really appreciated your dad giving me something to put it in." I put a tarp on the floor and added the bucket on top. "This should keep it out of the way since the gathering area is already renovated."

Joe set the blue spruce in the bucket and stood back to examine it. "You picked a great tree." His eyes scanned the room. "Didn't you say you needed something for this area?"

"Yes, I definitely need a desk or table."

"You saw the desk in my home office. I've never told you the history of that desk." He leaned his shoulder against the door frame. "Do you have a few minutes? It won't take long."

"I have tons of time. Tell me."

"Years ago, my desk set here in the original University of South Carolina at Hope. The men in my family sat behind it for generations until the new Hope extension was built. I inherited it."

"You're kidding me? That's such an awesome story and full of so much history."

"Would you like the desk?" His eyes glistened.

"Oh, Joe, I can't take your family heirloom. It just wouldn't be right."

"This is where the desk belongs." He took my hands in his and drew me closer. "Please take the desk. It'll mean so much to me."

I squirmed a little. "You should ask your mother and father."

"No, I shouldn't. The desk is mine and I'd be honored if you had it." He squiggled his brows. "Deal?"

I nodded and melted in his arms. "Thank you for such a glorious day. I'm so gratefully humbled about your desk." I squeezed him tightly. "I'll never forget your family including me in the tree search and taking me to that adorable restaurant."

Our lingering kisses made it more difficult to say goodbye.

Nothing more to say. Kisses trumped words. The professor departed in his truck. Although we'd see each other at church the next morning, it still seemed like an eternity.

***

I planned to tell Lauren the next day about my tree hunting venture and, of course, the historical desk. I couldn't wait to see her at church and afterwards at the monthly Fenster Haus meal.

Puffs barked when I let her outside before bed. I suspected Miss Doris's cat, Midnight, was on the prowl. Fortunately, there were no tree branches near the cottages where she could perch for the evening and keep everyone awake. The clever cat probably missed Puffs as a neighbor and made sure she harassed my pup upon her nightly rounds. Once Puffs did enough barking and exploring, she rushed back in and jumped on the bed.

With Puffs snoring softly, I fell asleep with visions of Christmas trees in my head—and maybe a thought or two of my knight in shining armor.

You will go out in joy and be led forth in peace;
the mountains and hills will burst into song before you,
and all the trees of the field will clap their hands.
Isaiah 55:12

Chapter Forty-Seven

Sunday. The organ bellowed familiar Christmas carols and goosebumps ran up and down my arms. Joe took my hand in his as we sang and listened to the pastor's message of redemption and hope. *Inspiring.*

***

Twinkle lights twirled around the scattered Christmas trees both inside and outside of Fenster Haus. Lauren and Mick waved as Joe and I walked toward the back of the restaurant.

Lauren patted the chair next to her. "Come, sit here, Rae. I have something to ask you before anyone else arrives." She took Mick's hand in hers.

Joe sat beside me as I waited. "Hurry. I'm all ears."

The church crowd poured into Fenster Haus before Lauren said another word. She glanced my way and shrugged her shoulders. We'd continue our conversation another time and place. Curiosity might get the best of me, though.

The chatter around the table centered on Christmas plans, final exams, and Christmas traditions. A few people reminded me they'd be glad to work at the Inn after lunch.

"Thanks, everyone, but there's no need because things are on track." I didn't breathe a word about Joe's desk. My stomach flip-flopped at the thought of telling Grace. "Plus, Dr. D and Mr. Dells never work on Sundays."

"She's right, folks," Dr. D said. "It's the Lord's day of rest." He nodded toward Abel Dells then continued an intense sports conversation.

Lauren and I had a chance to talk while everyone else had their own conversations.

She leaned closer to me and whispered. "Rae, my parents are definitely moving here and want to know if they can rent one of your cabins till the beginning of February. I wasn't sure if renting was an option." Lauren paused for a moment and quickly scanned the table to make sure no one heard. "I know Emily's wedding is January first and she's reserved some of the cottages. I wasn't sure if you had one available."

I, too, searched the lengthy table for any eavesdroppers but never had a chance to answer. At that moment, all eyes glared at Lauren and me. Grace straightened in her seat and looked my way. "Are you two talking about something that can't be shared with the group?"

Yes, and I'm not sharing it with you. I took a risk. "Miss Grace, Lauren and I are discussing the bed and breakfast."

Grace rose from her seat. "Well, you know we need all of the bungalows for the wedding."

I thought quickly and smiled. "Lauren's parents need an extended stay in one of the cottages, but that won't interfere with the wedding."

Lauren eased into the chair.

"I believe we discussed your family wouldn't be using my cottage for the celebration, because I originally thought

I'd still occupy it." I cleared my throat and guzzled half a glass of water. "It works out for everyone, because I'll move into the main building, Lauren's parents will slip into cottage number one, and there will be room for guests in all the other sweet dwellings." I wiped my flushed cheeks with the napkin.

Joe eased in. "Mom, Rae's got it under control." He squeezed my hand.

Emily slipped her two-cents worth into the conversation. "Mother, Rae and I have everything completed. Cottages reserved. No need to stress." She leaned in closer to Grace and whispered. "Mom, please be thankful Rae is gracious enough to allow you to be a part of the Inn at Hope. I hate to say it, but you've been a little snarky with her." Emily fluffed her hair. "I love you." She kissed her mom's cheek, then looked at Joe. "He has something to tell you about the desk . . ."

Joe's eyes widened. "Why did you bring that up?" *Glare.*

"Sorry, big brother, but I thought it best to get things out in the open."

Grace fidgeted on the edge of the chair. "Joe, what about the desk?" She grimaced. "Did you spill something on it?"

Everyone chatted amongst themselves, but I knew the Historical Society ladies' ears perked with every word Joe, Emily, and Grace spoke.

"Mom, the desk belongs at the Inn. Remember, that's where it originated?" Joe squeezed my hand again. "Rae didn't know it's historical, as well as a family item. I want her to have it." He looked at his mom. "If she spills anything on it that'll be okay, because it will be hers."

Lance stood and grinned. "Good going, Joe. You've made me even prouder of you." He pushed aside his chair and embraced his son in a bear hug, then looked over his shoulder at Grace. "Come on, honey, you know he's right."

Grace reluctantly joined the hug then pulled back. "Rae, I hate to admit it, but Joe's right. Since I'm the president of the Historical Society, and I know all about historical things, I agree, the desk should be at the Inn at Hope."

Emily maneuvered herself into the limelight, again. "See, Joe, it's always better to be up front. No need for hesitation."

He hugged his mom then scowled at Emily. "I'll remember that next time you share something confidential with me. Love you, little Sis."

The church friends meandered around the harvest table and let Grace know how graceful she was accepting the desk situation. After all, Grace Byer showed true southern hospitality to Joe's girlfriend. Albeit a Yankee.

As the meal ended, Grace stood abruptly. "Ladies and gentlemen, I just thought of something."

Victoria giggled. "This isn't a meeting, Grace."

"I know, but this is of utmost importance. I have an old picture of the bed and breakfast from years ago. It needs to be near the desk in the main building at the Inn, so I'll run it by your place tonight, Rae."

I didn't know what to say except, "Thank you."

Joe and I left Fenster Haus with lighter hearts. "Joe, I'm glad God worked out the desk reveal. Silly thing is, your sister got the ball rolling. Otherwise, who knows when we'd have told your mom and dad. I can't believe your mom's giving me a picture of the old bed and breakfast."

"Dad already knew about the desk. I think he'll rest better now since Mom knows, too. As for the picture, I'm glad she's giving it to you."

"Better yet, your mom is giving it to everyone. It's an historical picture, after all."

We laughed, hugged, and kissed. I returned to my place, and Joe to his craftsman-style home.

***

After changing into sweatpants and flannel shirt, I sorted through wallpaper samples, paint chips, and then poured myself a cup of hot tea. There were no guests in the cottages, but tomorrow they'd be occupied for a few days.

Mr. Tuttles had delivered and set up a small Christmas tree in each cottage. *Time to decorate the trees.* I carried a basket of white twinkle lights, tiny bows, and garland ribbon from cottage to cottage with Puffs, my happy companion, at my heels. At each cottage, Puffs rested contentedly on the floor next to me, and only budged when I finished a bow and placed it on the tip-top of the tree. She wagged her tail, approving of my masterpieces. Or at least that's what I hoped. *The trees—Simply beautiful.*

Back at my cottage, I poured Puffs' food into her bowl, and then nibbled on leftovers from Fenster Haus. A Christmas movie played on the television, and I thoroughly enjoyed the romantic comedy until my canine and I heard a knock on the door.

I peeked out the peephole and opened the door. "Grace, please come in."

She handed me the picture she'd referred to earlier at Fenster Haus. "Here you go, Rae. The frame is in pristine shape; hopefully it will stay that way." Grace turned and started to descend the porch stairs.

I gasped. "Grace, look."

"What's wrong?" She rushed to my side.

I pointed directly to two people in the photo. "My grandparents." I quivered just a tad and tears came to my eyes. "My Grandma and Grandpa Stone."

Grace took the picture from me. "I thought your grandparents' last name was Long."

"Dad's parents were Longs. My mom's maiden name was Stone. I can't believe it." I hugged Grace tightly.

"Oh, my goodness. My parents must have known your grandparents. It's unbelievable." Her eyes widened. "Well, I guess I'd better run and let the other ladies know about this discovery." She carefully walked down the steps. "It is unbelievable."

I immediately called Joe. "Hey, Professor, do you have a minute?"

"I have more than a minute. I just got off the phone with Mom. She told me about the picture, but I wanted to hear it from you."

"Can you believe it? Our grandparents knew each other or at least they shared a moment in time together."

"Like I told my mom, it's a God thing."

I love the simplicity and truth in his explanation. "Exactly, dear boyfriend. You bless my life."

"Good night, Rae, I'm glad you're my girlfriend and happy our family met each other years ago."

***

Exciting thoughts filtered through my mind. My grandparents would be a “part” of the Inn at Hope in more ways than one. *Sweet, sweet dreams.*

And rejoice before the Lord your God at the place he will choose as a dwelling for his Name . . .
Deuteronomy 16:11

Chapter Forty-Eight

"Ouch." I rubbed the crick in my neck and placed a warm washcloth on it as I ate my blueberry muffin. It was around eight so I knew Dr. D and Mr. Dells were on the job. I scurried as quickly as possible and dressed warmly. No reason to wear a hard hat inside, but I did need my winter coat and hat since the heat wasn't turned on yet.

I stomped the snow off my boots before entering the building and opened the front door. The foyer light illuminated the entryway and the beauty made me gasp. I greeted Dr. D with a broad smile.

"It's so good to see you this morning." My smile broadened. "I'm so excited."

"Excited? Why?" He wiped his forehead—with the infamous rag.

"Because everything looks wonderful." I slowly did a three-sixty.

"I'm glad it meets with your approval. I don't know if you'll like this idea or not, but I'll tell you anyway." He stuffed the rag into his overall pocket. "If you give us the paint colors you want, I think you'll be able to move upstairs next week. I know you planned on moving in after Christmas. Maybe after New Year's." He removed a bottle of water from his other pocket and took a drink. "What do you think?"

"What do I think?"

"Yes, that's what I just asked you."

I laughed. "I love that idea. As a matter of fact, I was going to ask you if I could move in sooner and paint later."

"Well, I guess I got my answer. Give us the paint chips, we'll buy the paint, and get started." He turned and headed up the stairs to the second floor.

I followed him and opened the double doors at the landing. Dr. Duntworth and Mr. Dells had designed them for privacy into my residential area.

I felt inside my coat pocket and pulled out my chosen paint chips. Dr. D stood inside the living area and I offered the samples to him.

He took them and grinned. "I see you're a prepared lady." He looked at the cards. "Thanks for writing on the back of them so we know which color goes in each room. I'll send someone today to buy what we need. Want to help us paint when the order gets here?"

"Of course. I thought you'd never ask." Toothy grin.

He put the paint colors in his overall pocket. Fortunately, not the one with his beloved rag.

I tiptoed between tools and hardware as I walked throughout the top floor. Sun streamed through the wall of windows facing the backyard in the master suite. The cream-colored crown molding added a touch of beauty.

"Does the second floor meet your approval?"

I grinned, "It more than meets my approval. It's magnificent."

***

I strolled to my temporary abode with a feeling of peace and excitement. A box from Buds and Blooms, filled with individual white poinsettia plants, sat on my porch. I loved the precious miniscule flower shop near Lauren's home. With a poinsettia in each hand, I made several trips to place a plant inside each cottage.

My stomach growled profusely as I put the finishing touches on each dwelling. Plumping the pillows on the king-sized beds and adding a cotton throw at the foot of each completed the preparation. I stood back and took a moment to absorb each Christmassy space. Above the beds hung a huge wreath covered in round pastel ornaments. As I began to close the door to the bungalow, I paused again and teared up just a bit. My grandmother always told me, "Rae, don't wait until the roses begin to wither, soak in their fragrance as they bloom. Enjoy life, dear." *Thank you, dear Grandma, for your soft words.*

After lighting the Christmas trees in the family cottage, I sauntered toward my place and noticed Molly's SUV parked in front of the Inn at Hope.

Molly waved. "Rae, I thought you could use some sustenance." She removed a serving tray and a couple covered containers from inside her car. "Hot tomato basil soup and a grilled cheese panini."

"Molly, you didn't have to do all this." I scurried to her.

"Enjoy, dear one. I heard the people who've reserved the cute cottages are out-of-towners. We can't wait to meet them and welcome them to Hope."

"I'm a little nervous, Molly. I hope they like it." I carefully held the tray.

"Oh, Rae, this is exactly what Hope needs. No need to worry, honey. God is in control even when Mrs. Persnickety is involved."

Mrs. Persnickety? What does she have to do with the bed and breakfast now that it's near completion? Thoughts quickly raced through my mind. *Is she going to do an inspection while my guests are here?* I didn't get a chance to verbalize my thoughts to Molly because the workers gathered around her SUV to help with the paninis, assorted soups, and of course, her famous chocolate cake. *I need to make sure Molly and her family have a weekend at the family cottage. Or perhaps, she and Henry might like a little romantic stay for just the two of them.*

I sat on the small front porch enjoying my meal. With phone in hand, I reviewed my to-do list for the upcoming occupants.

***

Preoccupied with last minute preparations, I placed thermoses filled with hot chocolate on the table in each cottage. Clear cellophane bags held two large Christmas cookies. *Delicious.* I switched on the fireplaces just before I returned to my place and forgot Molly's reference to Mrs. Persnickety. Thankfully.

I had an hour till guests arrived, so I changed into red corduroys and a creamy cowl-neck sweater. A plaid vest warmed my frame as I exited my little domain and the cottage dwellers arrived.

I walked each couple to their individual place. "Welcome to the Inn at Hope. I'm so glad you're visiting. There's a packet in your cottage containing information about the town. As you already know, breakfast is served at any location in Hope. Just let the restaurant know you are a guest of mine, and there will be no charge. After all, we are a bed and breakfast. I should be serving you breakfast." I realized I was rambling when one couple shifted from one foot to the next. "Oh, my goodness, you must be freezing." I opened their cottage door and welcomed them inside. "I'm in cottage one. Please let me know if I can help in any way possible."

I trotted toward the family cottage as a Chrysler van parked in front. An elderly couple carefully climbed out. The lady walked slowly to the porch and the man began pulling out suitcases.

"Welcome, Mr. and Mrs. Chambers. I'm so glad you're here. Come on inside." I opened the door.

Mrs. Chambers turned toward me and twirled her scarf securely around her neck. "It was hard finding your place. You should put a sign out by the road." She went inside.

"You're right. The sign will be placed out front when we complete all the construction. I hope you and Mr. Chambers enjoy your stay." I returned outside to help Mr. Chambers. "Let me give you a hand."

Mrs. Chambers came outside and stood on the porch. "Leave it to our daughter to not be here to help. She told us she'd be waiting when we got here." She turned and started back inside.

Mr. Chambers spoke softly. "Give Martha some slack, dear. She's a busy girl. At least she found this place for us to stay. It's nice being this close instead of staying out of town."

I heard what he said to his wife. "Martha? Does she live here in Hope?"

"I think you know her. She's the inspector . . ."

He and I halted in our tracks as a small car with an SHPO logo on the side stopped next to the van. The car door opened and out popped Martha Ingles.

Mr. Chambers started to walk toward his daughter; however, Martha moved quickly to him and gave her dad a hug.

I barely heard what Mrs. Chambers said to her daughter. Barely. What I did hear, kinda bruised my heart.

"Martha, it's about time you got here. We couldn't find this place, and you didn't tell us the bed and breakfast was off the beaten path. Where are the children?"

I nodded a welcome to Martha and moved aside as she and her parents entered the family cottage. Martha poked her head out the door when I stepped on the snow-covered ground.

"Thanks for helping my mom and dad. They're going to keep the grandkids here for the nights they've reserved." Martha's mother called her name. "Better get going."

As I walked to my cottage, my phone buzzed. "Hi, Joe."

"Want to grab something to eat?"

I hesitated and kept walking. "I don't think so." I gave a nervous laugh. "You're not going to believe who's staying in the family cottage."

"Who?"

"Martha's parents."

"Martha Ingles?"

"Yes. Now you know why I don't think I can leave the bed and breakfast and eat. I need to be at Mr. and Mrs. Chambers' beck and call."

Joe groaned. "I agree. You'd better stick around. I've made some of my famous lasagna. Mind if I bring dinner to you?"

"I'd love it. Bring Buddy, too. He and Puffs haven't visited in a while."

***

Some time passed, and I cleared off the tiny table in my cottage, put a Christmas tablecloth on it, and turned on the Christmas tree lights.

Puffs raised her head and barked at the faint knock on the door. "It's okay, girl. It's Buddy." I opened it, and Mr. Chambers stood in front of me.

"Miss Long, my wife wanted me to ask if you have a coffee pot that makes more than one cup at a time. I don't mind the kind of coffee pot you have, but she's set in her ways."

"Mr. Chambers, the coffee maker does make single cups but there is also a carafe in case you want a pot of coffee."

"Really? We didn't see it."

"I'll be glad to help you. Let me grab my coat. You're welcome to step inside."

He shook his head. "I'll go back to our place."

***

Mr. Chambers let me inside the cottage, and Mrs. Chambers sat up in the bed. I chuckled to myself at the sight of her spongy curlers.

She shuddered. “Close the door. It’s freezing in here. We’d like a pot of coffee. Not one of those single serve things.”

I bit my tongue as I moved to the coffee area. “This coffee dispenser makes either a single cup or a full carafe. There are small packets of coffee for one serving and larger packets for a pot. Shall I start some decaf for you both?”

Mrs. Chambers sneered. “Yes.”

I chuckled to myself as I thought of their grandchildren arriving in the morning. “I suspect tomorrow night you’ll want caffeine since the grandkids will be with you, and you’ll need all the energy you can get.”

Martha’s mother sat stone faced. Her father, on the other hand, released a belly laugh to rival all belly laughs.

“Good one, Miss Long. We will need the caffeine tomorrow. Thank you for everything. Our Martha told us you had a good heart. Now we see it firsthand.”

I left with a lump in my throat. Not because Mrs. Chambers didn’t say a word, but because of what Martha had told her parents. *Me—a good heart?*

***

Joe waited on the porch swing with Buddy sitting beside him. Crazy Great Dane wasn’t afraid of swinging. Buddy lifted his head and bellowed out his deep bark when I approached. He jumped off the swing and nudged me with his head.

"Hey, Buddy, come inside. Your girlfriend is waiting for you." I opened the door for Buddy to enter. Instead, Puffs ran out the door and the two of them romped in the snow.

Joe went to his truck, removed dinner from his passenger seat, and brought it inside. The dogs willingly followed us when they caught a whiff of the fragrant lasagna and garlic bread. *Memories of times gone by.*

Our meal tasted delicious. The lasagna warmed me from head to toe, and the porch swing kisses afterwards were sweeter than any Christmas cookies. Joe and I sipped our decaf while Buddy and Puffs remained inside curled in front of the fireplace.

Joe stopped the swing. "Remember when you came to my home for lasagna?"

"I sure do. You tricked me about using an old family recipe."

My phone played a Christmas tune. "I'm sorry, Joe. I need to get this." I pulled it from my coat pocket and saw the name. "It's the Chambers."

***

An anxious call to the family cottage had Joe crawling under the Chambers' bed with me scrunched down on the floor beside him. I aimed the flashlight in the direction Mrs. Chambers said she had lost her earring.

Martha's dad spoke first. "I'm so sorry for inconveniencing the two of you, but Mrs. Chambers was worried."

I chuckled when he referred to her as Mrs. Chambers. I wondered if he ever called her by her first name or a sweet nickname. *Probably not.*

Joe searched and searched and slid from under the bed. “I’m sorry. I can’t find it.”

She smirked. “I know it’s under there.”

I’d almost turned off the flashlight when the beam shined on a blingy, sparkly item under the table. I reached to pick it up. “Is this your earring, Mrs. Chambers?”

She sputtered. “Yes, I guess it is.”

Mr. Chambers shook my hand and then Joe’s. “Thank you both very much.”

***

Joe gave me an extra squeeze before he entered his truck. “Love you, Rae. Let me know if I need to bring a magnifying glass and detective kit next time I come over.”

I giggled. “Thank you for the wonderful dinner and for helping with the earring search. Most of all, thanks for the moral support. Guess we made a good team.”

When Joe started to enter his truck, we heard a deep bark coming from the cottage. Joe grinned, shut the truck door, and ran up the steps. “I forgot Buddy.”

“I can’t believe we both did.” I opened the door and Buddy plunged his huge canine body outside. Puffs tried to do the same, to no avail.

Joe opened the truck door, and Buddy jumped inside. “I’m kinda glad I did forget Buddy, now it gives me an excuse to kiss you again.” He took me in his embrace.

“I’m glad you forgot him, too.”

Joe paused before he stepped into the truck. “I’ve been wondering if you’d like to go on a date next Friday evening. I know you might be busy with guests, and I understand if you can’t.”

"A date night it is." I blew him a kiss.

"Love you, Rae."

"I love you, too."

My phone beeped. I shuddered at the thought the Chambers might need something else, but then remembered the Chambers didn't text.

Martha Ingles: Thanks for helping my folks. I apologize for my mom's unkindness.

Me: No apology needed, dear friend.

Do nothing out of selfish ambition or vain conceit.
Rather, in humility value others
above yourselves . . .
Philippians 2:3

Chapter Forty-Nine

Several toe-freezing days slipped by and the cottages were vacant. Martha Ingles came by after her parents left and apologized again for her mom's behavior. I reassured her there was no need to mention it ever again. *Never ever.* We talked of meeting sometime after the New Year for lunch.

***

The aroma of coffee teased my nostrils and drew me toward the main building. "Natalie, I saw your van out front. Thank you for delivering the coffee. It smells heavenly."

"Good morning, dear. It should smell heavenly because I brought your signature blend. Scones are in the kitchen." She handed me a cup of java. "Now, go grab one. You're going to need something delish to start your painting day." She winked and headed out the door.

I gazed into the living room area . . . completed. The Christmas tree was still propped against the fireplace mantel, so I checked the water in the bucket to make sure the trunk was damp.

Mr. Dells glanced in the room. "No need to check it, Rae. Joe makes sure the tree is almost saturated, or as he says,

'Gotta make sure the big guy gets a drink'." Mr. Dells chuckled and moved on to the dining area.

The professor never ceased to amaze me with his caring ways. My heart skipped a beat when I looked at that huge tree and remembered how much fun Joe and I had choosing it. However, my thoughts were interrupted when Mr. Martinez called my name and motioned for me to come into the dining room. He clung to a ladder near the fireplace. "Miss Long, what do you think of the paint color? Does it need another coat or is it okay?" He paused. "Since you're a professional painter now, I need your opinion."

"Oh, you're too funny, Mr. Martinez. I don't think painting a miniscule bathroom qualifies me as a pro. I'm almost afraid to paint the upstairs after seeing your fantastic work. You might have to put a third or fourth coat on the walls after I get through with them. By the way, the walls look beautiful. I love the pale yellow."

I continued through the main building. *Kitchen. Stunning. Completed.* Everything sparkled and looked how I'd pictured it, only better. The white cabinets looked fabulous with the shiny silver knobs and pulls. Emily and Lauren told me they'd appear too blingy, but I went with my instincts. I would refrain from telling the girls, "I told you so."

Scones, on a silver cake stand, embellished the marble island. The cranberry/orange delight tingled my palate. I relaxed a tad and took a drink of my coffee. Then the back door creaked so loudly, I jumped. *WD-40—a must.*

In walked Dr. D. "Bring your breakfast and coffee and we'll start painting upstairs. Follow me." He stopped abruptly. "By the way, I don't know what you said to Martha Ingles, but she came by early this morning, did a walk through, and signed all necessary paperwork for approval of the project. She even put a smiley face after her name." He started toward the stairs.

I smiled. "Before we start painting, I want you to know, I'm more than pleased with the first floor." I detected a slight blush on his cheeks, or maybe it was raspberry jam — I wasn't sure.

Music filtered throughout the upstairs while we all painted. Dr. D and Mr. Dells joined in the singing and kept us all on track. Abel reminded me making mistakes was the only way I'd learn. So, I kept trying. After I wiped paint-stained hands on my overalls, pulled a rag from my pocket and wiped my face with it, I realized I'd become a smaller version of Dr. D.

Dr. Duntworth patted my shoulder. "Good job, girl." He wiped his shirt cuff along his forehead. "Call it a day, Rae. The painting's done."

***

It dawned on me my lifelong friend, Lauren, would be heading to Maryland soon to pick up her stuff and drive her folks to Hope. I wanted to cram in as much time with her as possible.

Last-minute call. "Lauren, would you and Mick like to meet Joe and me at Gill's for dinner?"

"I'll check with him. What time?"

"Does 6:30 work?"

"It does for me, but I'll call him." She let out a nervous laugh.

"Are you okay, Lauren?"

"I am. Just a little scared." She laughed again. "I'm falling head over heels in love with Mick, and he doesn't fit into my ten-year plan. Remember the lists we made when we were in high school?"

"That was ages ago. I think it's about time we drew up some new ones. What do ya say?"

"I guess so." Lauren's sigh was anything but discreet. "I need to call Mick. I'll text when I get his answer." She hung up.

Lauren's message: See you at 6:30.

***

The snow fell softly as Joe, Lauren, Mick, and I stood in line at Gill's. People warmed themselves around the fire pit outside and sang Christmas carols. The multi-colored twinkle lights hung sporadically from gutters and dangled along tree branches near the restaurant. Some might refer to the mammoth blow-up decorations as gaudy and over-the-top; however, they seemed perfect for Gill's. No frills, no fuss. Just plain fun.

I huddled close to Joe. "Professor, I love you, and by the way, you smell wonderful." I kissed his cheek, "Oh, yes, wonderful."

He held me closer. "I'm glad Dr. D gave you the night off." Kiss to my forehead.

Lauren and Mick stood hand in hand. She glanced my way. "Rae, remember what we talked about earlier? I think you're right." She batted her lashes at Mick in a flirty way, then reached up and pulled his stocking cap over his eyes.

He removed his hat and pretended to grit his teeth at her. "Come here, Lauren. You're in trouble now." He held her by the waist and the two of them slow danced in place until Lou led us to our usual spot inside.

Lauren munched on her fries. "Mick and I are going on a sleigh ride Friday night. I can't wait." She dipped another one in ketchup and popped it in her mouth. "I've never been on a sleigh ride. Have you, Rae?"

"No, but it sounds like fun." I savored the warm ciabatta bun and juicy burger. "Have you, Joe?" *Hint, hint.*

Joe cleared his throat. "Sure. With my family."

Mick concentrated on his meal and didn't say a word—for a couple seconds. "You should take your girlfriend on one." He shook his head jokingly. "No pressure."

Joe wiped his mouth with his napkin. "All right, everyone. If you must know, the sleigh ride was going to be our date Friday night. Rae, I wanted it to be a surprise."

I shrank into my seat and took Joe's hand. "I knew we were going on a date, but I didn't know where. I'd love to do that, Joe."

Lauren gave him an apologetic look. "Guess I should have kept my mouth shut, but I didn't see your name and Rae's on the sign-up sheet."

I looked at Joe and our eyes met.

"Rae, our names weren't on the sheet for the large sleigh. I reserved a small one for just the two of us. That was my plan." He grinned and ate the last bite of his burger.

"I love your idea." I rested my head on his shoulder.

The entire evening was filled with chatter about Lauren's trip to Maryland, Mick's latest real estate endeavor, Joe's end of semester paperwork, and my excitement about Martha giving the stamp of approval on the bed and breakfast. However, all the while, my mind fluttered back to the thought Joe reserved a sleigh for just the two of us. I hoped he still wanted a date with me on Friday night, even though it was no longer a surprise. *I'll ask him when we're alone.*

***

Joe kissed me tenderly as we said our goodbyes on my porch. Soon I'd be moving into the main building and memories of porch swing kisses might fade. *Never.*

"Rae, if you'd still like to go on the sleigh ride, I'd love to take you."

Goosebumps. "Yes, I'd love to." I hugged his muscled waist.

May the Lord make your love increase and overflow for each other and for everyone else . . .
1 Thessalonians 3:12

Chapter Fifty

Grace drove Lance's humongous truck to the main building. The miniscule woman carefully stepped on the running boards and let herself down from the truck cab. I chuckled at the sight.

After smoothing the front of her red plaid coat and adjusting her faux fur hat, Grace slammed the door with every ounce of strength she could muster. "Rae, I couldn't trust anyone else with the sign. Joe will be here in a minute to lift it from the truck. Lance is coming with him."

"Why didn't Lance ride with you?" I quietly groaned. "There's no need to answer, I'm just glad you're here and we get to place the sign. I'm so excited."

"It's simple. If Lance, who is much heavier than me, rode in the passenger seat or driver seat it would unbalance the truck." She crossed her ankles and leaned onto the Ford. "Like I said, it's a simple explanation." She peered around me when she heard Joe's truck rambling down the driveway.

That lady drove me crazy with her craziness, but I knew her heart was in the right place. After all, she created the sign with such expertise I couldn't fault her for caring for it so much.

Joe parked and jumped out of the driver's seat. He slammed the door behind him, then wrapped his arms around me. "Good seeing you, girlfriend." *His kiss, woohoo.*

Grace punched his arm and demanded attention until Lance stepped out of the passenger side of Joe's truck and sauntered to her. "Come here, good-looking gal." He teased and flirted with his wife until she smiled a tender smile. "Now that's more like it." He belly-laughed and hugged her.

Grace melted in his arms and then refocused on the job at hand. "No more of that, Dean Lance Byer. We have business to attend to." She opened the tailgate carefully. "Use all your energy to lift my baby out of here, please."

Joe jumped into the bed and Lance stood on the ground near her. He picked up the sign with both hands and slid it to the edge of the tailgate. "Okay, Mom, get ready, because here it comes." He pretended to drop it from the vehicle.

"What are you doing?" Grace screamed, then realized he was kidding. "I swanny, you're in trouble, young man."

Lance laughed so hard he sat on the tailgate to catch his breath. "Joe, good job. I can't believe our plan worked."

I subdued a laugh. It wasn't easy, but I figured Grace wouldn't appreciate my giggling.

She walked to where Lance sat and jokingly put her hands around his neck. "You two fellas are really in trouble. I can't believe you'd scare me like that."

In the meantime, I stood and watched the entire scene. I loved the bantering and sense of humor the Byer family possessed.

The holes had been dug the day before and concrete poured for the posts for the permanent Inn at Hope sign.

The entire population of Hope arrived for the big reveal. Lottie took photos for the paper and website. I discovered Grace spread the word to a couple people and those folks told others via social media. As Joe and his dad hung the sign on the posts, Grace and I posed for picture after picture. Applause.

Tears flowed down Grace's cheeks as well as mine. We must have been quite a sight, but we didn't care. After Natalie wiped her eyes, she invited everyone for free coffee and cookies at Bitty's Buns. My new-found family left their cars parked at the Inn at Hope, and we walked to Bitty's.

Lauren grabbed my left arm and Emily my right. I was sandwiched between my lifelong sister and new friend. Joe, Mick, and Blake ran ahead of everyone and threw snowballs at each other. Friendly competition.

***

We pulled tables together at Bitty's Buns and munched on sweet delights with a sip or two of coffee between cookie bites. It was truly a magical afternoon.

Grace removed her phone from her pocket. "Look at the pictures Lottie took. She forwarded them to me. I swanny. My hat looks like a cat curled up on my head."

I saw my Pecan Street neighbor, Doris, sitting at the end of the table. "What's wrong with having a cat on your head? Midnight always curls up on mine when I sleep." She wiped her mouth and gave a slight smile.

Penny and Ike Woods sat nearby. Penny slipped out of her chair and came to me. "Miss Rae, I've missed seeing you. Is Puffs doing okay?"

"She certainly is. Maybe you and your Papa can come by the Inn sometime. I'll make sure I have hot chocolate waiting."

"Yes, ma'am, that sounds like a great idea." Penny did a little skip to her seat. The bright red bow bobbed up and down as I suspected she told Papa what I'd said.

Mr. Woods gave me a thumbs up. I'd have to make sure I stood by my promise of a hot chocolate visit for Penny.

***

The sweet time at Bitty's Buns ended and everyone returned to the Inn at Hope to retrieve their cars. Joe stayed to help me set up the Christmas tree in the foyer of the main building. Mick offered to help, but Joe assured him he was strong enough to do the job.

Lauren gave me a quick hug and bent down to whisper in my ear. "My ten-year plan has changed. Marriage just might be on the horizon. I love Mick and so do my parents. I'm so thankful for you, Rae." She sauntered toward Mick.

I watched as they moseyed to his sports car. I'd never seen Lauren so happy. *Never ever.*

She cupped her hands to her mouth. "Rae, see you tomorrow night at the sleigh ride. Love you."

"Love you, too." *Sleigh ride.* I couldn't wait.

Joe pulled me close. "Did you want to ride in the sleigh with everyone else?"

"Of course not, Professor. I'd much prefer to ride in a cozy sleigh for two." We strolled hand in hand to the main building.

Once set, the tree stood majestically in the center of the foyer. Lights and decorations of every shape and size set on a table nearby. The white twinkle lights sparkled against the dreamy, creamy, white ornaments. Joe placed a few more on the tree and left several for guests to add to the evergreen.

We stood in front of the blue spruce. Joe glanced toward the living room area on the left side of the foyer. “Rae, let me know when you want the desk.”

“Any time that’s best for you.” I kissed his cheek. “I’m so grateful.”

He placed his arm around my waist as we walked through the entire Inn. It looked fabulous. *A masterpiece.* He turned and looked into my eyes. “I can’t wait to see the desk and picture in their rightful place.”

I held his hands. “I’d like to move into the upstairs this weekend. That would free up a cottage for Lauren’s parents to rent for a couple months.”

“I think it’s a great idea. I’m proud of you, Rae. You stuck with a goal and completed it.”

I thought about the plan Lauren and I made when in high school. I’m so glad I hadn’t completed everything to a tee. Otherwise, I’d have missed out on Hope, the Inn at Hope and most of all, Joe. My thoughts steered back to him. “Thanks for all your help, Professor. I never could have finished if you hadn’t been so willing to assist.”

“Well, you know me, I had an ulterior motive. The closer you got to completing the renovations, the more I felt secure you’d stay.” He paused a second. “Right?”

I fluttered my eyelashes at him. *Lord, please don’t let my fake eyelashes fall off.* “Yes, Professor. I honestly know God led me to Hope and I'm glad He did." I squeezed his hand. "Mr. Byer, mind walking me to my little domain?"

His crooked grin tickled my heart as we walked to the cottage and kissed goodnight. I loved feeling his scruffy whiskers brushing my cheek as I drank in the fragrance of his aftershave. *Musky masculine.*

He gave me an extra hug and his embrace warmed my whole body. "Rae, I need to get a few things done before tomorrow night. How about I pick you up around five? I thought, if you'd like, we can go to Fenster Haus for dinner."

"I'd love to go there, and then the sleigh ride." I opened the cottage door and Puffs stuck her head outside. "Oh, no, you don't, girl. Buddy isn't here to play with you in the snow, and I'm certainly not going to." I turned to kiss Joe as he tipped his head and found my lips. "Good night, Joe. See you tomorrow."

"I can't wait."

***

I curled up into bed and dreamed about my beau. Maybe someday that handsome southern gentleman would be more than just a boyfriend. *Maybe someday . . .*

Praise be to the Lord your God . . .
1 Kings 10:9

Chapter Fifty-One

Sweetness and Sweaters had the cutest red sweater dress and evergreen tights. Sendy pressed me to try on earmuffs and mittens. “Give these a try.” She handed them to me. “The red faux fur is a must for sleigh riding and the mittens will keep you much warmer than those gloves you keep eyeing.”

I placed the earmuffs on first and then the mittens. “I look ridiculous.”

Emily pushed the store door open and blew in with the wind. “Hi, Sendy.” She looked surprised to see me. “Rae, I didn’t know you were here. Are you wearing those tonight on your date with Joe? I heard he’s taking you to Fenster Haus for dinner.” She giggled. “It might be a little hard eating with those gargantuan mittens on.” Emily grabbed a couple sweaters off the rack and stepped inside a fitting room. “Sendy, do you have any mittens like Rae’s wearing? Only I want chartreuse.” She laughed loudly and didn’t stop until she opened the dressing room door and modeled a snug fitting Christmas sweater. “What do you girls think? Will Blakey like this?”

Both Sendy and I laughed at the same time. She handed her a size larger. “Try this, Miss Em. No offense, girl, but I don't think you'll be able to breathe in the one you're wearing."

Emily took the larger size. "Okay, smarty pants. Good thing we're best friends or I'd walk right out the door." She flipped her hair in mock disgust and returned to try on the new sweater. Her voice carried through the door. "By the way, I wasn't joking about the chartreuse mittens."

Sendy placed a wrapped box inside my shopping bag. "It's a tiny something you might enjoy wearing. Merry Christmas, Rae. You'll look fabulous on your date tonight." She hugged me and handed me the decorative bag. "Enjoy the earmuffs and mittens."

"Thank you so much, Sendy. I'll let you know how the date goes and how Joe likes the mittens." I tapped on Emily's dressing room door. "Have fun tonight. I heard you and Blake are going on the sleigh ride."

She opened the door a crack. "How did you know Blakey and I were going?"

"Remember, there are no secrets in this small town." Giggle. Giggle.

"Thanks for all your help, Sendy."

***

Puffs cocked her head as she listened to Christmas carols flowing from my lips. "Hark the Herald . . ." I dried my wet hair and French braided it. I remembered Joe's comment a while back on how pretty he thought my hair looked when I braided it. Tonight, I wanted to look extra special. Long-sleeved sweater dress and wool tights felt soft against my skin and snuggly warm. After wiggling my toes into my faux fur-lined boots, I opened the tiny box Sendy had given me. A bangle bracelet fell onto my lap. Engraved in the bracelet were the words, *There is always Hope.* It slid easily onto my wrist as I picked up my phone and called Sendy to thank her. She was thrilled that I loved the gift.

I fed Puffs, patted her head, then stood on the cottage front porch to wait for Professor Joe.

His truck sputtered down the driveway. He parked in front of my place, escorted me down the porch steps, and into the awaiting chariot.

"Rae, you look and smell fantastic."

"So do you, Professor." I smiled and slid across the bench seat and sat next to him as we drove to Fenster Haus.

***

Christmas music filtered through the air as the filet mignon melted in our mouths. Our candlelit table, nestled in a corner near the fireplace, added an extra touch of romance.

"Joe, I love this place, but you know what? I love you more." I wiped my mouth with the cloth napkin and gave a little wink.

Joe took my hand in his as we sat across from each other. "I love you, Rae. I always will." He gave my hand a gentle squeeze. "We need to make a habit of dining at Fenster Haus. Is that a deal?"

My cheeks warmed. "It certainly is."

The two of us spoke softly with each other, shared a bite of our divine dinner, and even sneaked in a kiss or two. The evening couldn't have been more perfect. *Or so I thought.*

***

"Sleigh bells ring . . ." The music blared on the truck radio as Joe pulled in front of my cottage and parked.

"Joe, why are we here? I thought we needed to catch the sleigh out at Val's place. I thought everyone was meeting there."

"Remember, I told you we have a private sleigh ride. It should arrive in about ten minutes. Want to bring Puffs?"

"Puffs? Won't it be too cold for her?" I played with my bracelet.

"I don't think so, because I'm bringing Buddy. What do ya say?"

I must admit, my excitement meter kind of plummeted at the thought of two mammoth-sized dogs squeezed in between us on a sleigh seat. However, I agreed to the dogs coming with us.

I went inside the cottage while Joe sat on the porch swing, and I grabbed my red fluffy mittens and earmuffs. There was no way I was going to wear the silly things to Fenster Haus, so it worked out that Joe brought me back home. I clicked Puffs' leash on her collar, put on my earmuffs and mittens, and buttoned my coat. I opened the door and stepped outside.

"I do believe, Miss Rae, those are the reddest earmuffs and gloves I've ever seen."

"Well, I'll have you know, Mr. Joe, these aren't gloves. They're muffins."

"Muffins? I thought they were called mittens." He let out a belly laugh.

I stared at him in disbelief. "Did I just say, muffins?"

"You sure did." *Laughter.*

"No, I didn't, you're just making that up." I caught my breath as the most gorgeous white sleigh with twinkle lights aglow, glided down the driveway and stopped in front of us. It wasn't a tiny sleigh at all. There were two bench seats facing each other. Joe motioned for Puffs to climb onto the one with Buddy and then helped me step into the sleigh. He placed a fleece blanket across our laps and moved a basket from underneath the dog's bench seat.

"We'll have some hot chocolate later, if you'd like." He whispered in my ear.

"Yes, that would be nice." I petted Buddy on the head. "How did the driver know to bring Buddy?"

Joe winked and patted the side of the sleigh to let the driver know we were ready. The work horses lunged ahead and the sleigh jolted slightly. We held onto each other. What a nice way to start our adventure.

The sleigh slid easily down Beaufort Street and slowly around the lake. The twinkle-lit homes looked gorgeous as the chauffeur guided the larger-than-life sled.

Joe opened the thermos and placed two straws inside. "Be careful, beautiful lady. The chocolate shouldn't be too hot for your tender lips, but you never know."

I kissed his cheek. "I don't need to worry about you burning your lips, though. Since you do have the nickname, hot lips."

We both chuckled and sipped the warm chocolatey delight. The two dogs slept soundly under a cozy blanket and didn't raise their heads until the sleigh finished circling the lake and stopped on Beaufort Street.

Joe held the thermos. "Do you mind if I put this into the basket, so we can get out and stretch our legs?"

"That sounds like a great idea. Should we take the dogs with us?"

"Yes. I'll get their leashes."

The four of us walked toward the lake to our favorite spot. "Joe, this is our bench." I stopped. "You know it's my absolute favorite place to clear my head."

"Want to sit down before the dogs do?" He smiled that crooked grin of his.

Joe brushed the snow off the bench with a rag. *Nothing like Dr. D's rag. Fortunately.*

"Rae, thank you for tonight. You've made it extra special for me."

"I've made it extra special for you? You're the one who created this beautiful evening. Thank you, Joseph Byer."

He squirmed a little. "Remember how we met here?"

"I sure do. I couldn't believe Puffs jumped into the lake and Buddy went in, too. I was so afraid he was going to get my precious pup." I laughed at the thought.

"I know. You sure love that dog like I love Buddy." He turned toward me and took my mittened hands in his. "I'm in love with you, Rae. I hope you feel the same."

"Of course, I do."

He removed his hand from mine, pulled something from his coat pocket, then shifted off the bench onto one knee.

I tried to help him up. "Are you alright? You're going to get all wet."

"Rae, I don't care if I get wet." He shook his head and grinned. "I want to know if you'd mind sharing my last name with me?" He paused.

"Share your last name?" Tears quickly filled my eyes.

"Will you marry me?" He suddenly looked very serious. "You don't have to give me an answer right now. If you need to walk around the lake or something, I understand."

"There'll be no walking anywhere for this girl. The answer is yes!" I slid from the bench onto my knees and wrapped my arms around his neck.

We kissed passionately until the two dogs started licking our faces. We stood up and Joe brushed the snow from his pants while I quickly brushed the snow from my tights.

He opened a tiny box. "I love you."

The mittens flew off in an instant and landed on the snow. Inside the hinged box sat the most perfect engagement ring I'd ever seen.

Joe slid the diamond-cut solitaire onto my ring finger.

"It fits. How did you know my size?"

"Lauren told me."

"She knew you were buying me an engagement ring?" I rolled my eyes. "I can't believe she kept that secret." I gave my fiancé a gentle hug.

Joe and I embraced until we heard Christmas carolers nearby. We turned to watch and listen to them. Then I realized the large group of singers included Lauren, Emily, and all the townspeople of Hope.

Lauren left the singers and ran toward me. Tears streamed down both of our faces.

She looked at my ring. “Congratulations. It was so hard not telling you. I’m so happy for you and Joe.”

We hugged and cried like the two school girls we used to be.

In the meantime, Emily, Blake, Lance, and Grace left the group and gave Joe a family hug. Tears flowed from everyone’s eyes. Lauren and I joined the Byer family as Mick slid into the hug to steal a kiss from Lauren. Emily used her chartreuse mittens to wipe away her tears.

I noticed Dr. D and Mr. Dells waving. Dr. D pulled a bullhorn to his mouth. “Ladies and gentlemen, dessert will be served at 111 Charleston Street. Please follow us.”

I looked at Joe. “Did he say 111 Charleston Street? That’s my address.”

“Yes, he did. Ready to celebrate?” He pulled me close to his side.

“Let’s sleigh ride to the Inn at Hope.” Joe motioned to his dad. “Mind taking us, Driver?”

“Driver?”

“Yes, he’s the person who drove the sleigh while we were enjoying ourselves sipping hot chocolate. I guess the outfit Dad’s wearing was a great disguise.”

“You guys are full of surprises.” I held Joe’s hand with my left hand. It felt wonderful wearing his ring. “Joe, can we officially stop calling each other boyfriend and girlfriend, now?”

“Come here, my soon-to-be bride.” Joe carefully twirled me around, and we climbed into the sleigh. The dogs jumped onto the bench seat across from us. The ride to 111 Charleston Street was filled with kisses and more kisses, then barks and more barks. The dogs warned us of what was to come. Everyone stood in front of the Inn at Hope—and I mean everyone from the town of Hope. Candle-lit-luminaries lined the walkway to the main building. White lights decorated the outside and the beauty took my breath away.

Joe and I walked hand in hand to the large entryway doors and turned to face family and friends who'd congregated.

Mick and Blake blurted out. "Speech. Speech."

Joe nodded to me and I smiled my biggest smile ever. I had to regain my composure before I said a word. "I love every single one of you. My dreams have come true, and I can't even begin to thank all of you enough. I'm home."

***

Everyone meandered inside and outside the old university and chit-chatted their way through the entire building. *This is a night I'll never forget.*

Emily and Blake teased Joe and me and offered engagement advice. "Rae, you know that's why Sendy suggested you wear mittens instead of gloves. She knew you'd need quick mitten removal to put on the ring."

"She knew?"

"Well, of course she did, and so did everyone else. That's the beauty of a small town." Emily smiled, grabbed Blake's hand, and the two headed out the door.

The celebration went well into the night. When Joe and I gave our last goodnight kisses, we both floated on cloud nine.

He took me in his arms and squeezed me gently. "Good night, fiancée. I'm so glad you said yes."

"I'm so glad you asked, fiancé."

Our lengthy embrace ended with goodnights and see you tomorrows. *See you forever.* Puffs and I watched Joe and Buddy's truck drive down the driveway. *Someday it will be permanently parked in front of the Inn at Hope. Or at least until my Knight in Shining Armor trades it in for another chariot.*

***

Puffs slept contentedly at my feet. I pulled my comforter under my chin, slid my left hand from under the blanket, and stared at my engagement ring. Somewhere in the night, after talking to my Heavenly Father, I fell into a deep sleep. *Peace-filled contentment.*

Thank you, Grandma and Grandpa, for telling me about the bed and breakfast. Thank You, Lord, for giving me Hope.

Yet the Lord set his affection on your ancestors and loved them, and he chose you, their descendants, above all the nations—as it is today.
Deuteronomy 10:15

Just Beginning

Made in the USA
Columbia, SC
27 August 2019